A HOSTAGE TO LOVE

A ROPE MAY BIND HER WRISTS, BUT WILL
LOVE BIND HER HEART?

BRENDA MAY

A catalogue record for this book is available from the National Library of Australia

COVER by JAALA PEDLEY PHOTOGRAPHY & DESIGN.

A Hostage to Love is dedicated to a humble, intelligent, and
unreservedly kind person. I have only
known her this past year and have found great delight as the layers
of her personality were exposed,
and the depth of her knowledge uncovered.
Jeanette Smith, take a bow, you are an incredible person and I
humbly thank you for your assistance
and look forward to the day you produce your first book.

CHAPTER ONE

F or the first time in what seemed like forever, energy zinged through Kellee's body, enhancing the inner buzz that came from being physically and mentally healthy. Not just energised, but genuinely happy, and she couldn't resist breaking into a grin as she strode through the Cairns shopping centre. Rock climbing after lunch confirmed her back and shoulder were making remarkable progress under the hot tropical sun. Her inner euphoria stood testament to her mental wellbeing, and she glowed with empowerment from the massive step forward she had made in her recovery.

Normally she hated buying clothes, but today felt like a new beginning. She had enough time left after a fun filled afternoon to buy what she needed before her psychiatric appointment. There was no negative stigma associated with that word now. When her Captain stipulated the Police Department required she see a psychiatrist to help her adjust to the personal side of what happened, her stubborn streak emerged. She did not need a shrink. It had taken a few more weeks plagued by nightmares and jumping at shadows for her to place her badge on her boss's desk with the realisation she didn't have faith in her own judgement, or ability to work with a partner. Mentally she was a mess.

She stepped inside a beach themed shop; perfectly placed to catch the tourist's attention. The store muffled the busy hum of people going about their daily business, creating a background symphony to the two young customers laughing and chatting as they held up and admired items of clothing.

Kellee enjoyed the noisy banter as the friends helped each other choose garments and disappear to try them on. Her acquaintances were few, but she'd never embraced close female friendship, and after being on death's door just over five months ago, she was feeling the urge to become a little more social. To start, she should join the girls for Friday night drinks after work, to her 'step outside her square' tasks. Something to discuss with her psychiatrist. Was she ready to trust friendship again? Could she put the past totally behind her?

Kellee squared her shoulders and turned to the assistant. "May I try these on?" She lifted her arm to show a couple of t-shirts and a pair of brightly coloured bikinis.

"Sure thing, the changing rooms are just over there." The young woman waved her hand towards the back of the shop. "Just sing out if you need any help or a different size, my name's Ann."

Kellee drew back the flimsy print curtain in the doorway of the compact cubicle. Take a deep breath she told herself. It's not tiny. She looked at her reflection in the angled mirrors. Wow, that lighting would make anyone look good. Dropping her bag on the floor she reached for the first garment.

Oh my, she thought as she tied the final string on the bikini top, *this must be the most revealing thing I have ever worn.* Not that there was a need for this sort of outfit with her lifestyle. Even school swimming classes had been avoided with a cleverly forged note.

Muffled bursts of laughter from the two young girls filtered through from the next cubical, making her smile anew. The happy vibes were quite contagious, and she grinned into the mirrors believing that finally she was over the worst. These were well positioned, giving her a good all-round view, no need to crank her neck this way and that. She was still on the thin side, but muscle tone and core strength were returning with a vengeance. Six weeks staying on the Esplanade in Cairns, in the heart of Northern Queensland, had worked wonders, wrapping her in its magic.

Spring in the Tropics was pure heaven on earth, and the first seeds of a plan began to grow as she seriously considered moving away from police work. Finding employment in youth rehabilitation or something along those lines. The desire to assist troubled, underprivileged kids was growing stronger each passing day. An eight week all expenses paid holiday, with psychiatric sessions to help her emotionally heal through the trauma of being shot in the back by her partner, had been just what she needed. The doctor had worked wonders during the six weeks she had been in Cairns. She was no longer jumping at shadows and today she was taking the first steps to introduce her scarred body to the elements.

Sunshine her doctor suggested. Hence the bathers, the skimpiest things she would ever wear, even if only she would see them. They were for the morning sun which hit the balcony of her ocean front room.

The scars on her skin were not as horrific as the ones she carried in her mind. The bullet impacting high on her shoulder had done the most harm, going straight through her body, shredding the muscle as it went. The other three bullet holes on her back were nicely grouped around her heart, each one doing damage, but miraculously missing the vital organ.

The scarring wasn't that bad. Two to three centimetres of raised, puckered skin had not yet lost the pink, fresh appearance. In her mind the damage ran deeper, and she was working hard on repairs. She wanted her life back. At least she could acknowledge and examine what had happened to her now. None of it was her fault. She pushed thought of that day away. Today was for moving forward.

As if to agree, her stomach let out a deep rumble and Kellee laughed out loud at the genuine hunger gnawing at her belly. Her appetite had returned with a vengeance. She was recovering.

"I'll take these thanks." she placed her goods on the counter, before digging in her backpack for her purse.

"That will be sixty-four ninety-five." The shop assistant winked. "These are awesome bikinis; we have slip on sandals that match them beautifully if you are interested, and a sarong."

Kellee raised her eyebrows in interest. "I've never worn a sarong.""You won't regret it. Once you have there is no going back. You will love it. They are cool, comfortable, totally relaxing and give you such a sense of freedom."

"It looks so tropical, and the material feels soft and beautiful."

"And you can wear them in a dozen different ways." Enthusiasm bubbled in Ann's voice as she demonstrated how they could be worn.

"I'll throw in a second one for half price, the green one. It will really bring out the colour in your eyes, plus a booklet with diagrams on the various tying styles."

"Done." Kellee chuckled as she handed over her credit card. Tonight, after her walk, she would have fun trying on this oblong piece of material. She may even pluck up the courage to dip her feet in the shallow end of the impressive man-made lagoon style pool which graced the Esplanade. It was certainly warm enough.

"Do you want the sandals as well? They are only twelve fifty. You just slip your foot on the sole, cross the straps over and then around the ankle and up your leg a short way."

The shop assistant sure excelled at her job. They are a perfect match for the sarongs, Kellee thought as she looked at her wrist. Shoot, she was running out of time. "They sound great, but no thanks. I need to hurry, and I'm almost late as it is."

"Err... Transaction declined...refer to issuer"

For a moment Kellee couldn't believe what she was hearing. She shot a surprised look at the sales assistant.

"It usually means insufficient funds." she stated with a sympathetic shrug.

"That's impossible." Kellee deepened the two furrows on her forehead, ticking off her expenditure for the day. Coffee, lunch, rock climbing, a souvenir for the captain, a couple of odds and ends. By her reckoning she should still have plenty left. Remembrance hit. She had paid early for a reef trip in a few days' time. An irresistible special, pay up front offer that she hadn't hesitated to take advantage of.

She delved into her bag and dug out the cash she had drawn out for a splurge at the night markets. It would be easier to withdraw some more after her appointment, rather than taking precious time now transferring money via her phone.

"I apologise for that. " Embarrassment rode Kellee's tone as she handed over the appropriate notes.

"It happens all the time. Don't stress about it." Ann handed back her change and began to pack the goods.

Kellee checked her watch again and grimaced. It was bang on appointment time.

"Don't worry about a bag, they will be fine in here." she stuffed her purchases into her backpack, zipping it up tight.

Looping her arms through the pack so it nestled comfortably on her back, she grabbed her purse off the counter and took off at a sprint, calling over her shoulder, "Thanks for your help. I'm running late, but I bet I will be back to try on those shoes."

Dashing through the mall, she weaved in and out of shoppers who were strolling along at a leisurely pace. She hated not being on time. "I am so sorry," was a genuine response as she bumped into the trolley being pushed by an elderly woman, taking a few more precious moments to see if she was ok. The woman glared, snapping a grumpy, " Look out!" as she clutched her handbag tighter into her body before moving on.

Kellee raced to the automatic shopping complex doors, hesitating when they didn't open fast enough. Once through, the outside humidity slapped at her face, making her gasp; as much as she loved the heat, the thick syrupy air of the tropics still caught her by surprise.

Scanning ahead as she ran, she took note of the row of buildings that housed her psychiatrist practice, ignoring the blast of a car horn and the curse of the driver as she darted across the road and into the car park, weaving the straightest path possible through the crowded rows of parked cars.

Damn. The thought almost stopped her in her tracks. She'd foolishly left her credit card behind on the shop counter. She was sure the sales assistant hadn't given it back to her when she had paid cash instead. Pausing for an instant, she made a split-second decision to continue and phone the shop once she was at her doctors. The number should be on the receipt; she was nearly there, and it would be faster than back tracking. As far as she remembered, the complex was open until nine on a Thursday night. She would have plenty of time.

Choice made, she picked up pace as she rounded the corner of the building, squinting as the low afternoon sun flashed in her eyes. *I'm only a few minutes late* she thought as she sprinted up the half dozen stairs that serviced the four shops in the block, taking them two at a time.

Kellee let out a startled scream as she collided into a solid wall of a man. Arms failing like a windmill, she grasped whatever her hands reached, pulling the man back down the steps on top of her as she hit the concrete.

The air whooshed out of her lungs and as she gasped for breath, her hand went protectively to the healed wound on her chest as a sharp pain dug into her back. Spluttering an apology, she tried to rise when the weight of the man moved off her. He struggled to his feet. She lifted her other hand for assistance, realising she was clutching something black and woollen. Confused, she looked up into cold dark eyes glowing with evil intent. Her mouth went dry and opened wide in horror as she realised she held a balaclava in her hand.

CHAPTER TWO

C ursing, he narrowly missed colliding with the woman as she brought his partner crashing to the ground. The bulk of Matt's physically fit frame turned feather light as he leapt sideways at the last minute. A fast foot shuffle kept his balance on the stairs, and he ended up jumping the last two, landing in a crouch as he hit the sidewalk.

There was no time to voice the profanities that sped around his head. With lightening precision, he processed how to rectify what had gone wrong. In his peripheral vision he saw his mate Jimmy still floundering, not sure of what to do, his weapon held loosely in his hand. Jules, behind the wheel of the getaway van, had kept her cool and was yelling for them to hurry as she revved the engine. His partner struggled to his feet, his face, explosive red as he raised the gun ready to fire, point-blank, at the woman. Matt knew he had to keep her alive. Curse her interference, but being in the wrong place at the wrong time didn't deserve death.

Dashing forward he knocked Ed's hand upwards. The shot went wild as he pushed the woman into his partner's arms, screaming, "Use her as a hostage man, fuckin' cops."

He wrenched the balaclava out of the woman's hand, shoving the woollen garment back on Ed's head before racing toward the revving vehicle. Yanking the door open with a violent tug, Matt grabbed the stumbling Jimmy and tossed him unceremoniously inside, before turning to raise his own gun at the cop car screeching towards them, lights flashing and siren blaring.

Matt watched Ed grapple with the woman. They were almost the same height and with regained spunk she was putting up a struggle. Maybe she would escape, but his boss overpowered her, altering his position a little and gaining better leverage.

Ed had the woman in a strangle hold around the neck, his gun squashed into her temple causing her skin to crinkle. His mouth close to her ear. Whatever he said made her stop struggling and comply with his stumbling movement towards the vehicle.

He dare not interfere, but he might have to do something if Ed didn't let the woman breathe soon. As they drew closer to the van door, Matt could see her face take on a frightful shade of red, and her ragged breath as she tried to draw in air, rang painfully in his ears.

Terror stricken eyes locked onto his. The hold Ed had on her loosened, and he breathed a sigh of relief as her body visibly relaxed, allowing her to take small shallow gasps. She kept staring at him as Ed struggled to pull her through the door.

The siren's wail grew louder as it approached, rising and falling in unison with the spikes of icy adrenaline racing through his body. He turned away from the woman in distress, focusing on the police as their car screeched to a halt in a blaze of flashing blue and red. Two officers leapt out yelling "FREEZE."

Matt held his gun steady and took aim.

The sun sinking behind him gave him an advantage as bright rays glared in the officer's eyes. With a controlled squeeze of his fingers, two shots rang out loud and sharp in the air, and the policemen fell to the ground.

"Go, go go." Matt grabbed the woman's legs and shoved her hard as he dove in, slamming the door with a solid bang. His preference would have been to drag her out and leave her on the sidewalk as an unwanted complication, but with most of her body already inside, he was left with no choice.

There were no seats. The hostage struggling for balance, sprawled on her hands and knees on the hard metal floor. Matt scooted across and wedged his back against the van walls like the others for stability. He looked through the opposite window as they drove off, ignoring her wide-eyed horror as she stared at the scene outside. One cop clutched at his knee as he rolled around in pain on the ground, but the other lay motionless, as a mass of dark red flowed like a flooding river into the gutter on the side of the road.

"Throw this on over your top," Matt tossed a patterned blue shirt at the woman. Her expression was blank, and face drained of blood. "Now...Move!"

He held open a bag, and they all threw in their balaclavas, gloves, and their top layer of clothing before donning an assortment of wigs, glasses or beards, giving them instant new appearances.

"Do it quick, or I'll do it for you." Ed snapped as he stripped off his own dark shirt, to reveal a plain white t-shirt underneath, almost losing his balance as they lurched sharply round a left-hand bend.

Jules' laugher floated into the back. It sounded wicked and shrill as if overdosed with adrenalin. "We stickin' to the plan?"

"All the way sweet cheeks." Ed grabbed the back of the driver's seat as she sped through the car park behind the row of shops.

Matt's mind was racing, trying hard to work out what in the hell they were going to do with the woman. What would he do if it came down to her, or his plan?

Jules yelled, "bump."

He hung on tighter, along with Ed and Jimmy as they braced themselves for the speed hump. They had practised this so many times it was like working on auto. The hostage unawares, became airborne for a split-second, before landing heavily on her backside, flaying her arms as they searched to find some form of support. She was thrown this way and that as the van lurched and turned, finally crashing into his legs.

"Shit, shit." He muttered as he grabbed and pulled her close to his chest so her back and buttocks were nestled against his.

"Bump."

This time Matt held her tight and protected against his frame. She bounced again, but not as hard or uncontrolled. He didn't have time for her to be anything but compliant. This plan, if executed to perfection and carried out swiftly and with precision, would cement his position deeper into the gang. Timing was everything. Moving up in the gang was everything. That's where the big boys played, and the money was made.

"What the...," she spluttered against his cheek as she tried to pull away.

He had grabbed her hair, twisting it on top of her head before shoving on a long wig that covered her auburn colouring. "Shut it," he ordered, shoving her arms into the chequered blue and white shirt he had tossed to her only seconds before.

"Grab her shoes" Matt snapped to Jimmy. He almost smiled, admiring her spunk as she kicked out at him with her long shapely legs, covered only partly by her denim shorts.

"Y... yo...you shot the cops!" Jimmy's stuttering voice grated in his ears.

"Pull it together man. If I hadn't, they would be hot on our tails, and this wouldn't be working. We're still on track."

Ed laughed with malice, and Matt felt the hostage shudder when he said, "They don't call him 'The Reaper' for nothing, best hit man we've got."

The van lurched again, to the right this time, and began to slow to a normal pace. "Fuck it Jimmy, take off her shoes and shove them in the bag with the rest of the stuff. You know the drill. Keep your cool man."

"30 seconds" the driver called. "You ready?"

"Right behind you sweet cheeks."

"Now."

Ed clambered into the front, putting himself close to Jules on the bench seat. As they crawled down the ramp and into the underground car park, with practised ease Jules and Ed deftly switched places. She ripped off the wig she had been wearing and with an arrogant flourish, tossed it over her shoulder into the back.

"Put it in the bag. Don't leave anything behind." She demanded, sounding full of her own importance.

Matt let it ride. This was the most crucial element of the plan he had conceived, and his smile widened as Ed dug into his pocket and tossed Jules a decent sized velvet pouch. It chinked softly as she caught it, kissed it, made sure the opening was pulled tight before she looped the string around round her neck and tucked the bundle into her bra beneath her shirt.

Jules picked up the leather jacket that lay on the floor by her feet, sliding her arms through the sleeves and zipping it up over her chest. She blew Ed a kiss. And smoothly slipped out as the van slowed to an almost stop as they reached the ramp's end.

The vehicle slid to a halt in the quietest part of the underground car park. Matt waited patiently while Ed jumped out; it was his job to secure the area. He kept an eye on the back of Ed's head, smiling with relief when he gave the thumbs up to signify he had heard Jules' unobtrusive scooter putt putting its way up the ramp and out into the late afternoon sun. He remained alert, waiting for the 'all clear' knock on the door, keeping a sharp eye on the hostage as he and Jimmy packed away the last of the discarded clothing, making sure nothing incriminating was left behind.

It was eerily quiet. All Matt heard was his own heart thumping as adrenalin raced around his body. The next few moments were crucial and a lot more dangerous now they had a hostage. The noise of a fist thumping on the metal, although expected, made them all jump. He pushed the woman forward so she was behind Jimmy as the door slid open, cursing as he realised the woman's apparent demure was only a ruse as she tensed her muscles and sprung forward. Jimmy sprawled out, hitting the ground with a loud thump.

Matt reacted on pure instinct, with reflexes born from years of training. He dragged her back into the van, brutally clamping a hand over her mouth effectively cutting off her attempt at a scream. *Shit, she was strong.* He wrapped his other arm around her waist and applied more pressure, restraining her in a steel like grip against his chest. He hissed a warning into her ear.

Just as suddenly, she stopped struggling, as if she understood it was useless. Matt released the pressure and pushed her towards the door, manoeuvring so he was able to step out first, one arm kept around her waist, sliding his hand so it was still on her mouth, but more from front on, squeezing her cheeks. He could feel her breath warm as it hit the palm of his hand and for a split-second, he wondered if she would be able to bite it.

He tightened his hold. Her eyes stared at his, and he had no time to evaluate what she saw or how she felt as a low whistle signalled it was safe to move. Giving her no time to utter a word, he lifted her out the van and bundled her into the back seat of the Commodore, jumping in beside her so she was sandwiched in between him and Ed.

The door slammed behind him and the welcome cool of the air-conditioner whirled into life as Jimmy started the engine and sedately reversed out of the parking bay. Dark tinted windows shielded them from the outside world. The woman cringed and tried to duck as Ed lifted his elbow as if to smash it into her face. Matt's arm shot across in front of her to halt the action.

"Later, boss" Matt's voice was firm but respectful. "We still have a couple of changes to go, and a bloodied face won't help, unless..." he left it open to interpretation, "you want to leave her in this car, knock her out. We will be long gone by the time she wakes, or I could bump her off, strangle instead of shoot. No noise that way."

Flashing red and blue lights automatically made them flinch, then breathe a collective sigh of relief as it went whizzing past, sirens blaring.

"No, she comes with us." Ed's mouth lifted in a sneer, tapping her none too gently on the chin with his elbow as a warning. "I have plans for her." The wicked grin spread. "And I don't care how fucked up her face is in the long run, but for now you're right," he conceded. "The next change will be busier, more people. If she tries to escape, if she plays up in any way, I will shoot to kill anyone around her. You got that sweet cheeks. One wrong move and the bloodbath will be on your head."

The woman was shaking. She flinched as Ed jabbed his elbow in her ribs a few times, making his point. Her clasped hands caught his attention. They were a little contradictory to the rest of her subdued body. One was clenched in a tight fist, the other resting on top as if to stop it from lashing out. After a slight glance in his direction, she relaxed her hands and clasped them on her lap, head bowed.

The car veered steadily up the ramp to the top parking level. It wasn't particularly large. Open aired with some permanent undercover areas off to the side. People were milling about at the movie theatre entrance. It was quite a hive of activity.

"Stop just up there Jimmy, slight change of plan" Ed barked the order as he adjusted his fake beard and yanked his Akubra hat further down over his eyes.

Jimmy pulled over to the curb where other cars were dropping off or picking up people and turned to the back, resting his arm on the back of the seat. "Boss?" he questioned.

"We won't walk through the shopping complex, too risky with the bitch." Ed nudged her with his shoulder." Drop me and the baggage close to the car exchange."

He leaned forward, giving Kellee a look and sneering at the fearful expression staring back. "What do you reckon? act like a cosy couple for ten minutes or so. Give the people enough time to move on and new people to arrive."

"Yeah, that should do it. After that time, I don't think anyone will link us with the car swap." Matt questioned, "What about the clothing bag?"

"Plan stays the same. Jimmy can go inside and drop it off at the Opp shop, you keep the backpack. We'll have to burn that later."

"It won't take you long, but we can't risk walking her through the complex as planned. By the time you are back, we should be ready for stage three." Matt lifted his eyebrows, "What do you want me to do boss?"

Ed let out a wicked laugh. "You can get out near the entrance and just hang around as if you are waiting for someone. If she cracks a scene, let it rip. Got that sweetheart?" He grabbed hold of Kellee's chin and forced her to turn and face him. "You fuck up and a lot of these people are gunna die."

He smirked at Matt. "Make sure you watch us closely. If she fucks it, you open fire." He laughed again. "Just like the cops; that was quick thinking. They would have been on us like blue ass flies before we could even think about getting away. Use your key, take the new car and pick us up. Jimmy, if there's gunfire when you come out, or we are not here, just walk away. Phone the house and we will arrange an alternative.

CHAPTER THREE

Fear began to take hold. Kellee fought to stay calm and let her police training take over. Submit and wait for an opportunity. Avoid eye contact, keep the body small and relaxed. Make movements slow, hands visible, but observe everything. Keep civilians safe at all costs. Put your own life on the line. She had already done that and nearly died. Could she do it again? Oh, hells, what a mess.

Ed squeezed her chin harder, making her flinch, "I said 'got that sweetheart'?" She nodded her head, stealing a quick glance into his black eyes, suppressing a shudder at the hatred they held. A blast of humid air indicated Matt had slipped out of the car. He gave her a cold stare as he walked in front of the vehicle before blending into the milling crowd, hands casually in his jacket pockets.

Kellee noticed they all wore thin tight leather gloves. Jules had tossed hers to Matt, who had assessed her long slender fingers, knowing in an instant they wouldn't fit, threw them in the bag with the rest of the discarded clothes. This was a highly organised gang, and it was quite ingenious staying in the immediate area of the crime scene, totally changing their appearances and vehicle so quickly. Less than ten minutes had ticked by to this point. She presumed Jules was in charge of whatever they had stolen. Why else would she leave the group, and how inconspicuous a lady on a scooter.

What a mess she found herself caught in. Whenever she shut her eyes, she visualised the policemen falling. Memories flooded her senses. Blood, metallic, sticking to the back of the throat, coated with sulphuric gun powder. She almost gagged. Although she remained outwardly compliant, sitting still, internally she struggled not to panic, scream, and lose control. It was a continuation of the nightmare which plagued her since being shot only months before.

With more space in the back, Kellee desperately wanted to put some distance between her and Ed, but before she retreated to the other side, he threw his arm around her and pulled her back towards him. Her skin crawled where his hand touched her shoulder and for the first time since being taken captive, she reached utter despair, knowing the fate of innocent people was in her hands. She had no doubt the one called Matt would open fire if she tried to make a run for it. Her mouth went dry, and she started to shake as shock began to set in. How in the hells was she going to get out of this?

When Ed manoeuvred her from the car she didn't resist as he kept a tight grip on her waist. He walked her sedately towards a dark green station wagon, and leaned casually against the side, tucking her in close to his hip.

"Now isn't this a treat, take a gander at all these happy fuckers, going about their business." Reaching inside his pocket he pulled out a packet of cigarettes, flipped the top open and offered one to her. "Care for a nail in ya coffin?"

Not trusting herself to talk, a shake of her head was all she managed.

"Be a good bitch and light me fag, this arm is rather busy." He gave her a tight squeeze.

Unsteady fingers took the lighter and on the fourth attempt the flame stayed on for longer than a flicker. Ed pulled her hand closer to the end of the cigarette, almost burning her skin as he took a deep drag. Arid aroma filled the air, making her cough as she turned her head away. He purposely blew the next puff of smoke directly into her face, smirking at her attempts not to breathe in the greyish white fumes.

A car pulled in a few spaces down from them and a young couple emerged, laughing and talking about the movie they were going to see. He dropped the butt and stubbed it out with his foot, instantly alert, although his body still portrayed a relaxed attitude. He hugged Kellee a bit closer and in a pleasant voice turned his face to her and asked, "So what time did Jeff say he would meet ..." he let his voice trail away as they walked past without even a glance in their direction, obviously totally in love, with eyes only for each other.

Mixed feelings of despair and relief flooded through her as the pair ambled away, hand in hand, towards the entrance of the mall. She studied Matt as he leaned with casual grace against a pole near the curb outside the doors. He ignored the couple and stared intently in her direction, seeming relaxed, hand in pocket, but she knew he wouldn't hesitate to shoot if she made a wrong move.

Swallowing deeply she kept up her internal pep talk, which was only marginally taking the edge off the turmoil churning inside. Panic rose as Ed swung her round into a possessive full-frontal embrace. "You are a sexy little thing, aint' ya." His stale smoky breath wafted into her face. He was mocking her. For one, she didn't fit into the sexy category and two, at six foot she was as tall as he was.

CHAPTER FOUR

Three ambulances pulled in front of the jewellers almost simultaneously, finding room amongst the half a dozen patrol cars that lit the scene in a red and blue light show. Paramedics ignored the adrenaline filled buzz, shouts, sirens around them and with calm attended to the two fallen officers and the shocked jewellery staff, one who nursed a bloodied nose.

The man who had been shot in the leg was already being assisted by a fellow police officer, who had bound the wound and was applying pressure to staunch the flow of blood. The other was not so fortunate. His chest injury left him covered in a mass of deep oozing red, and it was to him the emergency services turned first. Two of the paramedics took charge of the body, quickly and proficiently lifting him onto a fold out canvas stretcher, then covering him with a sheet, before placing him into the nearest ambulance.

As the doors banged shut behind them, the man on the stretcher threw off the sheet and jumped up. Stripping off the soiled shirt and ripping away the almost empty blood pack attached to his chest as he bellowed, "Where in the hell did that woman come from? Who is she? And how did she slip through our team? I want answers!" He tossed the discarded items into the bin and looked around the interior of the ambulance that looked anything but.

The high-tech office was alive with computers, video screens and two employees working at the consoles. He grumbled thanks for the clean shirt that was tossed in his direction and sat in the offered chair a little more in control. It had played havoc with his nerves, pretending to be dead when things had not gone to plan. "What have we got, is the mission still operational?"

"Operation Killjoy still seems to be a go, Steve....err..sir"

"Drop the formalities boys, let's work out what we are dealing with."

The front passenger side door opened and the man with the bloodied face slipped quietly into the seat, swinging it around to face the activity. Breathing through his mouth he growled. "Hey, pass me some tissues. I think that bastard brother of yours broke my nose."

"I am sure you have given him worse in the past, since you went through training together. I remember a lot of rough housing." Steve replied.

"You should get that checked by the paramedics." said one of the guys at the console. "That's a shite load of blood, so don't come anywhere near my equipment."

Steve rested his chin on his fist, concern for the undercover mission his brother was on evident in his voice, "We are wasting time. Go and get that nose seen to, no big deal but you are out. Find the medical team, go to the hospital. Come back to headquarters when you are done, and we'll fill you in on what's been happening."

"Right, what are we dealing with? What we got?" Steve's voice was all business. "Tell me about the woman."

"We got nothing on her so far sir. Right now, they are still on the roof top car park," he fiddled with a few more dials and switches. "The cameras up there are more directed at the door and the drop off zone close by. We can't see anything from them. But we realised it would be a dead spot."

"Damn it." Steve swore as he watched the scenario unfold from the surveillance footage, observed Matt save the woman's life, seeing for himself that there had been no alternative but to take her hostage. He just hoped in hell his brother could find a way to set her free.

CHAPTER FIVE

Matt's eyes never left the hostage as she and Ed leaned against the car. The tension in her body was obvious. And while he held compassion for her situation, his mind jumped this way and that. Where the hell had she sprung from? Could she be as innocent as she seemed? Her attempted escape almost worked. Perhaps he should have let her go. Each time he thought about it, he came up with the same answer. No. Any other way would have jeopardised the mission and probably got her killed in the process. In Ed's hand a knife became a lethal weapon. There was always at least one tucked somewhere on his body.

He had worked relentlessly to make it this far undercover. This was the break he needed to work his way towards those who were at the top. Now he had to find a way to protect her, at least until he could help her escape without risk to him, his mission or herself. He couldn't blow his cover. Too much depended on pulling off this plan successfully. They would have no scruples in killing her, using her to put him through the grill to force information out of him. A shudder ripped through him. He was a hard nut to crack, proven through his training, but no one could predict what would happen in real life, and he certainly didn't want to test it. He might be tough, but he sure didn't like pain. Either to himself or other people.

Empathy rose again as he watched Ed blow smoke into her face. The impressive way she handled herself gave him a grain of uncertainty. Maybe they were testing him? Muscles tensed, ready to spring into action as the couple strolled near them. Staring at the woman he prayed she did not make a move now. If he fired on the crowd, it would all be over. The switch hadn't been hard. Loading the guns with blanks proved simple, as it was one of his duties to maintain the weapons. After this car swap, the weapons would disappear. With hundreds more at their disposal, a few would not be missed.

Matt breathed a sigh of relief as the couple walked past without incident. He willed the hostage to hang on tight, wishing she knew that if it came down to the wire, he wouldn't hesitate to take action to keep her alive. The hostage turned her head and stared at him, and it felt like a punch to the gut. Her beauty astounded him. Even with that wig and ill-fitting clothes, he imagined her hazel eyes would hold a hidden depth. He remembered the firm athletic feel of her body tucked against him and a bolt of unwanted pleasure flicked to life. Damn it, he really didn't need this kind of complication.

Out of the corner of his eye, he recognised Jimmy as he stepped across the road with his long-legged, loose armed swagger, ambling towards Ed and the woman. Resisting the urge to scratch at his false beard, Matt looked at his watch. Time to start moving. Timing was important. The longer they lingered, the higher the chance of someone taking notice. Most of the time, people walked around in their own little world, and wouldn't remember strangers with just a fleeting glance. Stay too long in one spot and the likelihood of a second viewing could leave a bigger imprint on the subconscious brain.

It was a risk, but he had to try to leave a message. The secret signs his younger siblings used to do flashed in his mind. The code itself was very subtle and rather ingenious, thought up by his sister, no doubt. Jo might be the youngest of the family of six, and the only girl, but she sure had a smart head on her shoulders. It had taken him and his twin brother Patrick months of observation to work out the basics of the slight hand movements his younger siblings Jo and Kevin used. His heart constricted at the thought of Patrick. Dead. Wiped out by the gang he infiltrated under the disguise of a boating accident. One thing that had been disregarded was his connection to his brother. They weren't identical twins, but somehow the feeling he was still alive continued to haunt him. He was not in denial, as his family and the organisation thought. He intended to expose the bosses. Find out what had happened to Patrick and bring this gang down. Stomping on those seeds of doubt that had begun to grow of late, he refocused on the task at hand. More than a year of not hearing a word didn't mean he was wrong.

He altered position slightly, angling himself towards the camera installed at the mall's entrance. Staring straight at it and with obvious movements, spelt out his message, hoping someone at HQ would question his actions. Contact at the best of times tended to be sporadic, an important part of what made his undercover work so successful. Backup was always there when he needed them. Like setting up this heist, the opportunity to infiltrate deeper jumped at him out of nowhere. One phone call and Steven worked wonders getting it all working the way he wanted. Every person in the vicinity of the robbery belonged to their team. Except the woman. And therein lay his dilemma. What to do about her, who is she and what is her part in all this? All he knew was he did not want to abort. There were more than just a few lives at stake.

CHAPTER SIX

K ellee watched as Matt slid into the driver's seat and adjusted the rear mirror. Ed pulled her close to his side, his elbow a constant threat, digging into her waist. Jimmy, in the front, looked rather sullen after being told he was not driving this time, but the final leg. Something to do with not trusting him to keep her quiet.

As far as she understood, Jimmy had accomplished his set task and then some. He had brought back a few extra garments for her from the Red Cross shop. She clutched the plastic bag, almost like a possessive gift. Stupid girl, she mentally kicked herself. It's probably for disguising her looks. Niceness had nothing to do with it.

Throughout her life, she had always made a point of not judging people on first impressions, or how they looked. While living on the streets of Sydney as an abused and unloved child, people judged her as a criminal, which couldn't have been further from the truth. That fuelled her compulsion never to judge others that way. These thugs were different. She didn't care what trials in life had bought them to this point. She'd witnessed what they were capable of.

Out of the three of them, Jimmy seemed to be the weakest link. A yes man. She could take him out. Matt, she didn't know what to make of him. Strong and assessing. Not much escaped his watchful eye. Ed was a different story. She shuddered. He radiated a pure evil which made her skin crawl.

Matt turned his head towards the back and raised a questioning eyebrow at the boss, totally ignoring her. He gave a nonchalant smile and tilted his head in an affirmative manner. Shrugging, he turned back, catching her eyes in the rear vision mirror. She looked hastily away, not knowing what to think about him.

Ed snatched the bag from her lap, rummaged through it and removed a floppy pink hat and a matching blouse.

"Put them on," he growled as he took off another layer of his own clothing, slipping on some tinted glasses and a cap adorned with blonde tufts of hair, giving the appearance he supported a healthy sprout of fair hair instead of the dark-haired wig he discarded.

"Take off the other shirt first, put it in the bag." In a matter of seconds, the two in the front had totally transformed their appearances with well-practised ease. Matt stripped away his loose clothing and now wore a white t-shirt. The bulk of his muscles rippled across his back and down the tanned length of his tattooed arms as the fabric clung to his skin. Her temperature rose a notch. His disguise was completed with a light brown hair piece that hung down over his shoulders, a couple of pieces tied at the back in a small ponytail. She much preferred short military style haircuts on men, but Matt looked appealing whatever he put on.

"Quit gawkin' and put the clothes on," Ed snapped, "plenty of time to play with the man later, bitch."

She looked hastily away, face burning with embarrassment and mentally kicked herself. She was a professional, a trained officer of the law. How could she stupidly get distracted by the good looks of a killer. That brought things back into perspective.

"Tuck ya hair under the hat," Ed reinforced his authority with a sharp jab to her ribs. "Jimmy, you thought of everything," he said rummaging through the goods from the Opp shop. "Here - use these clips, pin up your hair."

While she was still in the process of buttoning up the shirt with fumbling fingers, Ed impatiently grabbed hold of her hair, twisting and clipping into place against her head, plonking the hat on top. Large and floppy it concealed her face and hair beautifully.

"Ya did alright mate." He settled the round sunglasses over her eyes.

Kellee appreciated the protection. For some strange reason they made her feel safe, locked into a private world. Keeping her head still, her eyes scanned the surroundings, taking in as much detail as possible. Each time she glanced at the rear vision mirror, she saw Matt's attention turn on her, and she wished he would concentrate more on driving.

This trip was taking longer. No one in the car spoke. Eventually the rush hour traffic eased, and the sun hid behind a low-lying cloud making colourful mosaic patterns in the cloud scattered sky above. With the dying day's artwork on her right, she figured they must be travelling south. The three-lane highway out of town still carried a reasonable amount of traffic, and she almost laughed hysterically as they got caught at every set of traffic lights.

Something she had noticed about this city as she drove around in her rental. The lights, synchronised, annoyed the heck out of her. A green wave appeared impossible. She shook her head, what a stupid thing to think about. Ed kept his arm around her waist and pulled her tight to him every time they stopped. Not that it really mattered. No one even glanced into their car, everyone busily wrapped up in their own journey. The desire to keep moving was clearly visible in their faces as they pulled up next to them.

With some, the thumping vibration of the heavy music beat filled the air. Other vehicles held couples or friends who laughed and joked. Many sat in concentrated silence, lost in their own thoughts as they made their way home. One thing they all had in common, they were oblivious to her plight and there was nothing she could do to make them aware.

Kellee decided to concentrate not just on taking in every detail, but targeted anything that might come in handy for location identification if she ever managed to escape. *Out of Java* on the left, and further down *Piccones*, the small shopping complex on the right as they went through an outer town suburb. She either hadn't seen or missed the signage for that.

Compared to the rambling sprawl of urban Sydney, Cairns was small. In less than fifteen minutes they had left suburbia and were speeding through the countryside. Well almost. She could see new development taking place that signalled future urban estates and extensive road works to improve the infrastructure. Sad in a way, when you saw the beauty in the rainforest and the intrusion of the big fast food chain store. She wondered, not for the first time, why man created everything the same. Destroying the beauty of the natural habitat that drew people to the area in the first place. She also found it amazing how the farming land encroached so close to the city. Sugar cane, huge paddocks, a gold mine for the next generation as the suburban sprawl ate away like a slow-moving cancer devouring the landscape.

Matt kept the car at a steady pace, keeping to the speed limit, obeying the road rules, and doing nothing to attract the attention of the busy world outside. The car followed the curves of the road, past the golf course, only to slow down for another set of red lights.

Walsh's Pyramid loomed large and impressive, cloaked in green, with rock formations exposed as the peak rose upwards. Kellee wanted to run up all 922 meters of that rock and forest clad mountain one day. She knew where they were. Gordonvale, home of the Great Pyramid Race, held every August. A high-powered challenge to be the first to the top and back again, people came from all over the world to compete and raise money for charity. She'd been keen to try, as part of getting back to full fitness. Maybe she would come back another year at the right time and compete.

Ed's body tightened, his hand digging deeper into her waist, and she guessed the next change must be imminent. From their conversation before, she gathered they had one more switch to go. The car slowed to under the speed limit as it crossed the high bridge that spanned the Mulgrave River, before turning sharp left to sweep around the curved road that wound down to a large public picnic area. A rough, bumpy dirt track led to a spot under the bridge, where half a dozen cars were parked haphazardly around a BBQ that was in full swing.

"How are we doing this boss?" Matt's deep voice, startlingly loud in the quiet car, made her jump and Ed automatically pulled her closer to him.

"We need to modify the plan. I wanna be on the way in five, ten at the most, instead of the original half hour we planned. You and the bitch travel in the back of the Ute instead of you and Jimmy. He can ride with one of the others and make his way back to the house."

Jimmy's scowl deepened, and he turned to glare blame at her, but he must have known better than to disagree, "Yea, sure boss."

Matt nodded, got out and opened the back-passenger door.

Ed growled. "No use trying any fancy escape, all these people are with us." He got out of the car, half dragging Kellee to the door, then released her as he got out addressing Matt. "She's all yours" He glared at her, but directed his orders to the man in front of him. "If you can't keep her quiet...break her neck...she's disposable."

Kellee forced herself to remain outwardly calm in spite of the venom in his words and the hatred in his eyes, wondering not for the first time, how in hell she was going to get herself out of this alive. Inside she was a mess, and she couldn't help but let out a sigh of relief when he moved away.

Matt held out his hand. She avoided it, giving him a half shove with her shoulder as she alighted without assistance. "You don't have to pretend to be a gentleman."

Before she realised what was happening, he spun her around, using her body to close the door and pinned her against the car.

He spoke in a soft, drawling voice, "like before, we can do this two ways..." leaving the statement open, he placed his hands either side of her shoulders, moving in so close a feather wouldn't fit between them.

Where Ed terrified her, Matt confused her. He was a contradiction. His actions not matching his words. She had the impression that, although he would stop her, he wouldn't hurt her. That's what she couldn't understand. He was tough and a killer. She had seen it. That horrified her, yet why did she grasp there was an element of safety when he was near. It didn't make sense.

She found his size rather exciting. The norm for her was looking down at a person, or at least eye to eye. In fact, to look into his eyes required her to tilt her head. He was solid and well above the six-foot mark. The white t-shirt highlighted the tan of his arms and the bulk of his muscles. His breath held a slight tang of coffee, and it fluttered warm against her cheek as he bent his head towards her.

"Do what I say, and everything will be ok."

Laughter erupted around them. Matt moved, pulling her with him. Before she could process what he was doing, he had effortlessly lifted her up onto the tail gate of a nearby Ute and climbed up to sit close, their legs dangling over the edge. Kellee looked this way and that. The whole scene was very innocent, and no one paid any attention to her.

The group Matt had swung their car amongst were socialising in what appeared to be a family barbeque. They chatted happily. Some kids were down by the river playing, parents calling out to them to be careful, and everything looked happy and normal to the outside world. From what she could see, there were about ten adults and half a dozen children.

Soft music played over the radio, which was constantly smothered by the traffic speeding across the massive bridge high above them. Tantalising aromas rose from the cooking meat, activating the saliva in her mouth. Involuntary, she licked her lips as her stomach let out a rather loud rumble.

Matt laughed. "Throw us up a couple of snags mate."

"Here catch." The man pretended to take Matt literally and went to throw them, before handing them to someone close to him to pass them over. He laughed again, taking the paper plate and offering one to her as he called out his thanks.

Kellee looked at the greasy sausage and onions wrapped in bread, swimming in tomato sauce and almost gagged. She shook her head and looked away. Maybe the aroma appealed, but in no way was it edible. Her stomach lurched at the thought.

His tongue cleaned a morsel from the side of his mouth. "You should have some, really tasty, pure pork sausages, not fatty or greasy at all."

Kellee kept her head turned away "I don't want any, thank you". She groaned inwardly, why had she been polite? Get a grip she scolded, as safe as he might seem she was still a hostage, and she realised he had no intention of letting her get away. He is a cold-blooded murderer, she reminded herself. A criminal.

Further away from the BBQ, a caravan was parked near the amenity block and a couple of camper vans had found sheltered havens beneath the huge shady trees. "No help from there," she thought. The campers were facing towards the rainforest for privacy, well away from the hustle and bustle of the road and bridge. She couldn't see anyone near the van at all.

The sound of a siren getting louder set the hairs on the back of her neck prickling. The nearby group of people didn't stop their festivities, but she observed slight changes in their body posture and a sudden alertness in their attitude. Although looking relaxed, Matt was attuned to her every movement, as she instinctively tightened, ready to spring away, and he threw his arm around her and pulled her closer to him in warning. The wailing echoed around them, then sped away into the distance. Everyone visibly relaxed. Hands came out of pockets and a few who had moved closer to the open windows of their cars stepped away and resumed the festivities.

Matt and Ed locked eyes as the siren approached. Even though the moment passed, she still experienced the tenseness in his muscles, his arm now draped casually over her shoulder. She turned her attention back to Ed and caught him giving a small sharp nod. Her insides turned cold as he and another fellow sauntered towards them.

Before she had any inkling of what was about to happen, Matt drew his legs up on the tailgate and pushed back towards the middle of the Ute tray. Leaving her no time to react, he dragged her with him, twisting sharply, so they were both laying on their sides on the Ute's rubber matting. He tucked her back in close to his body, stifling her yelp of surprise with a solid hand over her mouth.

Daylight turned into a musky darkness as Ed quickly tugged the canvas covering over the top of the tray, then looping it into place with the fixed tie stays on the side. Matt threw his leg over her lower body when she started to struggle, effectively pinning her against him. Her heart started pounding and her breathing became erratic, shallow gasps of panic against the palm of his hand.

"Shhh shhh shhh" he whispered, releasing a little pressure from her mouth, allowing her to breathe easier. "It's a short trip to the house. We can't be seen, that's all. The neighbours are used to the Ute arriving home this time of day, with Ed at the wheel."

The smell of the greasy food on his hands, mixed with the fetid air slammed her panicking back into the past. She refused to go there, letting the tickle of his breath near her ear anchor her in the present. She was not in the terrifying dark chest her mother had locked her into when the men came calling.

"Shhh shhh. Everything is going to be ok." She let his soft words help her quell the panic. Her breathing slowed and the stale humid air thick with sweat and exhaust kept her in this reality. Kellee appreciated his gentle whispers for what they were, as it helped her control her fear. She pushed thoughts of being confined away, then worked at keeping the anxiety at bay. She had learned long ago how to wrap fear in ice and store it away.

It had taken her by surprise, that's all. She continued to concentrate on her breathing, getting it under control, fighting off the urge to claw her way to fresh air. The pressure of his arm lightened as he adjusted his position. Her half-twisted hat was removed, and he undid the clips, moving his hands through her hair. It shouldn't have affected her, but waves of pleasure passed through her body. She willed herself to relax even more, allowing his soothing whispers to calm her. Slowly he released the hand covering her mouth, continuing with gentle strokes and crooning noises.

Confusion flooded her mind as strange sensations inundated her body. It was as though he understood her claustrophobia and was helping her overcome it. Why would he do that? She was still jammed tight against his body, but the forceful pressure subsided as he continued to tease her hair, letting it fall playfully through his fingers, the strands dropping back at intervals against her cheek. He hugged her closer, soft and comforting.

Snug in a woven protective spell, her breathing ceased its erratic gasping; her heartbeat stopped thundering in her ears. Kellee hadn't realised how much she had relaxed into the cocoon of his warmth.

She suddenly froze. The air whooshed out of her lungs. That was definitely not a spanner pressing against her butt. She jerked away, but the jostling Ute making its way over the bumpy dirt road made it even more pronounced as he instinctively pulled her tight. The arcs of pleasure from his hand running through her hair was nothing compared to the fire that flared at this contact. His groan, deeply primitive, and all masculine quivered through her body.

This would not do at all. Taking him by surprise, she violently rolled away. He reacted remarkably fast, grabbing her hand before she was all the way over on her back, holding on tight. She thought he would use his strength to pull her back, but he cursed softly before muttering something about agreeing, and she was relieved when he let the gap between them stay.

Her brain searched for options. She wasn't stupid. The longer she was captive, the less prospect there was of remaining alive. And for the first time since being shot, it occurred to her, she actually enjoyed being alive. She had simply been going through the motions during the last few months and she realised Matt offered the best chance of survival, if only she could tap into the softer side she hoped he had.

"If you let me escape, I will put in a good word for you." There was no response as the vehicle rattled and jolted. "I promise I will do everything I can, everything within my power. I'll tell them how you helped me, how you saved my life." She didn't have to add a pleading element, it radiated through her voice.

Just as she was going to try again, he answered. "Not interested darlin'." The gruff finality in his tone sank her spirit. "Do as you're told, and everything will be ok."

Darkness devoured the silence as stale humid air turned as thick as syrup. She concentrated on a pin prick of light in the far corner where the stitching had stretched. It was only minuscule, but it represented the outside world, a fresh breeze and freedom. She figured the Ute must be back on the highway, because the ride was now a lot smoother, and she mentally counted as they slowed for what was probably another red light.

They must be going back the way they had come. Coming off the bumpy track they had turned sharp right, back onto the main road instead of left like she had expected if they were continuing south. She listened to the outside sounds, visualising what she remembered of the scenery. A train clickity clacking off to the right confirmed the retracing of their steps. She had seen those tracks to the left when they had fled the city.

Of course, she didn't really know if they had caught every traffic light, but the time frame felt like they had travelled back into town. She heard the indicator click and then felt the sharp swing left, followed by a couple of quick left - right turns. She found herself sliding down the Ute a little as the tray tilted. It was obviously going up a steep hill.

A wave of panic tried to take hold, and she fought the urge to claw at the thick canvas. Maybe her perception was wrong, and they were somewhere in the rainforest, and they were going to kill her and dump her body. She quickly regained self-control and made a pledge to never stop trying to escape. Reinforcing it with the promise to fight and put-up resistance at every opportunity. She was a policewoman; she had sworn to protect the weak and uphold the law.

Finally, calmness settled over her, and she decided to give it one more try, this time making a personal connection with her captor. Letting out a steadying breath, she spoke clearly, adding a soft sadness, making every word count.

"Kellee, my name is Kellee. I am twenty-six years old, and I am frightened. It is highly possible Ed is going to kill me, and I think you know that. Please let me go." Her words were whispered, not having to act the fear and vulnerability pounding through her veins. She desperately needed his help.

He tensed beside her, drew in a breath as if to speak, then let it out in a long-drawn-out puff. Moments passed as the Ute turned this way and that. Her sense of direction totally lost; from the angle they were at they must be climbing a hillside. She was about to plead again, when he began to rub small soft circles on the back of her hand with his thumb. If he intended it to be calming, or reassuring, it was anything but.

She took a deep breath, catching a whiff of his musky scent, which she allowed to dominate her senses. It was preferable to the oil and exhaust that permeate the thick humid air trapped under the tarp with them.

This was no worse than being locked in the trunk. Eventually the lid would be opened, and she could crawl away into a quiet corner. Except this time, she didn't know what to expect. Judging by the

way the vehicle slowed, turned, and crawled to a halt, she figured
they had arrived.

CHAPTER SEVEN

Activity in the operations room at MICO headquarters paused momentarily as Stephen strode in demanding loudly, "Someone talk to me, tell me what I want to hear." He stopped in front of the huge map on a high-tech computer screen. "Any info on the woman? What's happening with Operation Killjoy?" He hesitated a moment before continuing, "and any action from Matthew?"

"No leads as yet sir." The newest console operative flinched slightly, but stood firm against the aggressive tone of his voice. "I am still running what information we have about her through the database. We don't have much to go on, but there is a team on the scene trying to trace her steps to gather more Intel." She glanced up at her boss, "Someone is on their way with the footage from the cinema car park. In fact he should be here any minute."

"Ok, back to work. I want answers." He enforced the snappy tone with a dismissive wave of his hand. The half a dozen technicians and agents returned to their tasks with obvious relief. Stephen reigned in his frustration. In full bellow he was formidable, not quite as ferocious as his father, Sir Brennan, but close. Like father, like son.

The click of keyboards and the rustle of papers being shuffled blended with the drone of the air-conditioner overhead. A hushed silence fell as each member attended to their allotted task.

"Matthew's emergency GPS tracker remains silent sir." One of the support team offered. "That's a good start," he added unnecessarily, as they all knew about the built-in alarm that would automatically trigger if his heart stopped beating. They all appreciated the danger of Matthew's mission; they had been his backup and only contact for over a year as he infiltrated deeper into the underworld gang. Even though Stephen would not show any emotion in the work zone, Matthew was his brother. Five years younger, and at the age of twenty-seven he was headstrong, courageous and one hell of an undercover agent.

The phone rang, drawing everyone's attention. A team member picked it up and called out, "I am putting Tim on speaker sir."

"We are certain the woman's name is Kellee McGlover," the voice was slightly tinny over the speaker, but came across strong and self-assured. "Twenty-six years of age. We've obtained her home address in Sydney and where she is staying in Cairns. The psychiatrist next to the Jewellers, when interviewed by the local constable, said she had an appointment with him at the time of the robbery. The Description fits. Looks like the wrong time, and wrong place for her. According to the shrink, she made the appointment out of hours. He agreed as he saw it as important for her recovery. We checked him out before the operation. Usually he is shut at that time."

A drawn-out silence filled the room as everyone stared at the screen as her standard ID photo from the Police Force appeared. The console operative tapped the button again, and another picture flashed up. Taken a few years ago, but it was undeniably her on the police academy graduation day. Radiantly happy and carefree, she was smiling broadly, showing slightly crooked teeth, the sun glinting in her hair and her eyes. Arms high...tossing her hat into the air. Obviously, proud and in great spirits at her achievement.

Stephen spoke to the group. "Find out all you can. Why the heck was she seeing a shrink? We need to understand what sort of person we are dealing with...Now!" Everyone scattered to their workstations.

He turned towards the phone speaker "Keep it on the down low Tim. She's a cop and that puts her in a whole heap of trouble if she is found out."

"Right oh, we are at the bank checking her visa card transactions. We should be able to trace her steps, then I'll head over and check out her hotel room."

"Do that discreetly. Dust for prints, report back here with what you find."

"Yep. Oh, and boss, everything else went as planned. Ten mil in diamonds. Wow what a heist. The jewellery manager is running on overdrive. It's all in Matt's hands now. Over and out."

The buzz as the phone disconnected was loud in the busy room. Stephen stood contemplating how in the hell they could rescue this woman without jeopardising the mission which had been nearly a year in the making and wondering if Matthew was ok. How in the heck could he keep her safe, if at all? His nose twitched. Exactly what he needed. Coffee. He turned his head toward the delicious aroma and smiled thanks as he wrapped his hands around a mug of steaming pleasure.

"Sir..."

The woman who passed him the coffee had been the one who put up Kellee's picture. She pointed at the screen. He acknowledged her with a tilt of his head.

"I think you need to see this. I thought her name was familiar, so I ran a quick search." She flicked through a series of photos showing dead bodies and police reports.

Stephen took a mouthful of the much-needed brew and called the rest of the group over. Licking the froth off his lips, he acknowledged, this is one nice cup of coffee.

"Ahhum." Amy captured their attention, "I remember the story well. The internal investigation report said she was helping a young teenage girl break away from her drug dealing pimp, a boy in his mid-teens. Apparently, she called for backup, and when they arrived on the scene, the boy and the girl were dead. Kellee was lying in a pool of blood with gunshot wounds to her back. Later the ballistics report led to the hypothesis that the boy injured the young girl, then Kellee, trying to protect her, shot the boy. She was ambushed by her partner, who put four shots in her back. He killed the girl and came back to finish off Kellee, who, I might add, had lost a heck of a lot of blood by then. She is lucky to be alive. It was looking grim for a while.

"Holy shit!" exclaimed Stephen "When did all this happen?"

"About five months ago sir.'

"Great recall Amy." He was impressed that the newest member to the team had not needed to refer to the extensive technical report on the computer screen and had verbally broken the information down into the basic facts they needed to deal with. "Quite a memory you've got there. How long have you been with us?" He drained the last of the coffee, stared at the empty cup wistfully before putting it on the nearest desk.

"Almost eleven months, sir. I came in not long after Operation Killjoy was being activated."

Everyone gathered around Amy, watching the usually quiet woman's animated talk rather than the screen. Her shoulder-length, straight blonde hair bobbed enthusiastically as her hands spoke along with her words.

Amy's smile broadened at the praise. "I did speed read it before I put it up. To refresh my mind. The worst part is," her expression took on a concerned look, "she'd had a disagreement with her partner at the Station and he refused to go with her, saying that it was a waste of time. She wasn't authorised to go alone, but she had a reputation for being a bit of a hot head and went anyway. Apparently, she did call for backup and when it arrived, they found her partner standing above her, his gun aimed at her head. The backup took him out, but not before he got off a shot. Luckily for her it only grazed the side of her head.

"Good god, thanks Amy. Not an easy thing to come back from." Stephen puffed up his cheeks and blew the air noisily out of his lips." At least now we have an idea whom we are dealing with." He looked away, "Bert you..."

"Err... Excuse me sir..."

"You mean there's more?" His eyebrows raised in question as he turned back.He watched in fascination as her face flushed a deep shade of red over skin which, in his opinion, didn't see anywhere near enough sunshine. Hesitating, she sucked in her bottom lip before shrugging her shoulders and confessed with bright blue eyes that sparkled with guilty mischief.

"When it transpired, sir, the case piqued my interest, and I Facebook stalked her for a while. Her status said her relationship was 'complicated' which, after everything that happened, I found intriguing." She ran a hand quickly through her hair in an uneasy gesture, "so I...err...I... hacked into her account and discovered that she and her partner were lovers. They had a private group. I don't think anyone at the station knew."

"You hacked into her Facebook page?" Bert asked, eyebrows raised. "Should I be concerned?"

Amy smiled, tilting her head and pouting her lips slightly, "You're not that interesting Bert. She had the weakest password. So it was extremely easy. Besides, there wasn't much there, she only had a handful of followers, all which were work colleagues. Sad really, you can tell a lot about a person from Facebook; no family contacts, no friends, nothing, except some volunteer job notifications."

"Anything else?"

"Err...No sir."

"You sure now?

"Yes sir."

He stared at her for a moment. "Right, back to it team. I want to see what else we can dig up, and someone chase up what's happened to that footage from the car park."

They scurried back to their workstations and Stephen chuckled as he heard Bert muttering under his breath about changing his password.

"Amy, send a copy of the report to my iPad and get her Captain on the phone."

"Yes sir, and I have already sent it to you sir."

"Good job Amy. Welcome to the team, and it's Boss or Stephen. *Sir* sounds like my father."

"Thank you, Sir...err Boss."

There was not much to be done now they had compiled all the information they had about Kellee and her past. Hopefully, his call to Kellee's Police Captain would reveal more. He sat down at his desk "Ok everyone. Keep digging and remember, I want status updates on all our operatives, not just this case. As we know, things went haywire with the assignment Jo and Kevin were working on. We are fortunate it ended successfully, but we still need to find the cause of where things went wrong."

He took the phone from Amy with a nod of thanks, opened his iPad and pulled up the report. "Good morning Captain Russell..."

The elevator pinged as he put down the phone. He smiled with pride as his younger sister walked into the room. She was scheduled to come in for a debriefing after her first assignment had nearly ended in catastrophe, however, he hadn't expected her this soon. She'd been sent to Outpatients E & A. Other than some cuts and bruises, which looked like they were healing already, she appeared happier and healthier than he had ever seen her before. Maybe it had something to do with the man standing beside her. She glanced at him and smiled as she spoke.

"Axel this is my brother Stephen."

Her voice, usually on the tough side, held a note of softness that had him raising his eyebrows. Their father had said Jo trusted this man with her life, and he hadn't proved them wrong. Stephen liked the strength of the man when their two hands grasped. Not too strong, but firm enough to hold his own. He could tell there was a connection between them by the way she stood close to his side.

"Glad you both pulled through ok. You had us worried for a while. How's Kevin?" His team had set up an emergency extraction and all had ended well, except for a few loose ends they were still tying up. When the mission started to go wrong, the whole family had been on a razor's edge. Nothing had ever been the same since their brother Patrick had been murdered. He clenched his teeth and swallowed the pain of remembrance.

"Kev's doing fine. They are not sure of the prognosis with his knee yet. We left him chatting up the nurses as they were taking him for scans."

"Are you ok?" Jo seemed bright and chirpy, considering all she had been through. There was no time for further assessment. Amy called out that the video they were waiting for had been uploaded.

"Ok, gather round, concentrate on every little detail, the more eyes on this the better."

The screen sprang to life. It didn't really show a great deal. Mounted and stationary, the camera had done what it was supposed to do: capture people going in and out of the doors. Off to one side stood a disguised Matthew in a relaxed slouch against the pole. There was no mistaking who he was. Like his brother, he was tall, muscular, and self-assured.

"Is there any footage of the woman?"

"Err...No sir, the closest shot we found is of the back of the car and you can only catch a glimpse of her inside. Let me rewind...right there. Not much we can do.

It's poor quality. We didn't set anything up ourselves as we didn't think we would need it."

They watched the clip again. Matthew was staring intently at the camera.

Jo burst out laughing, asking him to stop the feed.

She looked up at Axel, a contagious grin on her face, then turned to Stephen," I do believe he is giving us a message - with his hands."

"Play it again," Stephen ordered, a frown deep on his brow. "What? These small random hand movements?"

Jo moved next to the screen for a better look. "Well, you are nine years older than me. Whilst you and Robert Jr were out chasing girls, Kevin and I invented a secret code. We used it for years. Obviously, Matthew picked up on it, being closer in age to us."

Stephen glanced at his sister. It saddened him a little that she had singled out Matthew and had not referred to his twin. The boys were inseparable throughout their younger years. Just because Patrick was dead didn't mean he never existed. He pushed the thought aside. He would talk to her about it during the debriefing. Until the beginning of her mission, Jo thought Patrick had been killed in an accident. Perhaps she was having trouble coming to terms with the fact he had died in the line of duty. Murdered. He squashed his own anger and sadness. He needed to talk to someone. Each day it seemed harder to keep his emotions at bay. Gathering his inner strength, he pushed those thoughts and feelings away. Time to concentrate on present problems.

"Alright, rewind. What is he saying?"

Jo asked for it to be rewound a couple of times before she said. "Not much, and he is certainly not being discrete, but I guess that's the idea. Basically, he's signing, 'stay plan, all ok.''

"Are you certain?"

"Pretty sure. He is using a basic form. Kevin and I used more intricate signs. Any chance of getting the clip over to him? It would be interesting to see if he comes up with the same message. Just as a double check."

"Good idea." He addressed his team. "Someone send that footage to Kevin and stay on plan. If he needs it, Matt will turn on his tracker. Keep alert."

"Any news about Kellee from her chief" asked Amy.

"She has only been out of hospital for a couple of months. She's better, but not fully recovered. The bullets did a lot of internal damage but missed her major organs. She is up in Cairns on recuperative leave and seeing a shrink to get her life back on track. To sum it up, her Captain reluctantly concedes she is like a sweaty stick of dynamite. Who knows what state her head is in now, after being held at gun point and witnessing Matthew shooting cops. It could send her over the edge. We have someone questioning her doctor for an opinion. He should understand her mental health the best."

"So can we trust Matthew to do what's right for her?"

They all stared at Amy in disbelief.

"Well," she threw her hands up in defence. "I have never met him. To me he is only an agent I have been following in the field. Most of what I know about him is on paper, but that does not tell me everything. His twin brother died a year ago. Sorry Stephen, Jo. You have my condolences and I mean no disrespect, but could he be unstable about Patrick? From all reports, he kept working, getting deeper into the gang. That doesn't allow time for grieving."

Stephen studied Amy. She had been the quietest employee up until now. He didn't want to admit it, but her point was valid. Matthew had refused to come in from the undercover assignment. He suspected some of Matt's grief was being worked out as he gained his reputation as The Reaper. The team had been kept busy with extractions and cover-ups. And when Jo and Kevin had been in danger, he had held back and stayed on standby. The gangs were all intertwined. Keeping someone on the inside would have been beneficial if the rescue had gone wrong.

"If anyone can get her out of this alive, I believe it's Matthew." It was Axel who spoke. "I am speaking from experience. MICO backs each other one hundred percent. They lay their lives on the line to protect innocent parties. As soon as Matthew gets an opportunity, he will take it. I have faith in him. I don't even know him, but I have trust in the family bond and the people they work with. We are his back up, and he needs our loyalty."

Stephen looked around the room. "Anyone else have anything to say. Now is the time, so we can move to the job at hand. Matthew might be my brother, but he is still a team member undercover, and he relies on us to watch his back."

"Not me. Trained with both Patrick and Matthew. He's her best shot."

"He can count on me. Bert gave Amy a pointed look. "I know he will do what's best for the hostage."

"Ok I'm sorry. I understand. I think it is better to be honest though and put things out in the open. As I said, no disrespect. It is good to know he is a man we can rely on."

Stephen turned, "Apology accepted. "Back to work everyone. I want to get this debriefing done. Axel, I believe you have some information about Ed... aka Thumper."

As they walked towards his desk, he called to Amy. "Any chance of another coffee."

Amy rolled her eyes at him. "Axel, Jo, you want a cup?"

"I'll give you a hand," said Jo grinning mischievously behind his back. "I know just how Stephen likes it."

Amy chuckled, "Oh, I have that area covered already, but thanks, I would appreciate the company."

CHAPTER EIGHT

K ellee breathed deep and controlled. She needed to slow her racing heart. Rushing blood thundered in her ears and perspiration trickled across her face, dripping down over the side of her cheeks. She lay on a hot metal sheet of filth, sweat and dread.

The Ute stayed stationary for some time before the engine was switched off. A strange noise followed by a slow, weird falling sensation, caused her to shriek and clutch tighter to Matt's hand. His whispered, *it's ok* a moment before they dropped did nothing tostop her rising fear and panic. She couldn't breathe. She wanted to scream. She wanted out.

The doors of the vehicle slamming shut added to the icy cold spikes shooting through her body. The cover of her prison pealed back, and shards of intense fluorescent lighting blinded her. She blinked rapidly, and once her eyes had adjusted, she wished for the protective veil of darkness again.

Matt kept a firm grip on her hand but allowed her to struggle to a sitting position. Ed scowled, signalling for them to stay put.

"Tie her up. Tight. So, she can't move."

Flinching as the bundle Ed threw almost hit her in the face, Kellee turned her head aside, looking into the eyes of the man next to her as he reached out and caught the corded bundle one handed. She considered herself reasonably proficient at reading people, especially through eye contact. Eyes told stories: truths and lies and fears. His espresso brown pools held her mesmerised. Drawn into those depths of the smooth liquid, she searched for some form of emotion, a spark to show he cared. All he gave back was an empty stare.

Nothing.

She couldn't read a single thing, neither hatred, compassion, nor hope. The dark orbs were expressionless, and sent a shiver of dread through her body. She had expected to see at least a hint of sympathy, because he had made her feel so safe and secure with his whispered words of comfort. Now suspicion crept in. Had he pretended to be kind just to keep her quiet?

Abruptly he broke eye contact and she mentally cursed herself for leaving her emotions so open and vulnerable. She fought to think straight. Vowing to be less transparent, she continued to stare at him with what she hoped was an expression which mirrored his emptiness.

He grabbed her other hand and bound her wrists. She winced as the abrasive fibres of the binding, as well as the callousness of his actions, bit into her skin. Denting her resolve. A traitorous tear spilling from one eye as he yanked her arms over her head, securing the rope to a metal bar behind her. For a moment he hesitated, hand in mid-air close to her cheek. She saw his jaw muscle move as it tightened in determination, his face stony as he tied the last knot.

After giving the ropes a final tug, checking on tightness, he squatted down beside her, leaning so close his breath tickled her cheek. He needed to clean his teeth; the stale odour of hot dog mixed with the day's adrenalin smelt quite unpleasant. It vanished as his silky words rippled through her body.

"Stay put darlin'. "His hand under her chin made the contact warm and sensual as he rubbed his thumb over where the tears moistened her skin. The action clashed with the situation she found herself in. She went to turn her head away, but he stopped her gently but firmly.

Espresso eyes flashed briefly, alight with mischief and he gave her a quirky, lopsided grin, causing her heart to leap. It completely altered the coldness of his expression, giving him an attractive, cheeky look. It took her breath away. She clenched her jaw and escaped behind closed eyes.

His, *I'll be back.* whilst the cliché made her grimace, held a promise she wanted to ignore. The Ute rocked as he jumped to the ground, causing her eyes to snap open. Craning her neck, she followed his progress as he disappeared out of sight.

His footsteps slowed to a stop. She heard a soft whirring noise, a small clunk, and a whoosh, then silence. She thought she recognised the sound, but couldn't quite identify it. One thing she did know, she had been left by herself.

She began tugging on her bindings, but they were tight and efficient. Nevertheless, she tried until her skin burned with pain and the energy drained from her body. Twisting sideways, attempting to manoeuvre into a crouch, only partially worked. She couldn't turn far enough to gain a position she could hold for any length of time. Long legs in this situation were a curse rather than a blessing.

Kellee forced herself to relax and take in her surroundings, trying her best to ignore the cold solid steel of the frame as it dug into her back, and the uncomfortable hard rubber matting under her backside. Instead, she concentrated on regaining her breath and strength.

Turning her head to the left, all she could see was a concrete wall. A metal ladder, its rungs glistening in the bright light, led all the way up to the ceiling. Up there must have been where they came from. She remembered feeling the going down sensation, but they'd been stationary ever since.

She moved her head to the right, her eyes opening wide in shock. Box upon box of weapons and ammunition, stacked in orderly fashion, were lining the walls. Not only guns. Each container sported a label with thick bold lettering identifying what they contained and stretched as far as she was able to see, reaching almost as high as the ceiling. Holy hell, a solid, underground bunker full of drugs and weapons. What had she landed herself into. The events of the day were suddenly too much, and her brain overloaded.

The monotonous drone of the air-conditioner and the ticking of a distant clock faded against the ringing in her ears. Her defences were down, the hard-won achievements with the psychiatrist over the last month fled before the on rush of remembrance. She relived the terror of a betrayal running so deep, it had made her lose confidence in both herself as a woman, and in her job.

∞

She had worked with her partner for over three years. They had both held the same morals and took a stand to make things better for the troubled teenage youth, the street kids. Young souls, some not yet in their teens, selling narcotics and prostituting themselves to stay alive. Trapped in gangs, never allowed to forge ahead in life.

Almost a mirror of her own upbringing; parents so dependent on drugs they barely remembered she existed. Independent by an early age, Kellee considered herself extremely fortunate. She'd been pressured into accepting help to leave a place she never wanted to be in. From her own experience, she knew, the first step was the desire for a better life. Having faith, accepting the assistance offered. The rest would follow.

She'd known a girl like that, Sweet Elsie. She'd made the first move with her cry for help. Kellee got the call late one night. Elsie's plea wrenched at her heart. Going against her Department's and partner's advice, she went after the girl by herself, with the intention of taking her into her own home. Anything to help get her off the streets.

Breaking rules was nothing new to Kellee. Her nickname of 'Rebs', short for Rebel, had stuck to her like glue throughout basic training and into the Force. Going against the Captain's orders was as natural as getting dressed. To be fair, of late she had tried to conform more. Her boss's reprimands were becoming tougher, and his recent threat of suspension had her toeing the line, as she had no wish to lose her job. But not the night Elsie finally reached out.

The dimly lit alley had smelt like bad choices. Rats scurried, hiding behind bloated dumpsters, where discarded food from nearby restaurants provided, not only the rodents, but the homeless, with food to keep them alive. A voice surrounded by darkness, called out in a desperate rasp for a cigarette. Kellee had ignored him, his profanities echoing the narrow span of the towering walls.

She'd kept her footsteps light and her body alert, as she avoided the rank garbage strewn across the uneven stone, continuing her search for Elsie. She hadn't worn her uniform, something else the Department hadn't understood. Street clothes gave her an approachable edge, made her look less official. Her near six-foot frame and confidant manner, along with her badge and weapon tucked into the back of her jeans, was all she needed.

Little had she known the events of that night would change her life forever.

She'd found a terrified Elsie, hidden deep in the twisting maze of the back streets. A boy, hardly old enough to be out at night, was holding her at gun point, ordering her to go back to work to make more money for him and his father.

Kellee had held up her identification, announcing herself as a police officer and commanding the youth to drop his weapon. Reluctant to shoot at a young kid, Kellee hesitated a fraction too long,

The boy fired.

The girl screamed, clutching at her side as she staggered and fell. The barrel raised again, this time straight at her. Instinct kicked in, Kellee fired and the look of shock on the kid's face imprinted in her mind as the impact of her bullet pushed him backwards before he crumpled to the ground, eyes vacant and lifeless.

Kellee couldn't remember hearing the shots that thumped with precision into her back. It felt like she was being shoved repeatedly. Then she stumbled forward. Her body no longer responding to her commands. The world was tilting on its side, and it took a moment for her to realise she had fallen, and the blood that was adding to the stains on the grimy stone was hers.

She heard feet rushing past her towards the girl who was trying ineffectively to rise and flee. Kellee tried to call out, but no sound made it through her lips. A shot rang out and the girl's head exploded into an unrecognisable mess.

The shooter's cry of anguish was heart wrenching as he bent and nursed the dead boy, crying *my boy, my son*.

Through a sea of agony, Kellee registered the moment the father turned his attention towards her and knew without a doubt she was going to die. Bloodied shoes stepped towards her with deadly intention. Gun held loosely in his hand, he kicked her over onto her back and his face swam into focus. An almost silent scream, a primitive guttural sound emerged, as shock and treachery drained all hope from her body.

Anger was plastered over his familiar features. Her trusted partner. Her friend. Her lover. A shock adrenaline rush gave her a lucid moment. She realised now why the Department was always one step behind. Why he'd refused to come to this alley tonight. He was the corruption link they had been looking for.

Her lover's head tilted to the side, as if listening to something. But all she could hear was the methodical beat of her heart, getting quieter. Slower. Her vision narrowed to the sight of his revolver as he raised it above her face.

∿

The echo of the fired gun reverberating in her mind brought Kellee back to reality with a jolt, and she sucked deep breaths into her lungs as she felt the phantom pain in her temple. She couldn't get enough oxygen and began to panic. Her face flooding with tears as she pulled frantically against the restraints. Abruptly she quietened, took a deep breath, and held it. Slowly she brought herself under control, using healing techniques learned over the last few weeks to stem her nightmares.

She was back in the present. Tied up in the tray of a Ute. Not safe, but alive. Her body was not deprived of oxygen, but overloaded and hyperventilating. Suppressing the urge to gasp in air by holding her breath, rationality started to return, and her heart began to steady into a normal rhythm. Her limbs were shaking, the surrounding air was so cold her teeth were almost chattering. Kellee began to breathe slow and steady, giving herself time to gain control as well as a mental kick in the pants.

Wiping her tears and nose on the shirt sleeves of her aching arms, she gave a final deep sniff. This time she would not go down without a fight, nor go back to a place of dark despair. The road to recovery had been long and tough. What had happened was not her fault. Falling in love with the wrong man did not mean she was a bad person. This was no time to be looking back. Now more than ever she needed self-control. Faith in herself rose. Her name was Kellee McGlover, and she would get herself out of this.

Twisting her neck to look back up at the ladder, she followed the rungs to the top. Off to the left a small control panel lay flat against the wall. Maybe a manual override to open the roof above her? A way out?

Her thoughts were distracted by an overwhelming desire to pee. Oh! God, she was getting desperate. Adjusting her position, relieved some pressure on her bladder. If someone didn't come soon, she wouldn't be responsible for the mess she would make. No way was she going let that happen. Yea. She was back and fighting, and here was oneway to gain attention, make a noise.

"Hey, anyone there?" Her strong, confident voice gave her the boost she needed.

From somewhere deep behind her, a muffled scratching came. "Oi, I need to go to the bathroom."

Nothing. All was quiet.

The rows of boxes seemed to absorb her words, leaving an eerie silence in their wake. Motionless she listened, pushing the sounds of the air conditioner and the ticking clock into the background, listening for any indication she was not alone. The sound came again. This time she could swear she was hearing a faint, almost indistinct sobbing.

Someone young in distress?

"Hello, can you hear me? Talk to me."

Silence. Was her mind playing tricks? If there was a child in trouble down here, she wanted to know. She would do anything to save it, anything. Tugging on her bindings only brought fresh blood and pain, and all she achieved was to pull the bonds tighter.

"Hi. My name is Kellee, can you hear me?" Her softer, friendly tone made no difference. Silence ruled. Maybe she had imagined it, a memory in her mind of the girl in the alley.

Kellee shivered, as if someone had walked over her grave. Cold and alone, realisation of her predicament crept in and hit home. Escape had to be her top priority.

Her gaze settled on the ladder, following its upward path until her eyes rested on the control panel high on the wall, deciding if opportunity arose, it was an option for escape. The thought gave her an element of strength. She would free herself of this mess and if necessary, rescue anyone else caught in this concrete dungeon.

Holy shit, Kellee leant uncomfortably against the steel frame. If she didn't get to a toilet soon, she would wet herself.

A repeat of the whirring sound and a light clunk had her senses jumping to full alert, as she realised what the sound was. The whoosh of the elevator door opening, and a waft of stale cigarette smoke told her she was no longer alone.

CHAPTER NINE

The house reeked of money. Not a place Matt would like to call home, everything gleaming white, decadent and sterile. The four of them had been living here, in what they called 'Granny's house' for the last couple of weeks, while they planned and practised for the heist. Whoever Granny was remained a mystery. By all accounts from Ed, she was the key element to getting more deeply involved in the gang. He needed to meet her. It had been a long and hard road to entrench himself into this position. All he sought now was the mysterious woman's approval.

"Cheers." Matt clinked bottles with Ed and Jimmy before taking a welcome swallow of beer. The bitter tang and the fresh fizz of the amber liquid hit the spot. Despite the hostage hiccup, the day had gone as planned. MICO sure knew how to execute a successful sting.

Ed clapped him on the back. "Brilliant plan." and raised his bottle in salute. "Jules should arrive soon with the haul."

Ed went over to a row of monitors by the front door, pressed a few buttons and brought up live feed, showing the hostage in the massive underground chamber they called the bunker. He sat sprawled on a white leather lounge. "Don't trust that fuckin bitch." In the same breath, he called out, "Jimmy, another cold one and a coaster. Granny will have a fit if I mark her coffee table."

Matt sank into the folds of the matching chair and positioned himself to keep an eye on everything around him. He wasn't a fan of leather in the tropics, but at least with the temperature adjusted the material felt cool and soft. Ducted air-conditioning kept all the rooms in the house, including the bathrooms, a comfortable twenty-four degrees Celsius.

"Quick thinking mate, with the cops," Ed laughed as he accepted the beverage from Jimmy. "Reaper strikes again. Granny's gunna be impressed."

Jimmy grumbled as he sat opposite them, "I reckon she'll be cranky that a pig is dead. Now they will be out after our asses with a vengeance."

Ed spoke to him as if he were a slow-witted child. "Killing the cop saved our asses stupid."

Matt relaxed, arms thrown over the armrest, legs outstretched, subtly paying attention to the monitor as he followed the conversation. The hostage. He didn't want to think about her name, that only made it more personal. Kellee. Her name rolled around in his mind. Her struggling had ceased a while ago. Now, she was turning this way and that, taking in her surroundings. He could almost imagine her brain ticking over. Not for the first time he admired her spunk.

"What are we going to do about her?" Matt asked.

Ed gave him a non-committal shrug. "Who is she? What did you do with her bag Jims?"

Matt let it slide and answered for Jimmy who deepened his frown at the shortened version of his name. The silly man bit each time he got provoked. If he ignored it, Ed wouldn't do it. "It's still in the garage. Want me to grab it?"

"Nar, we'll wait for Granny. What she says goes."

Ed got up and paced to the front door and peered out the side glass frame. "Where the fuck is Jules?"

Matt glanced at the clock on the far wall. Six twenty-two pm. "We're back early, it's not dark yet. We cut our time short at the BBQ."

"Well, I'm hungry and I want my diamonds." Ed sat back down again and snapped at Jimmy. "What's in the fridge? Granny said something about a stew." He leaned back and closed his eyes.

Matt watched Jimmy scowl and mutter under his breath as he got up to do Ed's bidding. His mind tossing over all sorts of plans, he turned his attention back to Kellee. She sat still now as if lost in thought. Her wrists red and chaffed from where she had pulled incessantly against her bonds.

Ed opened his eyes and stared at him briefly before closing them again. Matt consciously kept his face neutral, vowing to have faith in his ability to bring her out of this safely. How to do it still baffled him. His operational plan only went this far. The next phase would see him in uncharted waters. Easy enough on his own, just go with the flow. She certainly complicated things. But this was about more than one life. He wanted to see the whole drug gang on its knees.

After his brother Patrick's death, he had taken the opportunity to jump from his gang to the Hell Raisers, where Patrick had been undercover. After all, the smaller gangs were all connected to the same well spread organisation. Infiltrating deeper had proved easy. His club name of Reaper gave him a status that demanded respect. Hurt and angry, he allowed his grief to manifest in ways that added to his already deadly reputation.

His father. Head of the Military Intelligence Covert Operations had called him back out of the field when his twin had been murdered. For the first time in his life, he blatantly defied orders. A clandestine meeting meant to be a compromise failed. He stuck to his guns, not wanting to believe in Patrick's death. They weren't identical and didn't have a psychic connection, but he didn't feel it in his heart. He wanted to see this mission through and find out what happened to his brother. Although he expected a massive blowout, and the real possibility of going it alone, he was surprised to find his older brother Stephen backing him up, encouraging him to stay with the plan. It came with a price, and an extracted promise. If MICO deemed it necessary, he must abort, pull out and come home. He hadn't reached that point yet and prayed they didn't call him off because he was nowhere near done.

His mind churned over the facts, checking for missed chances since the woman had stumbled into the robbery. Could he have helped her escape? He came up blank. Should he have made an opportunity? Had he signed her death warrant by inaction? This mob played for keeps. She could identify them, and that already didn't bode well for her future. Matt was treading in unfamiliar territory here, gaining deeper access into the biggest organised crime gang they had uncovered to date. He had moved so far on from last year, when he had crossed across into the other gang, in no time working his way into their upper clan and beyond into this group, the steppingstone to the Compound. That is where he was sure he would find answers.

It hadn't been an easy road to begin with, but once MICO had stepped in to boost his reputation, it seemed almost effortless. Stephen, the brains behind MICO, and a master of deceit, kept up a supply of blank bullets, and perfectly well-timed plans. No one was any the wiser that most of Reaper's victims were still alive and in custody. Some of the innocent ones were in safe houses until this operation could be blown apart.

Now more than ever he wanted the big guns behind this organisation. In a recent undercover operation involving his younger siblings Jo and Kevin, it had been revealed there was a possible leak high up in their organisation, and, not for the first time, he appreciated the top-secret coding of his alias. The traitor might know of him, but would not know the who or where. Of course, there was always the chance of him being played, the possibility the woman below was a plant. They may even use her to prove his loyalty. He couldn't pull out now. He would simply have to stay vigilant. Things might get a little tricky if they ordered him to kill the woman. Provided he could do things in his own way, he should be able to help her. He just hoped she didn't get too roughed up in the process.

Jimmy took a swig of his beer and flopped back on the chair. "Stew's warming up."

Ed grunted, sniffing the air. Muttering, "smells delicious," Matt kept his attention focused on the woman. She was sitting quietly, eyes closed, but it looked as if the demons from hell were riding across her face. She jolted awake, eyes flung open in terror, sucking in great gulps of oxygen. He half rose from his chair, seeing the panic flare through her body with renewed vigour as she twisted and tugged at her restraints. Just as quickly, she stilled. Visibly shaking but in control. She had clearly outrun her horrors as she continued her visual assessment of her prison.

"Going somewhere?" Ed raised a questioning eyebrow at Matt as he started to rise at the woman's panic session.

"Bathroom...problem?" He went to turn away, then stopped hearing Ed's evil chuckle, and the excitement in his voice.

"I'll let you know if you miss any more entertainment. Maybe we should freak her out a little. She looks a feisty thing."

Matt's grin must have been believable as Ed laughed again. Walking to the bathroom, he heard him issue orders to Jimmy.

"Go bring the woman up here and don't forget her bag, I am sick of waiting."

Jimmy belched loud and long. Not even the delicious smelling stew covered the stench. The smell lingered and seemed to follow Matt into the bathroom. After relieving himself, Matt checked his own breath with the cupped hand test. He screwed up his nose and gargled with the mouth wash he found on the shelf above the mirror, then ran his fingers through his wavy hair. As much as he wanted to rush back, he figured it made his act more convincing not seeming to be in a hurry. He was halfway across the plush carpet when Ed's demanding voice yelled out, "get me another beer, this is a damn good show."

Before Matt could reach the fridge, Ed jumped up screaming, "Fuck, get down there. The bitch has knocked that useless git to the ground."

The elevator door whooshed closed behind him just as Ed finished speaking. *What in the hell has Jimmy done now,* was his first thought. His second was, he couldn't afford to let Kellee continue with an escape that was destined to fail. Stephen knew all about this place and its floor plan, he had made sure of that. But if MICO acted now, most of their past gains would be wasted. He hoped they would stay alert, ready to move in at the right time. Eye on the prize, they all wanted the head honcho and Patrick's killer. Now, with a possible traitor in the mix, things were getting dicey.

If things kept going this way, the communication system would be cut off for security. It fell to him to keep Kellee safe until they had more information. If the opportunity arose, he would help her escape, but only if he could guarantee her safety.

Jimmy's foul language followed by his fist banging on the metal rungs reverberated loud and angry throughout the massive concrete structure. Foolishly he must have untied her, instead of releasing the guide rope, and she had taken full advantage of his mistake.

A quick look at the monitor by the lift door revealed the woman almost to the ceiling. Jimmy was starting to climb after her, yelling about what he would do to her once he reached her. Matt shook his head at his stupidity. He opened a small tin box on the wall and flicked a switch down into the 'off' position. Safety shut down, cutting off both electronic entrances to the underground room sealing it tight. Jimmy should have remembered that. They had been given instructions on what to do on the day of their arrival. In case of a raid, fast track it to the bunker, cut the power supply. Sit it out. No way anyone would even suspect they were down here, let alone find a way in.

"Yo Jims, what you going to do when her feet connect with your face?" Matt stood close to the bottom rung, his hands on his hips, looking up.

Jimmy's foot stopped on the fourth rung and backtracked fast, muttering profanities.

"Didn't remember to disconnect the damn fuse." He sounded pissed off. "Stupid broad pushed me over. Too fucking tall that bitch."

"Don't worry about it Jimmy," Matt patted him in a friendly manner on the back, no use making an enemy. "Go and wait by the lift, I'll manage it."

Long shapely legs continued the climb.

"No point Kellee, power's off."

She looked down at him, climbed the last step, and reached over to press the button on the panel.

"I can stand here all day." He folded his arms across his chest and leaned casually on the Ute bonnet, giving a low whistle when she finally roused herself from her defeated position, deciding to make the descent.

As she descended, her lovely lithe body came closer. He appreciated the way her butt swung from side to side. The blue denim of her shorts hugged her cheeks tight, then hung loosely over the top part of her legs. Legs that went on forever. Legs that made him feel alive.

The skirt she'd been forced to wear before they stopped at the river, an obvious hindrance, lay crumpled on the floor. When her feet touched the ground, she kicked it aside in frustration and stood staring at him, arms loosely at her side.

"What now?" her voice sounded silky and strong even though a flood of emotions etched her features.

The trauma of the day was clearly sitting heavily on her shoulders, but he also admired the strength of character shining through as she stood waiting for his next move. She was stunning.

Even with her tangled, sweat-drenched hair, face red and puffy from crying, she plucked at his libido strings big time.

He stepped closer, nostrils flaring. He couldn't define it, but there was something about the way she smelt, her strong body language and the fact he hardly had to drop his head to look at her. She was almost as tall as his six-foot-three frame and it excited him to be standing almost eye to eye. It surprised him how much he found her height appealing.

She slowly stepped away, until her back bumped the wall, staring back at him boldly, using those intelligent hazel eyes to add strength to her plea. "Let me go...please."

A spear hit Matt's heart as her hand rested feather-light on his shoulder. The cameras were off. No doubt it would be annoying Ed not knowing what was happening down here until he turned the power back on. Jimmy was at the elevator. Could he dispose of him, set her free? His teeth clenched. No. Despite his reputation as the Reaper, killing never came easy.

"I promise I won't go to the authorities." Her eyelids fluttered as soft and delicate as her spoken tone.

He couldn't take his eyes off her face, devouring the sweetness and light.

"I'll walk away as if it never happened."

His heart kicked up a beat as she leaned closer to him with vibrant, sexy eyes and seductive mouth.

"I won't tell anyone."

"Sorry Kellee." Without conscious intent, genuine sympathy flowed with his words, as realisation struck how attractive he found her. She would go to the Police; he didn't doubt that. The boss would be waiting, anxious to have visual again. Even if he gave her the fuse and staged being overpowered, there was no other exit. As soon as power came back on, Ed would have visual and her attempt to flee would be seen. He would be out of that room in a shot and into the carport above. And he wouldn't be kind.

Damn it, she was a complication he didn't need. He pulled her close, whispering into her ear. "I can't let you go. I'm sorry."

"What's taking so long?" Jimmy came towards them holding out the rope.

Matt winced at Kellee's chaffed and bloodied wrists as he grabbed her by the upper arm and propelled her forwards, snatching her bag on the way.

"You better tie her up man."

"Fuck off." Slamming the lid into place he waited for the hum of electricity, grinned into the camera, and gave it a thumbs up.

Kellee started to shake once within the close confines of the small elevator. He held her hand steady, pulling her closer to him for comfort. She might stand tall and act tough, but he knew how she would be feeling after her failed escape. And there was nothing he could do or say to make her feel better.

CHAPTER TEN

E d noticed Matt nod at the camera before he pulled the fuse, so he would understand what he was doing before the screen went blank. Quick thinker that man, perfect to have on his team.

'His team.' The words made him smile. As a member of the Hell Raisers, he begrudgingly followed orders and put up with his stupid nickname. Thumper. He hated the name with a vengeance and had taken great pleasure in slitting the throat of its originator, Mad Dog, as soon as the opportunity arose. He told them killing was his only option, let them believe that. Them? He didn't even know who *they* were, just the name 'Mantis'. After his last failed job, he didn't have a contact for Mantis. Not that he was worried, a phone would appear when needed. And his bank balance reflected appreciation, bulging big time after he'd blitzed his orders and cleaned up their mess. Just a small snag when Mouse got away. At least he got his promotion. They 'requested' he still search for the cunning little bitch. He figured they would be looking as well. Not for the first time he wondered why they prioritised her.

"Come on...come on."

Impatiently he tapped at the blank screen. He didn't like not knowing the score. He laughed, pleased he hadn't had to go and re-capture the slut himself. Too fuckin' tall. He would never admit to fear, but dreaded the thought of being shown up by any woman. He liked his flesh feisty, but young and beatable.

Thanks to Wildcat, another bitch he would repay one day - along with her lover Phantom or Axel, whatever the fucker decided to call himself. Fuck the stupid nicknames. He pushed himself up from the couch, heading for the fridge for another beer. Jo Brennan and Axel Stone had ruined his last job and, in the process, helped Mouse escape. His memory was long and vengeful. He would kill them all, but Jo he would save for last, making her suffer for how she embarrassed him in front of his gang. He'd laid on the floor grabbing his balls in winded agony, his so-called mates laughing. Axel had warned him not to touch his woman. Well, they would regret messing with him, no matter how long it took.

The stew bubbled rapidly, the steam teased his nostrils, tantalising his taste buds. He turned the heat off as he passed, moving it off the ring. No point burning the meal. He opened the fridge, then shut the door again, deciding against more beer. Moving up came with rules. Not too much alcohol and no drugs. He missed his bike. Nothing better for letting off a bit of steam. Revving up and down the highway and partying hard at the clubhouse. That part of his life was over for now. Advancement meant leaving all the trippy highs and drunken parties for the crap below him.

Not all club members rode bikes. The gangs were the ones who lived to take the brunt of the law, to do the illegal shit, and risk getting busted. Most of them never got the chance, or even knew about the possibilities beyond the club rooms. Hardcore members kept clean, hidden behind a wall of rich respectability. After years on the ground in a lower level, he was now climbing the ranks, on his way to raking in the mega bucks. Nothing was going to get in his way.

The screen flickered to life, and a grinning face filled the darkness.

Ed was confident Matt would stick by him. He'd come from the Brisbane Chapter of the Hell Raisers about eleven months ago, with a reputation that made Ed smirk with approval. Today, Matt had more than proved he was ready to step above the protective cover of the bikie gang, leave the name of the 'Reaper' behind, joining the next level. He would give him a solid wrap up to Granny. He needed men he could rely on to take orders. Men to do things like keeping that fuckin' tall bitch under control. The last thing he wanted was to be shown up by a woman again.

The top was the only road to ride. He would use men like Matt and his brilliant plan to steal the diamonds to get there. He might want him on his team, but trust him? No. He didn't trust anyone, not Granny, not even his own mother.

CHAPTER ELEVEN

D read chilled Kellee to the bone. Her knees wobbled as though they were jelly as the confident hand propelled her towards a metal door. The size of the place rocked her senses. The area she'd craned her neck to see took up less than an eighth of what stretched before her. And she knew in that instant she would be fighting for her life. They would never allow her to see all this and still let her leave alive.

Her legs almost gave way when he jammed the fuse back into the power box, grinned at the screen, and did a thumbs up. He differed now from the man who had sounded so sincere when he'd whispered sorry. Brown eyes held hers, and for a moment she harboured the hope he would simply let her go. Compassion was there, she was sure of it, mixed with something else, something she needed to analyse. When his eyes deepened and became sensual, she felt drawn into them. It alarmed her. No way could she be attracted to a killer.

His hold was tight and unforgiving as he pulled her along. She didn't know what to do or what to think. His words sounded so genuine, his breath on her skin when he whispered close to her ear, sent shivers of pleasure through her, increasing her panic even more. Surely, she couldn't be falling victim to Stockholm syndrome. It was way too early for that scenario. No. Not

Stockholm. But yes, she admitted, she found him attractive, in control, and very much a man. She had glimpsed empathy; she was sure of it, so decided to keep working at him. So far, he seemed to be her best shot at survival, even though he was causing her to feel totally off balance.

She heard the whirring sound, and a steel door opened to reveal a tiny lift that surely no more than two could fit in at one time. Pulling back did nothing, as Matt easily manoeuvred her inside the confined space. Jimmy, squeezed in as well. Fortunately, Matt placed himself in the middle, so she didn't have to deal with Jimmy who kept shooting hateful looks her way.

She shrunk back as far as she could towards the cold comfort of the sidewall, her anxiety rising. Matt dropped his hand from her upper arm. She stilled as she felt the settling sensation of him rubbing his thumb in gentle calming circles across the top of her hand. She relaxed her palm into his, stealing a glance in his direction. He stared straight ahead, as if unaware of the action, of the comfort, he was giving. Why did she react this way? Each time she overloaded with panic he could bring her back with a whispered word or the soothing caress of a thumb. How could he make her feel so safe when all seemed lost?

Too soon the reassurance stopped. He re-tightened his grip as they exited from the elevator. Out the corner of her eye, she thought she saw him give a wry smile at her open reaction to the decadent luxury they had stepped into.

"What is this place?" Her voice hung empty in the air as she unceremoniously stumbled deeper into the room.

Matt kept a firm hold, but he allowed her a moment to look behind her as the lift whooshed shut, blending perfectly within the utility cupboards.

Ed strode over sneering, pulling the pantry door open to reveal a shelf full of canned and packaged food. His face took on a gloating expression "No way-out sweet cheeks."

She flinched as he lurched with intent toward her, her only choice being to stand her ground as Matt squeezed her arm tighter. Besides, where could she go? The kitchen opened out into a huge living area with wall to ceiling windows on the far side. The drapes were not yet closed against the evening sky. A quick scan of the room revealed only one shut door positioned centrally between the windows. She did something she had never done before during her rough and tumble life. She stood tall and proud, taking advantage of her height as Ed stepped in front of her. She almost smiled at how good it felt to look down on him. Her previous self would shrink into her frame, making herself small and appear less threatening. Not now, she could see his irritation, and while that probably wasn't wise, it still felt darn good.

"Why the fuck didn't you tie her back up."

Jimmy threw the rope on the table. "Told ya."

Ed picked it up and raised his eyebrows.

"She's staying put right now, I'll make sure of that." Matt held up her arm, bringing attention to her bloodied, chaffed wrist. "Going to fix that first. Infection. A sick hostage is a pain in the ass. Besides, if you're asking for money, you'll want her in ship shape."

"Who said anything about ransom? I got better plans for that bitch." Kellee didn't like the sound of the threat in his voice but found no time to dwell on his words, as the attention shifted from her to a loud crash as the pantry door flung open.

Jules strode through spitting anger, banging the door behind her. "What are you doing back already? the plan we agreed on... I arrive first. The garage entry must be playing up. I couldn't..."

She stood still when she saw Kellee. "What the fuck is she doing here?" Fluttering her baby blue eyes at Ed, she smiled provocatively. "Thought ya would have snapped her neck by now an' dumped her in the creek. Waste of croc food 'aving her here."

Kellee cringed as the scene unfolded.

With speed and precision, Ed lashed out a hand and smacked the young woman hard across the face, causing her head to fling sideways, and legs stumble back a few paces. "Don't tell me what I should and shouldn't do!" His voice cold and filled with malice.

Sniffling, Jules crept forward nursing her cheek, "Sorry darlin', I was just surprised to find her here." She moved closer, throwing her arms possessively around his neck. "You know best, always."

Ed pushed her none too kindly backwards, shoving his hand down her shirt, pulling out the black velvet bag. He nudged her aside, tossed it in the air then caught it again. "A nice little heist. A 'friend' deposits them, we steal them for him, and he gets both the sale of the goods and the insurance. Double or nothing."

He clapped Matt on the back. "Way to go, fuckin' brilliant man." He tipped the glittering gems out onto the table, "You can take your share now in cash, or hang around for the big stuff."

Kellee felt her arm pull against its socket as she was wrenched forward and shoved into a chair, forgotten now as Matt's eyes lit up with greed.

"I'll hang around." He curled up his lip, moving further away from her and closer to the stones. "I know a good thing when I see it." He reached out and grabbed a handful of sparkling stones, letting them slip through his hands. They clinked, bounced, and sparkled in the overhead light as they landed back on the polished wood table. "Simply beautiful." She watched as he picked up a large stone, his eyes wide and greedy as he held it up, fascinated as it glittered in his long fingers.

Keep it." Kellee didn't think generosity had anything to do with Ed's offer. "Consider it a bonus. I take care of those who take care of me. You hashed out the details and without your fast thinking with the cops, we never would have made it."

He shot a warning look at Jules as she opened her mouth in protest. "Shut up, turn on the news and finish cooking whatever Granny's left for dinner, I'm hungry."

Kellee began to squirm in her seat. Not only was she even more desperate for the loo, but she wanted to shake some sense into Jules as she jutted out her chest, pouting as she leaned forward, rubbing her hand up and down Ed's crotch as she whimpered, "I look after you."

"Sure you do sweet cheeks," Ed sneered back, pulling her up tight against him and giving her a rough kiss. Slapping her rump in a friendly manner, he scooted her towards the kitchen, grumbling. "Food woman."

Kellee saw the exchange and experienced a moment of pity. He was obviously using her. She clearly saw the coldness in his eyes as he watched the girl's departing back. And although she couldn't read what his eyes were saying, she didn't like his body language. Something sinister was lurking beneath the surface, and she had the sinking notion that Jules would find out sooner rather than later what that was.

Jules obviously took it all as a compliment. If she had taken a moment to turn back and catch the contempt on Ed's face, she would freak right out. Or maybe she wouldn't have seen anything. There was a lot of truth in the saying 'love is blind. Hadn't she experienced that firsthand?

Kellee rose slowly from her chair. If she didn't move, she would pee herself. They were so engrossed by the diamonds they were paying her no attention. A further step took her into the massive lounge, but she could see no doors leading off the pristine white walls to indicate a bathroom.

There was no entrance hall, just the kitchen and dining area and the richly furnished living room. White and pure, with artistically placed splashes of colour in paintings and artistic decorations. She took another couple of steps backwards, keeping her eyes on them as they laughed and played with their sparkling toys. No one looked her way.

The TV added a subtle background noise, and by the clock on the wall it was almost seven pm. A twenty-four-hour news program was running, and by the way Ed and Matt kept glancing at it, they were anxious to find out if anything would be said about them. For the first time she wondered if the Police had figured out her identity yet? What would happen if they found out she was an officer of the law? Would it be mentioned? She was still one unofficially. After handing in her badge, her Captain had shaken his head saying he would keep it for her, till after her holiday, strongly prompting her to make the final decision then.

Now she was in a hell of a mess. What was she going to do? She kicked herself for her failed attempts at escaping, for the fear ricocheting inside when she thought about the blood and the dead police officer, desperately trying to hang onto to the anti-stressing techniques she had been taught by her shrink. She should have tried to knock Matt out in the Ute, claw a hand through the side of the tarp, anything but be taken in by his bogus concern, and comforting touch. Even now, she was aware of his physical presence. He churned her insides, confused her thoughts, and so far, had deftly stonewalled any attempt she made to get away.

This was huge. She needed to get to the authorities. The guns alone in the basement indicated enough firepower to arm the whole of Cairns ten times over, not to mention the drugs. She must find a way to break free. The most important thing for her to do would be to keep her wits about her and be patient. Patience was not her best friend, never had been. If she had exercised more caution in Sydney, waited for approval and backup, maybe Elsie would be alive. But if the events hadn't unfolded the way they did, she would still be under the spell of her partner's lies and deceits, none the wiser.

Her back twinged at the thought. The wounds were physically healed now. What she felt was mental. The reality of that betrayal still lay heavy on her mind, settling deep into her heart. She had lost faith in herself and her ability to judge people. What a mess her life was in.

Again, her eyes came back to Matt. He was more than he seemed. He had gunned down the two officers in cold blood. She witnessed it, yet he also offered her a strange form of protection and kindness. She just couldn't fit him totally into an evil little package like

Ed, and true to her nature, it worried at her like a Terrier at an intruder's leg.

She took another couple of unobtrusive steps away, close now to a small table by the window, through which the city lights twinkled like faraway stars in the night sky.

A rich meaty aroma wafted from the kitchen, making her stomach rumble. It had been a long time since lunch and whatever it was, it smelt delicious. She couldn't understand why she was still alive. What did they want with her? There was no way she would be allowed to live after all she'd seen. She could identify them; they no longer wore their concealing clothing or wigs. Now it came down to two choices. Try to escape again now or wait for a better time. There was a solid looking blue vase just off to her right. She could smash it through the glass.

She took a hesitant step towards it. If she smashed it, then what? It didn't look as though there were any neighbours close enough to aid her escape.

Her eyes rested on the floor to ceiling glass windows that fronted the entire length of the house. Obviously high on a hill, overlooking, of all things, the shopping complex and the jeweller they had just robbed. Blue and red lights still flashed, indicating the authorities hadn't yet completed processing the crime scene.

Should she try the front door? What if she found it locked? Usually impulsive, her thoughts lay heavy on her heart. Her will to survive was strong, and for the first time in months she enjoyed the feeling of being alive and wanted to stay that way. The better decision would be to bide her time. They didn't intend to kill her straight away, otherwise she would be dead by now.

She wanted to bring this group down, expose them, make them pay to the full extent of the law. To do that, she had to set them at ease, fool them that she would not try to get away. Exercise patience and wait for the right opportunity to arise. Satisfied this was the best option, Kellee turned her back on the view and walked over to a deep burgundy leather lounge, chose the oversized armchair for personal space and settled herself into it, drawing her knees-up and clasping her hands around them. She still had bare feet, and they were so grubby; her whole body was filthy with accumulated sweat and grime. She scratched at some ground in dirt on her toes, wondering if she would ever see her favourite pair of runners again.

On the coffee table beside her was a vase, a holder with some coasters and a round snow cone. She picked the snow cone up, studied it, then glanced over at the kitchen. No one paid her any attention. It was solid and fit comfortably in her hand. An adequate weapon. In a swift move she let it drop onto her lap and re clasped her legs then sat for a while. Confident no one had seen her, she moved to sit in a more comfortable position, at the same time slipping the glass ball down the side of the chair, between the cushion and the armrest. Letting out a nervous breath, she closed her eyes. A weapon hidden for when she needed it.

CHAPTER TWELVE

M att kept Kellee in his peripheral vision, glad when she settled into one of the chairs. She was strangely calm. He would have expected some kind of hysterics, but her thoughtful demure kept him on edge. Could she be a plant from the organisation he was infiltrating? Unlikely. Her reactions in general, especially in the Ute, seemed genuine and his gut told him she had been in the wrong place at the wrong time, and his gut never lied.

Her words floated in his mind long after she'd whispered, *Kellee, my name is Kellee.* The soft lyrical voice still haunted him now. Smart and knowing or, openly vulnerable. Either way, the words clung to his heart and sent down roots of compassion. Hell, not just compassion, if he were truthful to himself. Her voice stirred a desire within him, and not only desire for her as a woman, but a desire to protect. He tried hard to push those thoughts away. Far too long a time had passed since he had confidence in his natural feelings. One thing he did realise, was he must keep her safe at all costs. It ran in direct conflict with the character he'd become, and he racked his brains for a way to save her without blowing his cover.

Still keeping an eye on Kellee, Matt picked up the TV remote and cranked up the volume.

"Breaking news." The announcer's voice held the appropriate note of shocked excitement. Looking straight at the camera, he paused for dramatic effect.

"Police hold fears for the safety of a woman taken hostage earlier today during a daring daylight robbery. Our reporter, Pamela Gordon, is at the crime scene. Can you tell us what is happening Pamela?"

There was a slight delay as the reporter stood off to the side of the crime scene. She tilted her head slightly as if listening and then spoke into her microphone, "Thanks Ken, yes, the city of Cairns is in shock this afternoon as the dramatic details of a brazen daylight robbery come to hand. Official statements are still to be obtained from the authorities, but I can tell you that one of the officers, who tried to stop the robbery, is being looked after at Cairns Base Hospital with a gunshot wound to his leg. The second officer, whose name has not yet been released, was pronounced dead at the scene."

"Three armed men, wearing black balaclavas, allegedly held up the 'Diamonds are Forever' jewellery store outside Maryland Shopping Centre. A fourth man, waiting in the nearby car park, drove the getaway vehicle. During the shoot-out, an unidentified woman, who was about to enter the building next door, was taken hostage and police hold grave fears for her safety. The men are considered armed and dangerous and not to be approached under any circumstances. Anyone having any information is asked to call Crime Stoppers on the number flashing across your screen. Back to you at the studio Ken."

"That was Pamela Gordon live from Maryland, Cairns. Stay tuned for further updates as they come to hand."

Matt's attention turned to Kellee throughout the news report, interested to gauge her reaction. When the announcement came on, she'd twisted in her seat to watch, her face expressionless, body loose and relaxed. It was ever so slight, but he could have sworn he noticed a small sigh of relief when they mentioned her as an unidentified woman. She stole a glance at him, almost as though she knew he was watching her, turning away quickly to avoid eye contact.

He turned the sound down and looked across at Ed as he finished packing the diamonds away into the black velvet bag. "Let's see what we can find out about her." He upended the contents of her backpack unceremoniously onto the table

"Move that shit." Jules placed a bowl of steaming stew in front of Ed, then Matt.

Ed gave her a glare before he snapped, "Mind the language sweet cheeks, you're in Granny's house," he dunked a chunk of crusty bread into his meal as he rummaged through the scattered paraphernalia.

"Look at these," Jimmy held up the brief bathers, "maybe she should model them for us."

Matt shovelled soup into his mouth. He wanted to punch the annoying twerp in the face, but let it ride, interested to discover what else her pack revealed. He glanced up at her. She was watching him, beseeching him with those intelligent hazel eyes. Why?

"Nothing much of interest here, not even a wallet with an id, no licence or credit card. Some cash. "Ed pushed the belongings back over towards him. "Put them back in the bag."

Matt complied, noting almost everything was new with the price tag still dangling. A couple of shirts, shorts, sunscreen, lip gloss, tic tacs, sunglasses, a worn and well-used Mp3 player. He dug in his pocket pushing an object towards Ed. "Her phone."

Jimmy picked it up. "Hey it's turned off. Won't find out nothin' that way." It was an older model flip top phone. He turned it around trying to find the on button.

"Idiot." Matt snatched it out of his hands and passed it to Ed. "It was in her pocket. I deactivated it in the van when we changed our clothes before the first stop. Turn it on again and her signal is going to ping off the closest tower. They are probably monitoring, waiting for it to be activated." He shot an annoyed glance at Jimmy. "Grow some brains."

Ed tossed it back to Matt. "Keep it safe; take the battery out." He tucked into his stew with gusto. "What's ya name bitch?" Small amounts of food particles flew from his lips as he spoke. He chewed noisily and swallowed. "Do I have to come over and smack it out of ya?" Ed started to sound pissed off when she just stared at him.

"Kellee," Matt interjected when she hesitated too long. "She whispered it sweetly to me in the back of the Ute."

"Kellee who?" Ed scratched his stubbly skin, before mopping the last of his meal with a piece of bread. He pushed the bowl away, belching loudly.

She remained silent, staring at them with vacant eyes.

As the stench of Ed's breath wafted in his direction, Matt turned his head away and made eye contact with the hostage. He must keep thinking about her in a detached sense. Already his desire to protect her was beginning to blur his rational thought, and, he had to admit, his libido. She was not the sort of woman he usually found attractive. Petite blonds were more his style. Easy going casual sex. This need to protect her was becoming all-consuming and not just from the situation she was in but in a broad sense. He wanted to wrap his arms around her and hold her tight. He found her height fascinating; she could almost stare him in the eyes, and the tight athleticism of her long legs were driving him wild.

"Oi, you listening to me?"

Ed's pissed off voice had him jumping back into the present. Shit, this was not like him. How long had he been staring at the woman.

"Yeah boss."

"Well, get to it. I told the bitch to come over here and she is still sitting on her ass, go smack her around till she understands she needs to do what I say."

Why in the hell didn't she do as he said? Matt knew only too well the temper simmering beneath the surface. It wouldn't take much to set Ed off on a violent rampage. She sat there staring like a gun was pointed at her head, and she had been told to freeze.

"My name is Kellee." The tremor in her voice betrayed her fear. Her chest rose as she took a deep breath, which seemed to steady her voice as she pulled herself up taller in the chair, before placing her feet firmly on the floor as she stood. "Kellee McGlover." Her tone held the same soft lyrical quality as when she had spoken in the back of the Ute.

He admired the way she held herself tall. Squared her shoulders, showing pride in her height. If Matt read it right, Ed almost flinched when he had tilted his head back at her approach. When he flickered his eyes towards him, Matt made sure his eyes were on the woman standing at the head of the table.

Ed sniffed long and deep before running a hand under his nose, looking at his fingers before wiping them on his shirt. He did a slow appraisal up and down her body. "Got plans for you, sweet cheeks."

"I thought I was sweet cheeks." Jules grumbled from her seat next to him, reaching out to put a hand on his arm.

"I call anyone that's fuckable that," Ed frowned towards Kellee, "but then again, this cow's lanky and old. I like my meat young and tender."

"Like me darlin'?" Jules smiled at Ed, sliding her hand down to the junction of his legs, rubbing seductively.

"Sure, keep rubbing at my prick and I'll forget you're getting on a bit."

Jules whined, "Don' say that! I ain't even tweny' yet."

Ed leaned forward, smacking her hands away. "Make yourself useful and clean up the kitchen."

Matt realised how much Ed was changing since he had been put in charge of this new gang. He had always been aggressive, but pushing Jules' advances away just now was not like the man he knew. In the past he would have let Jules go all the way and not just with her hand. He would have pushed her face to join the action, not giving a damn who was around while he got his pleasure. Matt realised he would have to watch his step around him as well. The power was going to his head.

The hostage remained standing, almost hopping from foot to foot like she needed to keep moving. She didn't know where to look and her face turned a deep shade of pink.

Ed's laugh was sick and twisted. "Sit down before I get 'the Reaper' here to make ya." He pointed to a vacant chair between Matt and Jimmy, banging his hand hard on the table when she didn't move.

"I need the bathroom," she blurted out in an embarrassed rush, looking pleadingly at Matt as she rubbed her hands up and down her legs.

"Shhh..." Ed reached for the remote and turned up the volume catching the tail end of the news update.

"...while no further details on the perpetrators of the alleged jewellery theft in Cairns have come to hand." A grainy picture showing the robbers clothed in dark balaclavas faded, and a photo of Kellee with a beaming smile appeared on the screen. "We have new information on the woman taken hostage. She is believed to be Kellee McGlover, a Grade 6 schoolteacher from Sydney. A tourist visiting Cairn on a recuperative holiday after being in a car accident a few months ago." Her name and statistics flashed bright and bold next to her picture. "If you see this woman, or the kidnappers, do not approach. They are armed and considered extremely dangerous. Please call Crimestoppers immediately."

Matt hid his interest as Kellee slumped in the chair beside him. Evidently the bathroom urgency seemed forgotten. What could have been in that news segment that had her catching her breath ever so slightly, and making her eyes widen with a hint of surprise? Ed and the others hadn't noticed it as they were focused on the TV. She had hidden it well by sitting down, but he could feel her energy and see it in the way she clasped her fingers together to keep them still. Something had captured her attention and sparked her interest.

CHAPTER THIRTEEN

K ellee did her best impression of a bland face. Inside, her emotions danced with elation. They had intentionally misspelled her name, identifying her as Kelly Macglover, changing personal details as well, twenty-seven years old...wrong twenty-six, and she was close to six foot, not six one. Most importantly, they reported her job as a schoolteacher. A great boost to her confidence. They were trying, and they were looking out for her, protecting her the best way they could.

Matt tapped away at his mobile. He looked up at her. "Google confirms the report. Has a Facebook page and is on Pinterest."

Kellee clenched her jaw to keep her elation hidden, thinking, "How in the heck did they manage that in such a short time?"

The shrill note of the land line on the side of the kitchen wall made them all jump.

Jules, being closest, lifted the receiver and said "hello." A look of apprehension flashed across her face as she held the receiver out.

"It's Granny."

Ed snatched the apparatus out of her hand and spoke, greeting the person on the other end in a deep, respectful voice, then listened intently. He moved away, speaking in hushed tones, settling into one of the oversized chairs. The way he watched her gave her the creeps and she knew the conversation included her. A more urgent issue pressed on her bladder.

Kellee's chair scraped nosily as she pushed backwards and placed her hands on the table. "I need to go to the bathroom."

Jimmy scowled, Jules shrugged, arms deep in soapy water and Matt ignored her. Totally engrossed in listening to the phone conversation, he didn't appear to have registered her plea.

"Please!" she put a hand on Matt's, the warmth of his skin sending feather light tingles racing along her arm. She pulled her hand away, rubbing her palms together. At her touch he had jumped as well, his attention back on her. "I need to go to the bathroom. It's urgent."

He shot her an apologetic look. Absently shovelling his stew into his mouth, his eyes darting back and forth between Ed and her. "Jimmy, take her to the crap house."

"Why don't you take her man?"

"Still eating."

"I wanted some more."

Jimmy maybe whining about it, but he still rose to do as ordered.

Kellee didn't care about the rough push Jimmy gave her indicating she move to the other end of the living area. Her full bladder provided enough motivation.

The alcove to the small recess blended perfectly, camouflaged behind a white wall covered with colourful paintings and potted palms, making it virtually impossible to detect. She made a mental note to check out the rest of the living room to see what else she might have missed. Maybe there were more hidden rooms. A possible avenue for escape.

Jimmy grabbed her arm pulling her to a sharp stop.

"In here," he said, shoving her towards a door which also blended perfectly within the walls. She experienced pure joy at seeing the little white seat. Turning to shut the door she was met with Jimmy's sadistic grin.

"Leave it open bitch," The degrading way he ran his eyes over her body, as if she were a piece of meat on display, made her extremely uncomfortable. He stuck his foot in the doorway, poked out his tongue making a disgusting lapping motion.

"Don't let me put you off. In fact if you spread 'em wide and give me a good look at what you got, I'll be nice to ya,"

Revolted, Kellee acted on instinct and with no thought to consequence, gave him an almighty shove away from the door before she slammed it hard with a bang. Ramming the lock home.

It wasn't an attempt to escape, she only wanted privacy. With shaking fingers, she dropped her shorts and got on with it. Halfway through, Jimmy started banging on the door, cursing, and swearing at the top of his lungs.

Oh gosh what a relief. She'd never in her life come so close to peeing her pants, she thought as she flushed, then washed her hands. She ignored the noise outside the door, checking herself in the mirror. 'What a mess.' Cool water splashed on her face and the act of straightening down her hair made her feel slightly better. She turned and sat on the closed toilet seat.

There were no windows, the only exit being the door. The pounding finally stopped, giving a few moments of peace to sit in the quiet without anyone constantly watching or hounding her. Oh my god. A million fearful thoughts raced through her mind. She didn't want to die. Who is this mysterious Granny? Why did Matt make her feel strange? She didn't know how to take him.

As if her thoughts conjured him, his soft honey tones drifted through the wood. "Kellee, unlock the door. Don't make it any worse."

Damn him, he sounded so genuine. Of course, she didn't intend to stay here, but taking that first step proved harder than she thought.

"Come on Kellee."

The sensation of being overpowered and helpless overwhelmed her. She went to open her mouth, but no words came out, instead she continued to sit, twisting her hands together. It seemed the safest option. She never should have pushed Jimmy. Once again, her anger had surfaced, landing her in deeper trouble. Face them she must, but first she needed a few minutes alone to gather strength. As a police officer, she should be better than this. It bothered her that she no longer held confidence in her ability to live up to her officer status. I am scared, she admitted. Really scared.

"Last chance Kellee. "Frustration and annoyance laced his words. She preferred it to his honey tones. She couldn't understand why he caused her emotions to race in all directions. No denying his looks set her on fire, and there were not many men who were taller than her. A man capable of kindling desire in her veins and who stood tall enough to look at her eye to eye. Matt looked down on her, not by much, but it was enough with his wavy brown hair and cheeky grin to send her heart into flip flops.

Maybe this was activating her fears. She seemed to fall for the wrong men. Attracted to the bad boy image. She must stop and clamp down on those feelings, face her current situation like the professional she claimed to be. They thought she was a schoolteacher. That must be a good start.

She didn't want to die. The only way to make sure that didn't happen was to keep her cool, plan her escape, and to do that she needed to bide her time and stay alive. As much as she didn't want to admit it, Matt was proving to be her best option.

"Kellee. You got ten seconds."

Ok, this was it. She steeled herself to get up, open the door, and face the man on the other side.

Without warning the door swung open with a crash. She screamed, pulling her legs up, curling herself into a ball on the toilet seat, her hands protectively shielding her head as a furious Ed stormed inside. A hand viscously grabbed her by the hair and yanked her out into the hallway, slamming her into a wall. Instinct took over and she used her strength and height to turn on her attacker. She wouldn't go down without a fight.

Ed stared at her, and she thought she caught a flash of fear in his eyes. "Fucking slut. Tie her up, break an arm if you must. I don't give a shit. Bring the bitch back to the lounge. Granny's on her way."

Matt stepped into her line of vision.

"We can do this hard or easy, turn around and face the wall."

An unwanted flair of excitement flushed through her body, and it had nothing to do with aggression. Pure instinct kicked in when confronted by Ed. Her reaction to Matt resulted in something else entirely. He stepped right into her personal space; she tilted her head slightly to look into his eyes and the action excited her. Tall, buff, and powerful and omg his eyes devoured her ability to resist.

Her hands went hot and clammy. His words *hard* or *easy* sang in her blood. He would do both to perfection.

"Haha, she's drooling over you Matty boy." Jules' shrill voice acted like a bucket of water tossed over her.

Matt scowled at the woman swinging the rope in her hand, "Don't call me Matty boy."

Jules took an involuntary step backwards, a flash of fear chasing across her features. "Fine." She held the rope out at arm's length, "Ed said to check her over to make sure she hasn't grabbed something and concealed it." With a toss of her hair, she walked away.

"You...you need a hand?"

"Fuck off Jimmy. Twice now she's got the better of you."

Kellee knew Jimmy glared at her, but she kept her eyes on Matt, willing him to...to do what? Let her go? Defeat set in. Her shoulders slumped, and she lowered her gaze. Good grief. Now she could see the hard ripples of his washboard stomach through his t-shirt. Get a grip girl.

Matt took a step towards her, reached out and took hold of a wrist, rubbing his thumb over the abrasions. In a low and controlled voice, he asked Jimmy to get the first aid kit.Back in the bathroom again, sitting on the closed toilet seat, Kellee suffered his applications of a salve against infection. He then proceeded to bandage the raw areas of her wrists, remaining silent, not once making eye contact.

"Rope."

Jimmy threw it through the door where he leaned casually against the frame.

"Make it tight." Jimmy's manic grin matched the high-pitched tremor in his voice, and she tried to relax as Matt uncurled her fingers when they automatically tightened in response.

Jules stuck her head around the door, "Ed wants to know what's taking so long." The sound of the admiration for Ed grated on Kellee's nerves. Men like Ed ate young girls like her for breakfast. She had seen it happen too many times.

Matt tested the rope attached to the one binding her wrists. " We're done." Without looking at her, he walked out the door pulling her along behind him.

Jimmy stepped closer. "You haven't checked yet to see if she hid a weapon. Want me to frisk her?"

"Fuck off Jimmy, you don't deserve that pleasure."

"I am not hiding anything."

"Turn around."

"How can I hide anything in these clothes?"

"You're not in a position to argue."

She found herself spun around, facing the wall, hands above her head. Matt's foot hooked in behind first one ankle, then the other, and the only option was to spread her legs and lean her arms against the solid cool surface.

His breath whispered warm against her cheek. "I am going to release you now. Keep still and don't move. If you do, I will have no alternative but to hold you while Jimmy frisks you. Understand?"

Kellee hesitated, then nodded, gritting her teeth as his hands slid in a gentle caress down her skin. Under her breasts and over her waist, hips and down to the bottom of her shorts, patting her pockets.

She suppressed a quiver as he started the upwards journey on the inside of her thigh, refusing to give him any satisfaction by moving away as he brushed his hand between her thighs. Cursing when he hesitated, as a bolt of pleasure made her jump, she hoped to hell he hadn't sensed it. His touch remained impersonal and thorough, and she sighed gratefully when he didn't linger.

"Every action has a reaction, there's nothing I can do to make this any easier. This will be rough. I'm sorry."

Why in the hell did he say that? His tone might be reassuring, but those words spiked fear. He tugged on the rope, leaving her with no choice but to follow. Even with the bandage separating her torn skin from the bonds, she cringed at the raw pain from the tight restraint.

Eyes darting around the living room, Kellee's vision bi-passed Jules and Jimmy, who were sitting at the table staring at her with quiet apprehension. Ed's narrow, cold eyes dominated his angry face and momentarily caught her attention. Finally, her eyes rested on a sweet little old lady standing by the couch, leaning heavily on a wooden cane. She exemplified everything a grandmother should be, right down to the neat white bun tucked up tight on the back of her head. Her tiny size and appearance offered comfort and security. You could almost smell freshly baked chocolate chip cookies, and an image flashed into her mind of small children curled into the safety of her loving arms, listening to her read them a bedtime story.

Granny's wrinkled eyes shone with compassion, as she took in Kellee's appearance in a slow appraisal from head to toe. A callus shrewdness crept into her eyes and pure malice poured out. The old lady's' withered lips became a snarl, etching deep wrinkles into a face that had seen at least seventy long hot summers.

Kellee stared, having trouble comprehending the change that came over the small woman. There was cruelty imprinted into the creases of her crinkly, leathery skin, and when she cackled, the image of a wicked old witch emerged.

Kellee automatically pulled back, not wanting to move any closer, but the choice was out of her hands as Matt tossed his end of the rope to Ed, who yanked hard, almost dragging her off her feet. Her cry of pain fell on deaf ears as the bonds cut deeply into her wrists. She stumbled closer, and he lashed out a hand that sent her head reeling, then threw the rope back to Matt.

"I got business with Granny. You watch her."

"Before we take care of business, I have something to say to Little Miss Flighty here. Bring her closer pretty boy." Granny's rasping voice matched the look on her face. "Do you know what will happen if you try to escape again?"

"I wasn't trying to esc..."

"Shut up!" Granny stomped her cane on the floor with brisk violence.

Kellee's mouth went dry. Fear crept into every corner of her mind.

Matt's deep voice rumbled from just behind her. "I think it was a privacy issue."

"If I wanted your opinion, I would have asked, pretty boy." Her voice, although harsh, sounded a touch softer, but she never took her eyes off Kellee's face.

The old witch moved as swiftly as a death adder's strike and Kellee cried out in pain as the cane smacked at her legs, catching her around mid-calf. Cackling, Granny hissed. "I repeat. Do you know what will happen if you try to escape again?"

Matt put his hands on her arms. He applied just enough pressure to keep her from moving backwards, holding her firm in front of the wicked old hag.

"What about you, pretty boy? I saw it in your pants when you walked into the room. You want to fuck her. You're in luck, don't want to sell this one just yet. I can tell, the two of you will make beautiful babies. Worth a fortune on the trade market, boy or girl won't matter. Bonus for you if she is pregnant by the time we arrive at the Compound."

The silence drew out, Matt eyed her shrewdly, before breaking into a wide grin. "No hiding the fact I like tall, feisty women. How much are we talking about?"

Granny cackled. "Tell me pretty boy, why did you bandage her wrists? Got no room for weakness where you are going."

Kellee felt a tremor flicker through Matt's body, his hands squeezed a little tighter on her arms, although his voice remained steady and bland. It gave her the impression there was a bigger picture at play here.

"From what I gather, good condition means money. Foolish not to take care of our asset now."

Granny lashed out again with the cane, catching the exact same spot as before.

Matt tightened his grip, refusing to let Kellee back away. As much as she hated it, tears formed in her eyes when the old woman hit out for a third time, snarling, "My preference is for teaching lessons, in a way that's not forgotten."

Granny's wicked laugh bounced around the room. "I like you pretty boy. Now let's see how good you are at obeying orders. Cut off her finger. The little pinkie should do it."

CHAPTER FOURTEEN

"Sick!, I heard he did it once before. Took a man's fingers clean off with a machete. One swipe, blood everywhere. Fuck did he scream."

Matt ignored Jimmy's excitement as his mind raced, seeking an answer for a way out. Kellee struggled wildly, trying to escape the bear grip as he tightened it around her waist. He didn't blame her. Granny's reputation already indicated what a nasty piece she could be, and he had the sinking feeling they were about to find out just how bad.

He lifted Kellee off the ground in a bid to stop her from kicking at his shins. Shit, she had strength. He used her struggle to give himself time to work out what to do. She was gulping air into her lungs as if it were going out of fashion. He needed to do something quick. Dropping her, he spun her around to face him and with a silent plea of forgiveness, punched her on the chin, enough to render her unconscious, but not hard enough to do any serious damage.

Catching her as she fell, he dragged her over to the kitchen and dropped her into one of the chairs, letting her head slump on the table.

Granny and Ed were laughing, and he knew he was left with no alternative but to tie her to a chair and possibly cut off her finger.

He harboured no doubt they would do a lot worse to her if he didn't do it and who knew what they would do to him.

Pushing Kellee back in the chair frame, her body flopping sideways, it took all his strength to sit her upright again. In the bathroom he'd bound her wrists so that one crossed over the other, looping the leader rope over them. At the time, his thought was, it would be less painful, but now it made it easier to bind them to the arm of the chair. Using the thickness of the cord to separate her little finger from the rest, it pushed them over the side, leaving just her pinkie rigid against the wood. He looped the left-over rope around her neck and tied it off on the back rung. If she struggled it would just pull tighter, effectively immobilising her.

An inkling of a plan flashed in his head. It might be weak and a long shot, but better than nothing. Whistling softly, he opened the kitchen drawers in search of a sharp knife. Trying his best to produce an erection to be proud of. This sort of thing rendered him cold but had proved useful in the past. Many times, when women from the Club House were being abused and he had needed to fake interest in what was happening.

He filled his head with soft images of his favourite kind of woman. Cursing, as instead, he remembered Kellee: the feel of her skin and the shape of her hips, the firm round breast as he patted her down. That jolt of awareness, as his fingers brushed the warmth between her legs. It worked, feeling as horny as hell, he turned back, putting his rock-hard bulge on display before it could disappear again.

He dragged her chair around to face the lounge and stood beside her brandishing the knife. "You guys coming to watch?"

Granny came forward and waved at his bulging crotch with her stick, "my, you are a big boy. This excites you, doesn't it?" She gave Ed a meaningful look. "He's certainly living up to his reputation, you picked well."

"Jules, get some towels, this is going to be messy and grab the first aid kit while you are at it." Matt looked at Granny. "It sounds like you want to keep her around for a while. I'll cut it off, that's not the problem, but we'll have to make sure infection doesn't set in. We don't want to lose money by killing her."

Ed's phone buzzed. He looked at the screen, then showed it to Granny and said something close to her ear. Matt couldn't hear what he said, but could tell their attention switched to the content, not the knife in his hand. Ed looked restless, the old woman as well. This diversion could work to his advantage.

This was it. Make or break time. The sad part was, he needed Kellee awake to make what he planned convincing.

"So where do you want it off?" He nicked just below the second knuckle, deep enough to draw a decent spurt of blood. "Or here?" he made the next slice just under the first knuckle. Jamming his free hand hard on her wrists to prevent her from moving as she came to, struggling in shock. He applied more pressure, causing the blood to flow faster, spilling over and onto the floor.

Kellee went into full panic mode; her eyes were wide in terror as she drew in a breath to scream.

He clamped a hand over her mouth. "Shit, we got a squealer. This is going to be noisy as well as bloody." Matt looked questioningly at Granny. "We can gag her, but then we miss the best bits. Shall we move it to the bunker?"

Jules threw the towel in his direction, "Matt, ya makin' such a mess," she rushed to the sink, "shit, think I am gunna be sick."

Jimmy looked rather pale; his eyes transfixed on the red mess which covered most of her finger and dripped to stain the white tiles below.

Granny smirked and moved closer. Matt's cool façade hid his panic. He didn't want to go through with it, but if it came down to the choice, her finger, or her life... This improvised plan had better work. He could sense Kellee's fear, taste the horrid tang of blood ripe in his mouth. As she came to, she probably thought her finger had already been removed.

To his relief, his voice came out cold and callous as he flashed the knife at Granny. "How do you want it off? Slowly? We can take our time, hacking away at the fleshy bits, leave it like a chicken bone sucked clean. Or I can use the meat cleaver and take it off in one swift chop. Just tell me what you would prefer."

Granny hooked her walking stick under Kellee's chin, watching her struggle to gain a breath. She smiled brightly at the stark fear in her face, touching a finger to the tears streaming over her cheeks.

"Are you going to attempt to escape again?" her voice grandma sweet.

Wide eyed, Kellee shook her head.

"Let me hear your words sweetie. Are you?"

"No." Kellee sobbed. "I...pro..promise...will not...try...to esca...escape again."

She cringed as Granny patted her none too gently on the head, "Good girl, but let me tell you sweetie, if you do, I'll get the Reaper here to hack off your foot."

"Fun's over pretty boy. Fix her up, you're right about infection. She's a long-term keeper and is worth a lot more kept healthy. A baby a year for the next ten years...if she survives that long."

Matt shrugged. "Easy money. I'll find another way to get my kicks."

"Oh, you won't be short of those where you're headed." Granny cackled as she walked back towards where Ed stood still, flicking through his phone. When he looked up at her approach, his face flushed, and his eyes filled with a lustful gleam.

Matt's ears were straining as he kept a watchful eye on the couple. Something important was going on and he itched for more information. The words he overheard from Granny's low voice, as he untied the rope from Kellee's neck, just made him more frustrated. "Remember, these are 'look' only. Whet your appetite with them, and when you have finished here, I have someone special lined up for you."

Kellee flinched, trying to pull her hand away when Matt touched her. Her face devoid of blood and her erratic breathing almost broke his heart.

Pretty shaken himself, Matt, torn in two, wanted to reassure that her finger was still attached, and stay within earshot of the conversation between Granny and Ed. This could be the long-awaited next step in his climb to the top of the scumbags that ran this operation. Drugs, guns and hell...slave trade. Everything about this place played a key role in the movement and distribution of whatever came across Granny's territory.

This house, now marked by MICO, would not stay operational for much longer. They couldn't afford to let the goods in the bunker be dispersed, but knew it was unwise to move too soon either. Timing was everything.

Hardly any details about the human trafficking business had surfaced yet, apart from kidnapping the children of customs officers to enable contraband to be smuggled into the country. It was only a week ago, his sister Jo and brother Kevin had been instrumental in bringing that operation to its knees. His heart filled with pride. At this stage he only knew the bare details and was looking forward to hearing all about his younger siblings' first dip into undercover work. Who knew when that would be? Sooner rather than later he hoped. He desperately needed to pass on information about Granny.

Kellee's soft whimpering brought his attention back. A weird look from Jimmy made him realise he'd been staring off into space. It had taken him a long, hard, few years getting to this point. To gain access to the next level he couldn't do anything now to jeopardise his position.

He pulled himself together and paid attention to her finger. The bleeding stopped once he released the pressure, and he held her hand up so she could see it was still intact as he put a Band-Aid around the two thin lines. Her shudder of relief shot an arrow of regret straight to his heart. All he wanted to do was pull her into his arms and give her a reassuring hug to let her know everything would be ok. Not that he could really promise that.

With only himself to look out for, gang life, although not easy, was reasonably relaxed. He went with the flow, putting his personal feelings in deep storage, working his way deeper and higher, willing to give his life as he gathered information to aid in the protection of his country, and the freedom of its people. Now new responsibilities surfaced, his empathetic side demanding he keep the hostage safe. His long dormant, passionate side wanted...hell he didn't know what he wanted. It seemed like forever since he sported a genuine interest in the opposite sex. Personal feelings aside, there was one thing he knew for sure. He urgently needed to contact his Team.

Matt pulled lightly on the rope, indicating to Kellee she should stand. Ready with a steadying hand, he suppressed a smile when, with a gutsy shrug, she brushed off his assistance and stood tall on her own.

"Jules. Clean up this mess."

"Aww, Ed. Do I have to? Blood makes me sick."

"Do it sweet cheeks. And smack her one Matt if she gives you any trouble."

Jules pouted at Ed, turned, and fluttered her eyelids at Matt. Moving around the table towards him, swinging her hips from side to side. As she got closer, she slipped out her tongue and slid it sensually round her lips. "Why don't you let Jimmy do it?"

"Just do it Jules." Matt threw her a cold, threatening look. Hating himself for the fear that flashed in her eyes. He towered above her. She was a small slip of a woman, who needed more than a bit of meat on her bones. Skinny, he could see her collar bone well defined against her skin.

Girls like Jules never learned. Always thriving on the authority of men, accepting abuse to get attention. Young women like her needed help. Shown how to stick up for themselves, to know their own self-worth.

Ed and Granny finished their discussion and sauntered back over to the kitchen. Ed shoved his phone in his back pocket and Matt vowed he would get his hands on it at the earliest possible moment. He doubted it would be tonight. It looked as though Ed wanted to be away from here quick smart. Kellee tensed as they got closer and she kept her head bowed and subdued.

"Good job today. You're proving to be a great asset, Pretty Boy. Don't let me down now." Granny poked her cane towards Jules. "You girly, make sure to clean that blood up good and proper, and look after Jimmy and Matt. Ed, finish up here, then you and I have some business to attend to. As for you guys, you are on your own for now. Be ready to move in forty-eight hours.

"Let your hair down, have a few more beers, have a foursome." She cackled again as Kellee looked up at her in horror. "I told you what I would do if you try to escape again, but sweetie, you are more than welcome to fight off any advances these boys might make."

She reached out a gnarly hand and patted Matt on the arm, winking boldly at him. "That should spice things up for you pretty boy." With that, she walked down the length of the lounge room toward another hidden alcove, her cane clicking on the hard tiles.

"What did she mean 'look after these boys'? I am your girl," Jules placed her hand possessively on Ed's arm, looking up at him imploringly, "aren't I?" The crack of Ed's back hand echoed as he sent her sprawling and crashing into a chair, setting Matt's temper on edge. He willed himself to relax.

Ed stood staring at Jules on the floor nursing a bloodied lip. He grinned, flashing his nicotine-stained teeth. "I don't care if one, or if both of you fuck this old slut. I've finished with her. If she tries to leave the house, tie her up. No-one leaves." He nudged her none to gently with his foot. "Relax, the fun's just beginning, you're in for the ride of your life sweet cheeks."

Matt's mind reeled. Forty-eight hours. He desperately needed to get word out to MICO. He'd been so intent on his own thoughts, and trying not to interfere in the interaction between Ed and Jules, he didn't see Jimmy make a move on Kellee until the rope pulled against his hands.

He almost wanted to see Kellee deck the bastard. Casually stepping forward, he placed himself in between them. Jimmy's aggression accelerated, and he could see the situation getting quickly out of control. The only thing he could do to keep Kellee safe was to stake his own claim on her.

"Back off, she's mine. You can have Jules."

Matt put his Reaper persona into the face off. "You can fuck off unless you want to fight for her."

Jimmy scowled at him. Eyed Kellee, standing protectively behind him, and back, as if weighing up his options.

Matt took an aggressive step forward "Come on... outside... you and me."

"There'll be NO outside" Ed intervened, a smirk spread across his face, "If ya game Jim's-me-boy, take it down to the bunker. Don't want the neighbours callin' the cops now." Ed's chuckle, low and sinister, indicated he would personally like to see a bloody and brutal fight.

"The bunker then. Come on."

Jimmy hesitated and broke eye contact, then turned away muttering "Go fuck ya self, that sluts not worth it."

"Well, I won't be fucking myself." Matt chuckled, easing off a little. But there remained one thing he could do to help Jules. He stepped right into Jimmy's space and poked him on the shoulder. "And while we are at it, if you don't look after her nicely, you won't be fucking no-one, I'll make sure of that."

Ed got cranky. "Enough of this shit. I got things to attend to. Jimmy, take care of Jules. I still want her in one piece and not banged up. Matt, make sure you always keep that bitch tied up. Swap if you want to, I don't give a fuck." A knife appeared as if from nowhere in his hand. "You'll both regret it if I have to come back and split up a fight." He spun, stomping off in the same direction Granny had taken.

CHAPTER FIFTEEN

K ellee was feeling remarkably cool-headed. When she had jolted awake to the knife slicing her finger, panicking, she thought it had been hacked right off. Looking back now, the pain seemed minimal. A smart sting like a paper cut. The amount of blood made it look worse than it actually was. His words though, had been a different matter. Even now, recalling them, they chilled her to the bone. She was certain he would have done it.

Now, he confused her again, by playing the protective game. Keeping Jimmy at bay. What in hell was he up to? No way would she play games with any of them. She could hear the jerk in the background whining about a foursome. Matt continued to ignore him and turned his intense gaze on her. She put up her hands to ward him off, taking a step back, shaking her head.

Matt grabbed hold of her bindings with ease. "You can protest as much as you like. I love it feisty. I prefer to take it long and slow, but darlin' feisty works just as well." He pulled her to his body.

"Trust me," his whisper floated like liquid silk against her ear, so light and gentle she almost thought she was imagining it. The soft words came again, "trust me." Rationality disappeared to sensation as his breath led a trail down to the base of her shoulder, where he planted a delicate kiss, moistening the skin with the tip of his tongue.

She wavered and leant into him, then mentally kicking herself she stiffened, ready to pull away. Her emotions were flipping topsy-turvy. How could she feel this way when she knew he was a criminal? Why so aroused and feeling protected, yet wanting to escape and stay all at the same time? Thoughts vanished as he suckled deep into her neck, spinning a silky web of desire. She automatically leaned into him, unable to suppress a sigh of pleasure as she angled her head to give him better access.

It only encouraged him. He rested warm hands on either side of her cheeks, his thumbs offering a feather-light caress. With infinite tenderness he tilted her head until she gazed up into his face. He seemed to be drinking in the sight of her, and she was mesmerised as his eyes, strong, hot and inviting, darkened into rich pools of espresso brown.

His hands turned to fire, not one that burned, but the kind that smouldered welcome warmth into all the parts of her body, flooding her with sensations never felt before. His maleness surrounded her, drawing her in closer, wrapping her in a world of his making. The spacious room shrunk as lust flooded every cell, and she parted her lips in invitation. He accepted, and, at the first gentle touch, she knew, no way on this earth could this man be evil.

His lips hovered like a butterfly over a flower before they touched, and then, like a fire brand they teased. Short and light kisses, gently tugging on her bottom lip. Releasing it, he started again, small undemanding tender kisses that caused her to want so much more.

She went to move her hands, the restraints forgotten. He stopped, then gently lifted her binding, placing both of her hands over his head. It bought them closer together and for Kellee sensation exploded into overdrive. She'd never looked up into a man's eyes before kissing him. Matt's encompassing embrace offered safety, and the admiration he showed made her feel beautiful. And when his mouth came down again, she opened to him and greeted him with her tongue.

He responded with an energy that engulfed her as he deepened the kiss. She melted inside, moving against him, encouraging him to kiss her with more flare and passion. When his hand dropped to her hips, she moved against him, pressing in hard. A perfect height and a perfect fit, and if they shucked off their clothes, they could make love without hesitation.

How and when he'd manoeuvred them down the narrow hall unnoticed eluded her. She found herself up against a wall and responding to the erotic motions of his hips. Wildfire sensations devoured her, and she embraced the moment as each thrust of his tongue matched hers. She ached for his touch on her body, her breasts tingling as she rubbed herself against his rock-hard chest.

Only when the wall gave way did she realise they were leaning against a door. He swung them through, spinning her around so her back met the interior wall, and he cocooned her on either side with his arms. She protested as he released her mouth, his breath coming in deep gasps, caressing her face as he rested his forehead on hers. Her hands were still tucked over his shoulders, and she used them as leverage, trying to press against him and bring him back into contact.

"I'm sorry," his voice sounded shaky as he lifted her arms over his head, letting them fall between them. She closed her eyes as she felt the orgasmic feeling slipping out of her grasp.

He stepped back a pace. Her breathing and heart rate were matching the erratic pace of his. She was hovering on the edge of an orgasm without barely being touched. All he had done was kiss her, and she willingly kissed him back. Desire flooded through her again, as she imagined what she would feel if he touched her where she ached for his hands to be and how she would react.

The need to say anything vanished as he let out a curse, reaching sideways in a bid to shut the door as it began to swing open. Before she could scream, he threw her on the bed, arms over her head, spread her legs and lay on top of her, his body flush with hers. Oh shit. She kept perfectly still, willing him not to move as she instantaneously found herself back on the precipice. His sexy arousal nestled deliciously right where she didn't need it, and their clothes didn't make an ounce of difference to what she was feeling.

"What do you want Jimmy?" Matt's voice sounded deadly as he turned his head to look at the open door.

"A foursome," Jules giggled. She wasn't missing Ed at all as she shook her boobs at them.

"Fuck off. I don't share – close the door behind you."

"Come on man, it's fun time."

"Get out and take her with you." Matt half turned and growled at the couple.

"Your loss." The door banged and rocked the elaborately framed picture on the adjacent wall.

"Sorry, I heard them coming." When he turned back to her, she knew she couldn't conceal what his movement did. So she clamped her teeth, squeezed her eyes closed and let the waves of ecstasy wash over her in silence.

He jumped as if a taser bolt had shot through him as she shuddered beneath him. Muttering an oath under his breath, he grabbed the lead rope and looped around the head of the bed and fled into the adjacent bathroom, his face as red as a furnace.

Mortified, Kellee pulled herself up into a sitting position. His expressions screamed louder than words. Astonishment, shock, and then horror had crossed his face. What had she done? From the moment his whispered "trust me" snaked its way into her heart, his spell began to weave its magic around her. When she ripped her feelings apart, analysed them, she knew she trusted him. She just couldn't understand why.

Trying to sit up was uncomfortable and constricting. He had been slap-hazard when he tied her to the bed, and she had it undone in no time at all. The bonds around her wrist were another matter altogether. She moved off the mattress and sat with her back against the door, crossing her legs and leaning backwards. Without a lock, there was no way Jules and Jimmy would be getting back in. She gritted her teeth, determined to give them hell if they tried.

At the sound of the shower she began to relax. If he was under the water, she would be left alone. He still invaded her thoughts. Looking at the clock on the bedside table, she could hardly believe only five hours had passed since she had been taken hostage. It seemed like a lifetime. Mulling over the events, it dawned on her she did hold a certain amount of faith in Matt. He had stopped Ed from shooting her straight up, consoled her panic in the Ute, and protected her from Jimmy. She shook her head, still coming to terms with it... he hadn't cut off her finger. And his self-control just now, she'd felt the hardness of his arousal. Goodness knows, there had been no resistance from her.

A glance down at her hands showed an element of care. He could have bound them behind her back. Leaving them in the front offered her more movement. She wiggled her fingers, reliving what had probably been the scariest moment in her life. Even when her partner had callously aimed the gun at her head, all she felt then was a deep betrayal. She knew her rambling thoughts were being ruled by her head, her logical side. She preferred it that way. Forget the heart; trouble, indecision and pain followed that route. Stay rational.

He had shot two police officers in cold blood. He had stopped her from escaping both times she tried. Bringing her wrist up to her face, she twisted them towards her, so she could tug at the band-aides with her teeth, wanting to see how bad the cut really was. A nick below each joint. The lower one was deeper, longer, no doubt the one causing all the blood. It should heal in no time at all. Neither of the cuts were serious. Would he have followed through? She shivered, remembering the cruelty in his voice. Yes. He would've. She was sure of it.

It was more important than ever to get away. Maybe now she could convince him to let her go, come with her even? She remembered the greedy gleam, as he had drooled over the diamonds, and her heart sank. Time and time again money proved to be the route to all things horrid.

Oh, gosh. What about her feelings for him? Did she have compassion for him, or was it Stockholm syndrome setting in already? Surely not. She snorted out loud at her stupidity, knowing she couldn't use that as an excuse. She was angry at herself for the fact he turned her on, and she was finding him irresistible. His quirky, lop-sided smile changed his harsh face, enhanced his looks with a cheekiness she found impossible to resist. She cursed. Was she destined to always be attracted to the bad guy? Pushing the memories of her first teenage boyfriend and her traitorous lover out of her mind, Kellee drew once again on her inner calm.

Years of Police training had flown out the window the day her partner turned his gun on her. The twinge in her back, a daily reminder that life could be snuffed out in a precious second. She didn't want to die. In the last few weeks with the help of the psychiatrist, she stopped jumping at every shadow and began to enjoy life again, sleeping without the plaguing nightmares. A corner had been turned, but now she felt she was being dragged back down and into the dark alley of despair again. She couldn't afford to let that happen.

Using a relaxation technique, the psychiatrist had taught to help her sleep, Kellee tried to calm the torment of her mind, concentrated on her breathing, and relaxed her muscles one at a time. Her eyes shut and she summoned a mental picture of her peaceful safe place. She internalised sitting on bare rocks opposite the top of a high waterfall. Rainforest-clad mountains rose on either side, and she could see the Tully River as it tumbled over the falls to the ground below, before it wound its way through the valley. She had been there on an organised tour when she first arrived in Cairns. Beautiful, stunning and majestic, she couldn't wait to go back. For now, she used the vision to provide her with a mental sanctuary.

To her despair, this time the waterfalls proved to be no haven. The invading visions from the other room, kept her well and truly in the present.

CHAPTER SIXTEEN.

Matt let the pounding water cascade over his hair and down his back. The cold water brought no comfort to the raging inferno inside. He needed heat. He added a little, then some more, until the temperature offered a steamy comfort as well as a cleansing. He turned his face into the stream. What in the hell had happened back there? He'd been so intent on controlling his own roaring urges, stopping from taking her up against the wall, he had failed to see just how much his actions were arousing Kellee. He'd been taken totally by surprise when she orgasmed under him. He had been darn close to coming himself. Her silent rapturous expression filled his vision and for an instant, a part of him had wanted her to cry out in delight. He'd wanted to fill her need and urge her on to greater pleasures.

Given it had been a long time between his own physical relations didn't help much. Too long. He felt himself grow hard again at the thought of her. Resting his head against the wet ceramic tiles, he let the water pelt against his neck, hoping for some relief. He opened his eyes, looking down at his penis. It was swollen, throbbing and demanding attention. He reached out, running his hand over the length, the heated sensitive flesh jerked at this touch. His balls, hard and full, responded as he worked them like spheres of putty. A deep throaty growl rumbled as he clasped tight.

Her faint underlying perfume played on his memory and the remembered sweetness of her voice sang like music in his ears. Her lips pliant under his, demanding more each time the kiss deepened. He almost swore he could feel her mouth, warm and inviting as it closed over his erection. His hands moving in time to her sucking motion. Down and up, down and up. It was as though he felt his hands running through her sexy hair, encouraging her to move faster and deeper, faster and deeper.

Eager fingers cupped his balls, squeezing, and moulding, rubbing along the sensitive line between them. He saw her on the bed, long legs open to him, her arms reaching up as he plunged deep inside her. Her muscles clamping around him, pulling him into her warmth with each thrust. His hand gave one final pull. Bucking and jerking he threw back his head, suppressing his own cry of passion as he spouted creamy white jets of empty pleasure against his stomach.

The aroma of bitter almonds filled the air, and it was some minutes before he could breathe properly, soap up and rinse off. A little shocked at the intensity of his sexual self-gratification. Shock waves still racked his body, and he made a mammoth effort to put other, less stimulating images into his mind. He had to maintain control. It wasn't the first time he'd needed to do that, but it was the first in a long time. What he found most surprising was the surge of pleasure that continued to swamp him, even now as he pictured her hands tied to the bed. Never in a million years would he have thought she could turn him on so much. Those long legs. Water droplets sprayed the mirror as he shook his head, trying to clear his mind.

"What in the hell are you going to do?" he asked his reflection. Thoughtful brown eyes stared back, not supplying him with any kind of answer at all. Running a hand over the day-old stubble on his cheek and chin, he contemplated a shave. He hung his head, knowing he was simply delaying the inevitable. He would have to face her sometime. *Get a grip man, she'll be feeling a hell of a lot worse than you.*

Matt tucked the towel around his hips. He needed clean clothes, and they were in the wardrobe. Stepping out, he shivered slightly as the chill from the air-conditioning swept over his damp skin and wet hair. For a brief second his heart leapt into his throat when he saw the bed empty. To his relief, she was sitting on the floor across the opposite side of the bed, her lower back against the door. Raising her head off her drawn up legs as he entered the room, she turned toward him, her troubled eyes connecting briefly with his. She turned away, a slight flush gracing her cheeks as she bowed her head, resting them back on her knees.

Glancing down at his bare chest, his washboard abs and the towel riding at a dangerous level on his hips, he knew he looked alright. He loved and cared for his body; it was a vessel to take him through life. He cursed under his breath. No wonder she flushed and turned away. What in the hell must be going through her brain? She didn't know he had no intention of taking this sexual connection between them any further.

"Only getting some clothes." He intended his words to be comforting, but they echoed sharp and strange as they invaded the silence. Almost like it wasn't his own voice. "I'll be back." he rolled his eyes and look heavenward, cursing at how stupid he sounded. Who did he think he was, Arnold Schwarzenegger?

Matt pulled on a dark tan t-shirt, tucking it into the waistband of his olive-green cargo pants and did up the belt buckle, transferring the contents from his dirty trousers to the ones he now wore. He checked himself in the mirror, looking at his wavy hair. It needed a cut. It was much longer than he would usually wear it, but that was part of his undercover appearance. He found the unruly curls were easier to manage if he didn't fight them. Taking his sister Jo's advice about what to do with wayward hair, he ruffled it up and let it do its own thing.

Delaying tactics over, he walked back into the bedroom and stood in front of the woman still sitting on the floor, deciding honesty was the best policy.

"I'm sorry," he said. "Not just for before, but for your being dragged into this mess. Especially your finger." He reached out and took her hands in his, pulling her to her feet. He didn't like towering over her and again admired her height as she stood almost as tall as him.

"Would you have cut it off?" Her words were blunt and her face expressionless as he inspected the place where she had removed the band-aides.

"I was doing everything in my power not to. If it came down to your finger or your life, then yes, I would have." Matt pushed away any feelings of guilt. He couldn't afford them in this business. The fact she was alive and unharmed would have to suffice. Keeping his mind positive proved to be more productive.

She stared at him long and hard. Assessing him with intelligent eyes. He easily held contact. Her eyes shone like green gold gems, framed with thick dark eyelashes that closed and opened in slow motion as she accepted the sincerity in his words. She gave him a simple nod as she turned her head to the side. Her tongue came out and moistened her lips, and she swallowed deep before turning her eyes back to his. "So, what now?"

"I must keep you tied up. Granny's orders." He dived into his pocket and took out a knife which flicked out a six-inch deadly blade as he released the switch. Instantly regretting the thoughtless quick movement as she flinched, seeing her eyes grow wider.

It's OK." He reached out and pulled her to him, grabbing hold of her bound hands, noticing the bonds were damp and slightly frayed. "I need to know you won't try and take off if I untie your hands so you can have a shower. The back of that Ute was filthy." He shook his head. "Are you trying to chew your way through? You'll break your teeth doing that darlin'. Only way to get these off is to cut them, but first I need your promise."

Her eyes narrowed thoughtfully. "OK, I will not try to escape, as long as I am showering alone, with the door shut."

He couldn't help but smile. "Fine by me. Do you give me your word?""Yes, I thought I just did that."

The ropes fell apart once he sliced through the top strands. He unwound the rest, removed the protective bandages, gathering them together and tossing them in the bin by the desk. His body remained alert in case she tried to bolt for it. After all, she was under no obligation to keep any promise to the man who held her captive.

She rotated her wrists, then shook them, flinching a little as the blood supply flooded back. He moved, so she could walk past him and around the bed to the bathroom. When she turned to close the door, he was right behind her, reaching out a hand to stop her.

"A fresh towel is on the side of the bath. You can give me your dirty clothes. I'll get your pack. At least that way you can put on something fresh." He moved aside and let her shut the door with force. Smiling to himself, he appreciated the feisty glare she gave him. He shouldn't really get any amusement out of the situation, but it was impossible not to. Her mind was clearly running erratic; fearful and quiet one minute, aggressive and annoyed the next. Funnily enough, he believed her when she said she wouldn't try to get away. Her words held a solid truth. And if he guessed correctly, she may have a wicked temper under normal circumstances. The door opened a fraction and her arm appeared holding out her shorts and shirt.

"Any undergarments? All I am going to do is throw them in the washing machine and dryer."

She shut the door.

"If you want to put them back on dirty, it's your choice." Silence. He could visualise her leaning against the other side of the door chewing on her lip, indecisive about what to do. He tried not to imagine her naked.

"You could always rinse them out in the shower. I promise not to look as they are drying."

The door opened wide. With a towel wrapped tightly around her chest, she threw her undergarments into his arms saying, "Bastard," slamming the door hard behind her.

Matt couldn't help but chuckle to himself as he walked away. Yep, she had a gutsy temper on her. He admired that quality. So far she had shown her anger at appropriate times, which showed a natural control. He suspected there was more to her than met the eye.

Closing his bedroom door behind him, he slid the bolt into place, effectively locking her in. All the bedrooms were like this, no lock on the inside, but could be bolted from the outside. Not for the first time he wondered what other things went on this this house and he wished the walls could talk. The drugs and guns were horrific enough, but now he had risen higher in the gang, he realised human trafficking would be a primary part of the operations and it sickened him to the core.

Once out in the hall, he took a left turn and left again almost straight away, back into the bathroom Kellee had locked herself in before. The toilet and hand basin were off to one side, the other end held washing equipment. He tossed the clothes into the machine, checked his watch and set the alarm. Thirty-eight minutes, then he could transfer them to the dryer.

He returned to the living room. Rummaging through the fridge, he found the stew, and placed a decent portion into a microwavable bowl and set the timer. While the seconds counted down, he cut off a couple of chunks of bread, whistling softly.

"Finished already Pretty Boy?"

He prided himself on his cool composure, but when the raspy voice emerged from within the shaded depths of the living room he jumped, dropping the knife on the counter with a loud clang.

"Fuck Granny, I didn't see you there." He picked it up and placed it on the sink, pulling himself together quickly. "Want some stew?"

"No and watch your cuss words boy. I have washed more than one young man's mouth out with soap and water. Now come here and assist an old lady up out of the chair."

Matt complied, holding out his hand offering support. Realising as she stood easily, she didn't need his help. The muscle tone he could feel beneath the looseness of her weathered skin was rock solid. He filed away this piece of information but kept his voice and movements casual as he loaded up a tray with the meal.

"Where's Ed?"

"If you want to keep in my good books, you had better cut it with the questions." Granny stomped her cane hard on the tiles. "I like my boys to do as they are told."

"Understood. I can take orders."

"You're also good at avoiding answers. If you want to put it to the test you will see how good I am at getting what I need. I asked if you had finished already?"

Matt turned on his charming smile, one that never failed to get a result. One corner of his mouth lifting, eyes sparkling with mischief and a lustful hint to his voice. "Hell no." He gave her a broad wink. "First time hard and fast, second time slow and steady."

"Hell is still a cuss word." Granny chuckled deeply, no reproach apparent in her words. "You're a cheeky one alright. Your soft edges are a concern boy." Instantly she transformed from sweet old lady into formidable old grouch. Her eyes narrowed, and features became stern and cruel. "I want you to understand one thing. I'll shoot you myself if I think you won't fit into the Compound. Just because you are in my good books does not guarantee your safety. If you are a threat or a loose cannon in any way, you are dead. Once on our turf, your life belongs to us." She stared at him long and hard.

"I am who I am Granny. Can't be anyone else. Will get what I can, anyway I can. I have a lot to offer and want to be where the big bucks are earned. This world owes me jack sh... Nothing. Absolutely nothing."

"You have come to my attention now pretty boy. I want you to realise something. We don't let any old riff-raff in. Once you are inside, there is no coming and going. You're either in or you are out. No phones, no communication with the rest of the world. We will be your world."

"As long as I am paid well, and get a chance to spend it every so often, I don't give a..a hoot where I am." He hadn't realised how much bad language had become second nature. Watching his p's and q's around Granny kept him on edge and by the gleam in her eyes she enjoyed his discomfort.

"Might have another little job for you." She looked around, leaned forward, dropping her voice low and conspiring, "Jimmy's getting to be a nuisance. Not sure if he is suited to compound life, and he knows too much to let him walk away."

Shit, this was going from bad to worse. He desperately needed to contact his back up team. Aware of Granny's shrewd eyes watching his every move, he grabbed a couple of beers and put them on the tray.

He turned and held her gaze, giving her a sharp nod. "Just say the word."

"That's my boy."

His mind kept racing. Could he achieve it without actually killing Jimmy? So far, he had been put on the spot only once. His other 'so called' killings had been manipulated set-ups, which kept the victims not only alive, but a useful source of information. When he had killed a man outright, his own life had hung on the edge. If he'd failed to react first, he would have been a dead man himself. That the man was selling ice and amphetamines to kids as young as ten, helped to ease any guilt. This was social warfare after all, and he wasn't going to get anywhere by playing nice.

"Granny, I am done here. Need me for anything else?"

"Maybe if I were twenty years younger." She cackled with laughter. "Go on with you boy."

."Goodnight Granny." He thought it best to be polite.

She called after him. "I am locking the house up for the night. I'll be in the bunker and don't want to be disturbed, I have some private business to attend to."

Matt turned and nodded to indicate he understood. Wishing like hell he knew what that business entailed. He had his suspicions all right, but like the turtle, he intended to play it slow and steady to win the race. He was one step closer to finding the traitor, and who killed his brother. The organisation was huge. This promotion was only middle ground. Patience proved to be so darn hard at times.

As he went to turn into the hallway Granny called out again. "Keep her restrained at all times, pretty boy. Never trust a woman. They will always double-cross you." she cackled again. "And I may just come and check to see if you are being a good boy."

CHAPTER SEVENTEEN

Granny studied the giant of a man as he sauntered off. She didn't trust anyone. This one oozed a certain charm that stirred her stagnant hormones into life. Ahh, if she were twenty years younger, she would take great pleasure in pushing him to his limits, seeing the capability and stamina of his muscular athletic body. Alas, those days were past. Her mind may be willing, but her body, old and withered inside, grew closer to its expiry date.

She lifted her finest Waterford crystal out of the cabinet, appreciating the way the glass sparkled and danced in the overhead light. Her favourite wine added liquid sunshine as the Ramonet embraced the glass, producing swirling aromas of fresh citrus, rich acacia honey with an undertone of mint.

Instead of having Jimmy killed before they got to the Compound, it would be exciting to organise a fight between these two, see who came out victorious. Nothing like a bloody brawl in the death pits. She shrugged off the thought. No doubt Pretty Boy would come out on top. In fact, it would probably prove to be disappointing, over before she could blink. They were no match, but it would be a great test of loyalty. The more she thought about it, the more she despised Jimmy for being a weak link. She hated any chinks in her chain. A chuckle escaped her lips. Better still, pit

Jimmy against the hostage. Now that would be something worth watching.

With care, she placed the wine on a coaster, cursing at how her hand shook. Her cane clicked methodically on the tiles as she headed back for the rest of the bottle; sacrilege to leave a Ramonet unfinished. So much still needed to be done. At this age you realised life was far too short. The business she had nurtured and built up over the years, supplied her with a lifestyle she felt owed by society. Like an addictive drug, she clung to dreams still possible. Money...pfft...not an object. Glory be, she never would be able to spend her wealth in ten extravagant lifetimes. Might be fun to set the cat amongst the pigeons and leave her fortune to Pretty Boy. She cackled, wicked and dangerous, as an evil thought flashed into her head. Devious, murderous, brutal games to lay claim to her money. That would be one hell of a fight to watch. Not that it would be happening any time soon; plenty of life left in her yet.

A sigh of relief escaped her lips as she sank her tired bones back into the chair and reached for her wine. After a long luxurious sip she chuckled softly, feeling down the side of the cushion and pulling out the round snow cone from its hiding place, placing it neatly back on the polished surface. She couldn't help but admire the girl's spunk.

Ed, on the other hand, persistently annoyed the crap out of her. He thought he connected well with the hierarchy. If she had her way, he would soon find out they ate puny cretins like him for breakfast. Expendable after the job would be the best way to describe him.

Think of the devil, and he is bound to show up. She heard the hiss as Ed opened another beer while he made his way to the lounge. She enjoyed his annoyed grunt as he sat opposite her. Patience was definitely low on the list of his virtues.

"Got sick of waiting for you to come back." Ed grumbled as he took a long swig of the beer.

Granny never explained her actions to him or anyone. She narrowed her eyes as he blurted out.

"When do I see your latest acquisitions?"

"Plans have changed."

"Oh." He paused. "What! You said I could at least see the young girls."

His frustration rang happily in her ears. She felt a little sadistic, annoyed at his impatience.

"Well, what about that girl you promised me?"

"Wipe the scowl off your face. The prostitute has been paid and sent packing." She reached for her cane, thumping the floor to emphasise her point. "You want to go back to being one of the boys, 'Thumper?' If you do, just say the word?"

She saw Ed's jaw tighten as he gritted his teeth at the use of his old gang name. Such an easy man to control. No way would he wish to go back to being a club member. The greedy man craved all she offered, and more. He wanted to climb right to the top. So, he missed out on looking at the sweet souls she had procured. He understood the strictly 'no touching' rule. She needed their innocence intact for the sales organised from the Compound. Pure and in immaculate condition meant mega bucks. She would kill anyone who jeopardised that.

"Fu..." He remembered the no swear rule just in time. "No way Granny, disappointed that's all." He licked his lips and absently scratched at this groin. "So, what are the new plans?"

She picked up her wine and took a delicate sip. "Ahhh nothing nicer than to relax with a glass of quality wine at the end of a busy day." She leaned back with contentment, knowing the action would drive him to the point of frustration.

Ed took a mouthful of his beer, not caring about her love of expensive wine. Ten dollars or fifteen hundred, to him they all tasted like vinegar. He waited an appropriate time before asking. "Do you need me to hang around?"

"Yes," she said, studying him from over the rim of her glass, thoroughly enjoying the way he squirmed restlessly in his chair. She didn't need him, but her ego thrived on making him sit and wait for his dismissal.

Even though she had been waiting for it, the telephone's loud shrill still caused her to jump and set her heart pounding. Five loud rings before falling silent. She waited, not minding the secrecy, the code names, the caution, and protocols that must be strictly followed. These precautions had kept them safe for years. She glanced at Ed when the strident sound came again. He went to rise, but stopped when she signalled for him to stay. Her hand trembled as she lifted the receiver on the fifth ring.

"Butterfly," a nostalgic note graced her tone. In her youth she had been as beautiful and elusive as a rare butterfly.

She moved the phone slightly away from her face as the gruff wheezy reply of 'Mantis.' grated on her eardrums.

"You don't have to yell. My old lady's ears are a bit delicate these days."

Mantis' softer tone caused Granny to smirk as she settled deeper into the chair. The stupid old coot, she still had the power to control him. She listened intently for a while, then asked him to wait a moment. She covered the mouthpiece with her hand and spoke to Ed.

"Go down to the basement. We have visitors, men that Mantis has sent. Let them in and give them a hand, do whatever they ask. They are in charge." The protest forming on his lips died as he saw the malevolent look she gave him. He simply nodded and walked away.

Granny waited until Ed stepped into the elevator and closed the door before she spoke again. "Now, what is this about Mantis?" She reached for her wine, listening to her long-term business partner's croaky voice.

"Your home's compromised. You need to take refuge within the Compound. The men I sent are to clear out the entire bunker stock and the latest acquisitions. I have had word that MICO is planning a raid in just over forty-eight hours from now."

She kept silent, letting Mantis tell the full story without interruption. The phone grew sweaty in her hand and her arm began to shake so she switched sides, nodding in agreement every so often. Age sat heavy on her shoulders, the aches and pains of arthritis grew worse, becoming harder to block out. "Do you trust your source?" she questioned.

"Yes." He mumbled as a bout of coughing interrupted the conversation.

Granny sighed. Fool of a man not taking care of himself in his ageing years. She waited until the fit passed before she queried, "There is one thing I don't understand. We were due to leave in two days' time. Why is MICO conducting the raid after we depart? Why not why we are still here? It doesn't make sense." Even good wine could turn sour sometimes. But she finished the last drop, resisting temptation to throw the glass against the nearest wall in frustration. Her sharp mind assessed the problem at hand. His next words caused her to sit up straight with attention.

"The hostage is a policewoman, and judging from MICO's reaction, totally unplanned. They sound worried about her."

This is going from bad to worse she thought, squeezing the bridge of her nose in a bid to clear her head. Finally, she spoke, confidence and decisiveness ruled her tone. "I agree. I don't think she is a plant. More a wrong place, wrong time issue. Don't worry, this is an interesting turn of events. I have a plethora of contacts will pay handsomely to lay their hands on an officer of the law. Maybe I will sell her instead of her offspring. I'll ask Matt to check her out again, make certain she is not bugged in any way, and remind him of the need to keep her secure at all times."

She shook her head as Mantis continued. "Go to the Compound for safety. Surely you have enough stashed away to set yourself up again if necessary."

Stupidity did not feature on her list of attributes. She might be getting on in years, but her brain still fired on all cylinders. "I am too old and tired to start over. I suggest you do the same. You won't like it, but you are going to have to trust me like I trust you. We know each other's identity. I have taken precautions in case you hatch any nefarious plans which will interfere with my existence. As you, no doubt, have done with me. I feel it is the right time for me to bow out now. Thanks to MICO, my operation is irreparably compromised. I will stay in the Compound while I finalise a few retirement plans."

She gathered her strength, noting the unhealthy weakness in his voice as he rambled on about trusting each other. She took satisfaction in knowing his age affected him much more than her. Age might be creeping up, but she kept herself healthy and fit.

"Mantis, my old friend! I have no intention of spending my last years behind bars and I don't want you too either. I can handle everything here. I will ring once I arrive. Do not worry, I will tell you my plans when I see you face to face." She hung up, not giving him a chance to challenge her authority.

Compound be damned. She possessed more brains than that. If she went there, Mantis would make sure she never left. Her time with the Organisation was over. Safeguards were in place, time to implement them, so they couldn't find her, let alone touch her.

Hands resting on her chin, she sat quietly thinking as she formulated a plan. She possessed enough money to do anything she pleased.

The clunk, clunk of her cane on the tiled floor made her stop mid stride, causing her to smile. Tempted to wildly toss the thing across the room, she stopped herself just in time. Not yet. She couldn't afford to let anyone see the real her. She proficiently faked needing the support after she healed perfectly from her hip operation, overplayed to everyone the frailty she endured. Her wig, worn for so many years, had been a permanent fixture for so long, she doubted anyone really knew her original hair colour anyway. The blue/grey, granny bun was so far removed from her natural style she looked totally different without it. Younger in fact. Even her stoop was exaggerated.

The men from security should be well into clearing out the bunker by now. It was time for her to take charge. She walked to the bookshelf on the far wall, and pulled out three adjoining books, laying them in their places, but on their spines. The shelf slid silently about half a meter to the right, exposing a small panel. She placed another two books onto their spines and the panel slid downwards revealing a keypad and a compact lever.

With deft fingers she tapped in a sequence of numbers, hesitating momentarily before pulling the lever into the up position. Her fail-safe switch. If the power went off, the battery backup held enough charge to keep the countdown running and to detonate the explosives at the time she coded in next. Anyone still inside would be shattered into a million pieces along with the house. She timed it for maximum damage to MICO's operatives, as they made their grand entrance. A pleasant thought popped into her head. She hoped to blazes it took out the stupid old hag in the house closest to her. Fucking bitch, always attempting to make friends.

She walked through the lounge, touching favourite pieces of artwork and furniture, remembering each purchase, and the pleasure in finding the perfect place for them. A huge fortune helped created this house, and she would miss its luxurious charm. Mantis would be busy for a while, tracking a leak within their Organisation. He had resources of his own. His government contact willingly informed him of an imminent raid by MICO. Some sadness crept in. Her dear home would be no more. The clearance and evacuation of the bunker would be well under way, done and dusted well before MICO's arrival. There was more than one way out of her underground haven.

Something still bugged her; it was eating away at her logic. What advantage could be gained by MICO taking action after their original departure time? Alarm bells clanged. It made a lot more sense to attack whilst she and her people were still here. Why let us absconder scot-free? Could the traitor be one of them? Logic twisted that theory upside down. If the informant was in the house, why hadn't they used their insider position to their advantage and assist MICO. Her smile failed to reach her eyes. There were too many variables. What would it matter to her now anyway? Time to pack up a few of her personal belongings. Soon she would leave by the front door, walk down the hill to the main road, stripping off her wig and changing her clothes as she went. A new person would call a taxi to the airport. First though, she needed to pay a visit to Pretty Boy, let him know about the bitch cop. She didn't know why, but felt she owed him that much.

CHAPTER EIGHTEEN

K ellee leaned back against the bathroom door, the sound of it slamming still ringing in her ears. What in hell was she meant to do? He had shocked her by asking for her underwear, then outsmarted her with his logic of leaving them to dry in full view, versus having them back promptly. One thing for sure, clean clothes and undergarments would improve her inner strength.

In the next breath, she cursed herself for being impulsive. Now she had nothing to wear after her shower. *Stop and think girl,* she chided. He said he would bring her backpack, didn't he? There was no lock on the door, not much she could do about that. Scanning her surroundings produced nothing sturdy enough to jam under the handle. The room, white, elegant, decadently generous and, like the rest of house, wearing splashes of vibrant colour with style. A spa bath snuggled in the corner, off to her right. The frameless glass double shower took up a large portion of the wall. A marble bench with a raised multi-coloured, crystal-like bowl sat off to her left. And behind a lattice panel nestled the toilet.

Alongside the elaborate mirror above the sink were cabinets. She opened one to find it was full of male toiletries. The other side revealed dozens of women's items, all unopened. Without wasting any more time, she grabbed the nearest bottle of shampoo and conditioner, some liquid soap, turned on the shower, adjusted the temperature, dropped the towel within easy reach, and stepped under the spray. Pellets of steaming hot water pounded her skin, giving instant relief to the tension in her shoulders. Not wanting to linger, she resisted the urge to stand under the spray and wash away her fears.

At first the hair products smelt a little flowery for her liking, but as she worked up a rich lather, she found the aroma refreshing and quite invigorating. Rose and Geranium, the label supplied. A pleasant combination. She soaped up and rinsed off her hair and body, ignoring the sting on the chaff of her wrists and the cuts on her finger, until one of the cuts started to bleed. Red droplets diluted by water pooled near her feet before swirling down the drain. Mesmerised, she couldn't take her eyes off the cut. Her vision darkened, and she was almost consumed by the memory the tangy aroma evoked. Once she gained control, she pushed the thoughts away. This was not the dark alley, and she was not covered in blood. She couldn't see or smell the deep red life flowing out of the young girl, who had been laying barely a few feet from her. This is only a tiny cut for goodness' sake. She pulled herself together, sucking on her finger in a bid to staunch the flow, turned off the water and slowly became attuned to the intense quiet surrounding her.

The silence rang in her ears. Turning her head to one side, she listened. Nothing. Letting out a sigh of relief, she stepped out onto the thick bathmat, securing the towel and wrapping it around her tight, tucking the ends in at the side of her breast. It made her feel less vulnerable. Her finger had almost stopped bleeding. She checked every so often as she searched for some Band-Aids, but there were none to be found.

Perched on the edge of the spa, she towel dried her hair as best she could, applied some moisturiser and combed out the knots, flicking the strands back behind her ears. Never had she grown her hair so long, and she harboured a twinge of regret she hadn't had it cut once it started to become annoying. Her desire to look different, be different, had won. A kind of physical recognition she was no longer the same person as before the shooting.

Kellee considered herself to be one of the fortunate ones, her cry for help, not only heard, but answered. She wouldn't be who she was today, except for Harry's intervention, the grandfather figure who had taken her on as a rebellious teenager when no-one else would.

Life had been rough as an unwanted child, with only the collected welfare payment to give her any value. Being raised in a home of abusive, drug addicted parents she became an angry, hard to understand child. School had provided her with an outlet. She found the classroom a place to flourish in peace and solitude. She excelled at her studies. Once she hit high school, problems arose with not fitting in with the cliquey structures of the groups and she found herself bullied incessantly.

Her gangly height and scruffy appearance made her the butt of many jokes, and she'd retaliate in the only way she knew how, with her fists. The teachers, overworked and underpaid, missed the tormenting that led to these skirmishes, only seeing the end result, and the headmaster's office became her second home.

Her peers found inventive ways to continue their torment. The local heart throb came on to her, and she fell for his highly attractive bad boy image and the attention he lavished upon her. Flattered by his interest, and overwhelmed by her own raging libido, she failed to see the wicked prank until it was too late The video clip he showed his friends of taking her virginity and the subsequent laughter and ridicule that followed, sent her plummeting into deep depression. It hadn't stopped there. Foolishly believing him when he said he would return the footage if she helped him with a robbery. It was a set up, and she had fallen into deeper trouble, only this time with the law.

Time in juvenile detention had made her tougher and more self-reliant. Not long after her release, she came home to an empty house. Her folks were gone. She was only fifteen and she never found out what happened to them. Keeping quiet about it, she struggled to survive, dropping out of school, and managing to find part-time work as a waitress. It was not enough to live on. She got caught stealing the perfectly fine but wasted food from the restaurant bin. This time, when she appeared in court, she fronted a Judge who cared. Seeing potential in the young girl, he arranged placement in the home of an old, retired policeman, who helped her continue her education and give her the lift she needed to steer herself forward in life.

Recognising her quick anger, her foster parents rigged up an elaborate climbing wall in their garage, setting hard and challenging courses. By channelling pent up aggression against her own strength and dexterity, she learnt a personal form of self-control. The next logical step was to join the Police Force, and from there she never looked back. She loved her job; she knew instantly she wanted to help young girls in need.

Her thoughts came back to the present, mulling over all that had happened since she was taken hostage. Something niggling in the back of her mind came to the surface. Subconsciously, she'd been suppressing the thought, while struggling for her own survival. Now, she had time to think. Pin pricks of fear shuddered through her body. In the basement, alone and afraid in the back of the Ute, she was certain she heard a young soul crying. Was there a girl who needed her now? What would happen if she confronted Matt about it? Would she be able to judge anything from his reactions? Maybe it was time for the policewoman to emerge.

Kellee stood, pulling the towel tighter and readjusting the corner so the tighter tuck made her feel secure. She also felt pleased her thoughts had taken her back to a part of her life she usually ignored. Realising, perhaps for the first time, the grudge held towards her parents no longer weighed her down. The psychiatrist not only reconciled her to the aftermath of the shooting and her fiancé's betrayal, but he'd also helped heal the pain of her upbringing. The last of the resentment for being born into such a family drifted away. Her past created her persona today. For the first time the load lifted about her childhood, finally that mountain of neglect stood behind her. Now she just needed to move out of its shadow.

Where were her clothes? Should she venture into the bedroom? He had promise to bring them to her. Adrenaline buzzed as she opened the door a fraction and stuck her head out. She jumped back as his hand, clenched ready to knock, pulled back. His face broke into a huge grin and her insides flipped into jelly.

He pushed the door open wider and held out her backpack. "Here's your bag. Your clothes are in the dryer, half an hour and they should be ready."

"Thank you." Kellee kicked herself as she snatched the pack and clutched it close to her chest. Why in the heck did her natural politeness have to surface? Her breath caught in her throat, as his eyes turned serious, and a frown appeared on his forehead. Intense and brooding, he was no longer looking at her face but downward, at the bullet wound on her shoulder. The heat of the shower highlighted the puckered red scar, and she instinctively hitched her towel up higher, hoping the other three were not visible. Before she could move away, he reached out and traced a soft path around the circle shape, moving towards her to inspect the entry point on her back. His hands dropped and he looked questioningly at her.

She didn't know what to do or say. Her mouth opened to talk, shut again as she took a step back, still clutching her bag. The movement caused his eyes to drop again. But this time they lingered on the long length of her legs. Something sparked between them as his eyes locked onto hers, and again she enjoyed the fact she looked up to meet his gaze. She could see the bright flame of desire dancing within the brown depths. They held her mesmerised, like a rabbit caught in a high beam. All too soon he broke contact, cursing under his breath. He backed out and shut the door behind him.

Her school crush may have used, abused, and ridiculed her. Not a nice memory, but she could push that away easily now.

Concentrate on the positive elements he had awoken in her. She'd felt alive and in awe of her body and what it was capable of feeling. And she treasured the feeling of being desired and creating desire. And to be honest, her relationship with her fiancé over the three years of togetherness had been happy and caring. She'd felt loved, cherished, and safe in the comfort of his arms.

Through her therapy sessions she realised most of the time she had instigated their lovemaking, failing to see the tell tail signs indicating his attention wasn't one hundred percent devoted to her. Her psychiatrist helped her to understand; he was the one lacking and at fault, not her. And for the first time since the shooting, she felt relaxed and openhearted about the good person she was. Her fiancé's betrayal was not her fault. Neither was the situation she found herself in now. She vowed to keep her head together and get out of this mess. She would find a way to escape.

Keeping up her pep talk as she sorted through the items of clothing in the bag. Using the bikini as temporary underwear, and with a sarong tied around her bust, she wiped the steamed glass over with a dry towel. Twisting sideways and craning her neck to look at her back in the mirror. No way could she go out into the bedroom wearing just this. All her scars were visible, and she was showing far too much skin. No way. She needed the type of clothes that offered comfort and protection.

Rummaging through the backpack she pulled out the Barrier Reef t-shirt she bought for her boss. Ripping off the price tag she pulled it over her head; big, baggy, and perfect. Wasting no more time thinking about what she might find on the other side of the door, she stuffed the rest of her belongings back into the pack, hung up the bathmat, opened the door and walked through. One thing she had never done, and didn't intend to start now, was hiding from her problems.

The first thing that hit her as she strode into the bedroom was the mouth-watering aroma of stew riding on the cool air. Rich and inviting. Her attention went straight to where Matt had placed it on the small desk.

"Sit." he commanded. "You must be hungry."

"I need a Band-Aid for my finger."

"Here, let me have a look at that." He pulled her hand in for a closer inspection. "I didn't think it was that deep. It should really have a stitch or two. It might leave a scar." He never said anything, but his eyes went back to her shoulder before he moved away to rummage through his pack in the wardrobe. He came back and applied some antiseptic before placing a bandage on top. "That should fix the finger, now let's take a looked at these chaffed wrists. They really need re bandaging."

Her stomach let out a loud rumble as she sat in the chair indicated. She looked across at him, but he moved back to the bed and picked up his gun and began to clean it, completely ignoring her. Suited her fine. She didn't need him gawking at her while she ate. If she could eat. The first mouthful played and danced on her taste buds. Strength came from food. She devoured the lot, mopping up the remnants with a bread roll.

Two beers sat on the tray, dripping condensation into small pools on the wood. She didn't drink; never wanted to after seeing her parents wipe themselves out night after night using welfare payments to fund their addiction. The whole system needed to be shaken and tipped upside down, weed out those abusing the benefits and only help those who genuinely needed it. Many times she had endured going to bed on an empty stomach and waking up to nothing.

Matt leaned across, grabbed a bottle, and twisted off the top. He offered it to her, she shook her head and turned away. He shrugged, went back to his job on the bed, taking a sip every now and then and putting it on the bedside table. The silence felt uncomfortable, at least to her. But be dammed if she was going to fill the void with pointless chatter.

Out of the blue, two things popped into her mind. She needed that drink, and she wanted some answers. She got up and turned her chair, so she could see him better, sat back down, reaching for the beer and twisting off the top. It gave off a hiss and a small puff of compressed gas burst out. Not taking her eyes off him, she took a sip and almost spat it back out again. It tasted worse than it smelt and destroyed the pleasant aftertaste of her meal.

"I gather you don't like beer." It was more of a statement than a question and the laughter that shone from his eyes suggested her expression amused him. Her cheeks began to burn. She turned away, taking a second tentative sip, finding it tolerable, keeping it in her hands to give them something to do.

"Would you prefer a glass of wine?"

There it was again, the suspicious kindness. "Thanks, but no, I never cared much for alcohol." She twirled the bottle in her hands before taking another swig. "This will be fine."

She watched as he turned back to reassembling the gun, looking up at her as he reloaded it, checked the safety, and placed it on the bedside table. Her mind automatically judging the distance and time she would need if she decided to make a grab for it. What would she do if she succeeded? Everything here appeared to be locked up tighter than Fort Knox.

Kellee subconsciously took one hand off the bottle of beer and rubbed the Band-Aid on her little finger, deciding when she made her escape, she would make one hundred percent certain it would be a success. Granny would indeed cut off her foot. Of that, she was sure. Would Matt do it? She couldn't work him out. He obviously looked unconcerned that she might try to grab the gun, although she could feel him watching her. Avoiding eye contact seemed the best option. It helped her think clearer. Almost. The thought of those smouldering coffee eyes following her every move sent her thinking skewwhiff. If she connected with them, she knew one simple gaze would light up her emotions like party time at Christmas. Unable to put a reason to it, except perhaps, her fatal attraction to the bad boy. She must get away before they moved to the Compound. Wherever that may be. She had a feeling it would be a place of no return.

Maybe she could use the physical spark between them to her advantage. But how? She was not going to sleep with him. A bolt of awareness flashed through her at the thought. Well, she would have to live with the attraction, utilise it, overpower him and get the hell out of here. No point trying to go through the lift to the bunker, she needed a quick easy exit. Pick up a kitchen chair, smashing it through the window by the front door could work. There had to be a path leading away from the house, with neighbours close by. If she made enough noise...she jumped, almost dropping the bottle of beer as he stepped right into her personal space.

"You don't have to drink it." His voice was soft and mellow, a tone you would use to soothe a frightened animal. A strong hand reached out gently, tucking a strand of damp hair behind her ear before pulling her to her feet.

Looking up into his eyes proved to be a big mistake as bolts of raw energy ignited in her blood. Oh! He was hot. Her bottom lip began to quiver, so she clamped her teeth on it. His eyes were mesmerising, deepening from chocolate to deep rich coffee. His lips parted as he leaned forward to kiss her. She let out a small breath, opening her mouth to lick away the dryness.

Holy moly she wanted him. Using her beer as a barrier between them, she stepped back, took a long deep drink, and finished the bottle in half a dozen large gulps. Alcohol should give you courage, shouldn't it? Even with a bit of distance between them, she knew there was no way she could overpower him, with his formidable height and muscles stretched against sun-bronzed skin. His warrior stance oozed alpha male.

Needing a barrier between them, she blurted out. "I am a policewoman." If you help me, I promise I will do everything in my power to help. I'll put in a positive word for you, hell, I guarantee you, I 'll do whatever I can."

He didn't look surprised at her outburst. He tilted his head and looked thoughtful. She thought momentarily of the dead policeman before pushing the negative image away. This was about getting away. Her superiors needed to know about Granny and the bunker underneath the house and the Compound, whatever that may be. Possibly people smuggling. She was certain she hadn't imagined a young girl crying.

"I will turn my back while you run." she lied, realising there would be nothing she could do to help him. He had broken the law in the worst possible way. "Please, let me go."

"Now why would I want to do that, when I have everything I need right here?"

If she thought the sexual chemistry was strong before, now it exploded into a million scorching fragments. Backing up, the desk hit her legs, leaving her nowhere else to go. It only took a split-second for Kellee to realise, by coming around to her, he had separated himself from his gun. It was closer to her by a short dash across the bed.

Ensuring he couldn't see any tell-tale signs in her expression, or what flashed through her mind, she dropped her head. When she deemed him to be at his furthest point, she leapt at the bed, turning it into a sideways roll, reaching out with her left hand as she completed the move, coming up gun in hand.

He stood stock still.

Kellee swung her feet onto the floor, keeping the weapon steady and pointed at his chest. Why was he standing there so relaxed and calm? "Lay face down on the bed, hands behind your back." Glad her voice came out strong and firm, a total contradiction to how she felt inside.

She almost panicked when he shook his head, with a tisk tisk expression on his face.

"Now!"

"And you will do what if I don't?" He moved around towards the end of the bed.

"Stop right there."

Slow deliberate steps kept coming her way.

"Last chance." Kellee released the safety catch, her mind in a turmoil. What in the hell was he thinking? What in the hell was *she* thinking?

"Don't come any closer, I will shoot you." To her own ears her voice lacked the conviction drummed into her during cadet training. She fought to steady her shaking hand, realising she didn't think she could do it.

"Come on. " He goaded. "Don't stand there quivering like a blinded rabbit. Toughen up, pull the trigger."

They both jumped out of their skins as the door flung open and Granny stood just inside the room. "What in the blue blazes is going on here?"

"Just having a bit of fun." Matt walked the last couple of steps and took the gun out of Kellee's hands. "It's not loaded. I wanted to see the disappointment in her face when she realised she was playing a fool's game."

"Put that sadistic streak away Pretty Boy. I have been informed she is a cop, an officer of the law."

"What?" He spun around to face the old lady.

Kellee didn't think it possible for someone to move so fast. Matt dug into his pockets and loaded his weapon in record time He turned his head to face her and took steady aim. Strength deserted her legs as she jumped back against the wall, sinking to the floor, hands protectively covering her head and body.

"Don't fuckin' move."

Granny cackled.

No way did Kellee want to. She was not only terrified, but totally confused. Why did Matt act so surprised, when only a moment ago she had announced she was a Policewoman? And why on earth did he wink at her when his head turned away from Granny. Whatever game he was playing, she didn't like being a part of it.

The stew sat thick and heavy in her stomach and for a horrid moment Kellee thought she would lose the contents. Swallowing the bile that rose to her mouth, she willed herself to stay calm. Kellee listened, missing Matt's question, but Granny's answer came through loud and clear.

"No change of plans. She will bring in a better price. Lots of buyers I know would love to get their hands on a cop."

"Me included." Matt laughed. "Maybe I will buy her myself, but then again, I would probably be bored with her after a few days."

A jangling noise caused Kellee to risk a fugitive look.

"No more games, Pretty Boy." Granny held out shiny handcuffs. "I want her cuffed to you at all times."

"You ever slept in these things? Can I cuff her to the bed, so I can get some sleep?"

"Cheeky boy. Lucky for you I am in a pleasant mood. Do whatever you see fit, but she must always be locked onto something solid. When we are on the move however, I want her linked to you so there is no chance of escape."

"Consider yourself fortunate, copper." Granny's harsh voice filled her with fresh panic. "No time to cut off your foot, too busy tonight."

"Anything I need to know?" Matt questioned.

"Nothing to worry your Pretty Boy head about." Granny pulled the door closed behind her, with finality.

"Come on, up off the floor."

He clearly used a different voice with her when they were alone. Gone was the aggressive stance and tone, and he was back to that relaxed, confusing, sexy bad boy.

"Get a grip." she muttered under her breath as she stood to face him, hands on hips. She had just about had enough of not knowing how to react to his games. She could have sworn he had loaded the bullets back into the gun before he placed it on the bedside table.

"I don't know what you are playing at. Getting your kicks letting me think I can escape?" She kept her voice quiet and controlled, under no circumstances did she want Granny coming back in. For some reason, she harboured no fear of Matt when he was away from the others. Wary yes, confused, and angry. You bet your bottom dollar! But frightened? Strangely not. She shook her finger at him as she hissed. "Did it make you laugh? Give you a big enough thrill to let me think..."

"Right now, I need you to have trust that I am going to get you out of this alive. Both of us." he interrupted, clasping her waving hand.

"You expect me to have faith in you..." again he cut her off. This time by pulling her into his arms and covering his mouth with hers.

CHAPTER NINETEEN

He kept the kiss light and tantalising, pulling back before he got lost in her sweetness, almost caving as she began to melt into his arms. A Policewoman. It fit the calm strength he saw when her steely resolve surfaced. His attraction ran unparalleled to anything he'd ever experienced. He stepped back, studying her face.

"Sorry," he started. "Not a good idea with the empty gun." He traced his finger over a bruise beginning to blossom on her cheek. "Truth be known, I wanted to teach you a lesson. You need to be extra vigilant if you are going to get out of this alive. You shouldn't take half-cocked risks based purely on emotion."

He liked the way she glared at him. She shone like a beacon of light in this world of dismal crime. "Make sure you observe everything. Stay alert always, and, if you are going to pick up a gun, be prepared to pull the trigger. Hesitate and you're dead."

Kellee's face turned even paler, and he thought for a moment she might faint. Then, like magic, her colour returned, anger flaring as she fired the words at him. "Would you have shot me? Would you, if Granny gave the word?" She didn't wait for him to answer. She shrugged off his hands and confronted him. "One minute you are ice, then you are fire. I don't know what to make of you, or how to take you. And you want me to trust you?"

"Shhh..." Matt glanced towards the door, making quietening motions with his hands as her voice began to rise. "I don't want Granny to come back." He took his own advice, lowering his tone. "Honestly, I never know what I am going to do until the moment hits. It's the way I work. I act on pure instinct and quick thinking."

"So, you would put a bullet in me."

Wow, she radiated rare beauty. He stared at her. She stood tall and proud, crossing between a tiger protecting her territory and a gazelle, unsure of whether to stand its ground or flee.

"Don't you have any moral sense at all? Are you always looking out for number one?"

The spoken words knocked him for a six. Of course, he held morals. He never put himself first. He could see how it would look to her though. Not much he could do about that now. Her strength and composure astounded and impressed him, but her vulnerability, when it surfaced, displayed a raw insecurity, and it held him back from telling her about his undercover assignment. The less she knew about him, the safer she would be.

"Well, are you going to answer that or not?"

He chose his most charming grin, one that never failed to win a person over. "I do what's right at the time."

"That still doesn't answer my question."

"Well, I can't give you` an answer, as it never got to that point." His smile deepened, but she stood her ground, staring at him blankly, before she spoke.

"Looked like a close thing to me. Guess we're at a stalemate then. Do you mind if I go to the bathroom? I need to clean my teeth and then sleep. It's been a long day." She didn't bother waiting for a reply. He admired the swing of her backside as she strode away from him. On her tall frame the baggy t-shirt added a sweet mystery to the shape beneath. At the door she turned and paused, asking in a sarcastic tone, pushing him as far as she could.

"Am I entitled to privacy?"

He grinned, something he seemed to do a lot around her, "entirely..." His grin broadened as she didn't bother to wait for him to finish, his words hitting the closed door..."up to you darlin'."

While she secluded herself in the bathroom, he took the opportunity to rush the crockery back to the kitchen and throw her clothes in the dryer. He arrived back a scant moment before she stepped through the door to stand uncertain before him.

Matt dreaded the next step. He didn't want to see that look of vulnerability on her face deepen. She may not believe it, but her safety was his highest priority. Should Granny make another entrance, and he had neglected to comply with her order for the restraints, he didn't think he would be let off easily. It would indicate how soft he treated her. At this stage he couldn't afford the risk and her life could depend on it. He had to keep her by his side, to help her escape when the opportunity arose.

The cuffs clinked as they dangled off his fingers. Prepared for a battle, she surprisingly made it easy for him, going over and sitting on the side of the bed and holding her wrists towards him. Her tight-lipped expression, the only hint she was acting compliant on the outside only.

He snapped one cuff around her right wrist, the other to the lowest horizontal railing of the frame before making his own way to the bathroom. Torn by the desire to ease her stress, he wanted to explain about his undercover work. He knew it would be detrimental to her and him if they decided to apply any pressure to see what she knew. Now they held Intel on her being a Policewoman, the unpredictability of what they might do to her weighed heavily on his mind. Hells, they may even think she was a spy.

Bottom line, the less she knew the less they could force out of her. Basically, the more ignorant of his affairs she remained, the safer they both would be. For now, he just needed her to have faith in him as a person, one who would keep her safe, protect her from the evil clutches of Granny and the organisation.

Each step he took got him closer to nailing the bosses. Imagine what closing the Compound would do. True, he only held a basic understanding about the place. He gathered from their talk it involved human trafficking, as well as drugs and guns. As a Police Officer, she was sworn to uphold law and protect the citizens of Australia. Surely if she knew his reasoning for keeping it under wraps, she would understand.

By the time Matt came out of the bathroom, Kellee lay on the far right of the king-size bed, her back towards him. The cuff on her right wrist gave her the chance to pull right away from the left side he would sleep on. Hopefully they would both get some shut eye, although the way the sheet she clutched tight under her chin hugged to her curves, had him thinking of things other than sleep.

He slid into bed and turned off the switch, shrouding the room in deep black. Kellee's breath caught in her throat, and he remembered her aversion to closed in spaces, and realised total darkness would trigger her fear. He threw back the cover, padded to the bathroom, turned on the light and propped the door ajar, so a light glow illuminated the room.

"Thank you." Her soft appreciation floated across the expanse of the bed.

"You're welcome."

He could hear her steady breathing over the faint hum of the ducted air-conditioning and knew she lay awake. He relaxed, trying to clear his mind, but his thoughts refused to settle.

He wanted to set her more at ease, to have her believe he intended to see her safely out of this quandary. To do that, he needed to take care not to put her in any more danger than she already was. Hell, what a mess. He steadied his thoughts, finally able to relax enough to mull over the day's events. Could he have let her escape? A rewind of the events confirmed that at no stage could he have pulled it off without either jeopardising his mission or her life. Running through each part of the day, he felt satisfied he had accomplished all he could under the circumstances. At no time had there been a chance to help her escape successfully.

The handcuffs rattled and scraped along the wooden rail as the woman next to him rolled over. He could see her outline in the dim light.

"If it was up to me, I would take the cuffs off."

His quietly spoken words floated in the silence.

"Granny will think I am too soft if she sees you unrestrained."

"I know."

"She will let Ed take control if I don't comply. I don't want that to happen."

"Me neither."

The silence held for a while, and as he thought to speak again, she spoke first.

"Would you have shot me?"

He shut his eyes and shook his head, a wry smile gracing his lips. She didn't let up. Deciding to be as honest as possible he answered, "Let's say, I wouldn't have killed you."

"I'll take that as a yes."

"A flesh wound would be the first step towards convincing Granny not to kill you."

Silence again.

"Why did you pretend you didn't know I am a Police Officer?"

Matt rolled on his side, so he faced her. "I reacted instinctively. I always do. It felt more productive, than saying...yes, she just told me."

"More dramatic."

"I suppose. I didn't question it; I went with my gut. It worked, you are here, still safe and unhurt."

"Hmm."

"That's it? Hmm."

"Well, what do you want, thanks?"

He chuckled at her sarcasm, enjoying her sassy approach. "No. Care to tell me about the bullet wound in your shoulder."

She replied short and sharp. "No."

"Wounded in the line of duty, maybe?"

This time the silence stretched out for such a long time, he thought she finally slept. The rise and fall of her chest remained even and steady. Every so often he caught the subtle fragrance of whatever shampoo she had used. He found the faint scent enticingly pleasant, and it triggered images of how her body would feel under his. He felt his cock hardening, let out a soft groan and turned on his back, not wanting his thoughts to go in that direction. Her voice when it came barely reached his ears, and her words sent a wave of sympathetic horror washing over his soul.

"Yes, in the line of duty. I failed to save a young girl, who depended on me. My...my partner... put four bullets in my back." The sentence trailed off..." S...s..so much blood...I... I can still smell it."

He went numb with shock. What she said was near impossible to process, let alone give him the ability to formulate a response. His analytical brain became clogged with unaccustomed emotion and minutes ticked by before he could articulate a simple un-personal reply.

"How long ago?"

"Almost six months. I came to Cairns to see a...um... specialist and to recuperate."

"Where are you from?"

"Sydney. Lived in the city all my life."

"It can be a rough place." His brain finally kicked into gear. He needed to clarify the point that was giving him the most trouble getting his head around. "Did you say your partner shot you in the back?" Once he asked the question, he made himself relax, allowing her the time and space to answer when ready.

She let out a long heart wrenching sigh. "Yes. I didn't know, he was a dirty cop. He is dead now. One of my colleagues killed him as he went to finish me off with a bullet to the head. He still got off the shot, but lucky for me, it only grazed my temple."

Once she began to talk, the words flowed, like a burst dam in full flood. He reached out and took her hand, rubbing her soft skin in comforting circles with his thumb.

"You wouldn't recognise me a few weeks ago. A total mess. Couldn't sleep, go out in public, overpowered with guilt. Literally jumping at shadows."

He sighed as a shudder went through her body and his heart filled with compassion.

"The psychiatrist my boss made me see, worked wonders. The constant nightmares began to disappear over the last few days..." Kellee's voice hitched as her words tapered off. He could feel her struggling to get under control. She was obviously implementing breathing techniques she'd been taught to use in times of stress. Slowly the sharp rapid breaths became deeper and more controlled.

"I am so tired. I keep smelling the blood mixed with the stench of the alley. I am too scared to close my eyes. All I see is that young girl's face. And blood, so much blood, hers and mine running towards each other. It's all coming back. My doctor helped me put it in the right compartments, now it is jumbled again. I hear the gun exploding near my ear. I smell sulphur and the sour tang of life ebbing away, and I am engulfed in a darkness I can't get out of."

The room fell silent again. Matt didn't know what to do. Overcome with so many emotions, he wasn't sure which one to focus on first. What would help her most? He continued to rub circles on the back of her hand and squeezed it slightly to let her know he cared.

"Can you hold me?"

Soft words, barely audible, tugged at this heart.

"...like you did in the back of the Ute."

He scooted over to her side of the bed in a flash, unlocked the cuff on her wrist and tucked her in close against his chest. Her back nestled against his front like perfect puzzle pieces fitting together. The closeness of her body, the fresh fragrance of her hair filled his senses. Inhaling deeply, he felt himself being wrapped in a web of emotion, so alien, it felt like coming home.

He thought they slept for a short while, but he couldn't be sure. The light blanket cocooned them from the cool breeze coming from the air conditioner and he felt deeply content. The transition from comfort to awareness grew as he fought to keep his desire under control. No way did she need that kind of attention from him.

She stirred in his arms.

"I guess we were the last people you needed to bump into today." Matt wanted to lighten the mood. He figured she was close to being overwhelmed and he wanted, desperately, to bring back her fighting spirit, to give her courage and the hope he would get her out of this alive.

"I am a bit of a believer in fate. The past few months really taught me a lot about myself. This holiday, talking to Dr Whitman, I realised some things you can't control. You must gather the pieces and move forward. Thank you for giving me time to get my head together. Today's been a day quite like no other."

She turned to face him. "Your spanners back." She chuckled. Soft, feminine and alluring, it sent his heart pounding to match hers. A tentative finger reached out and traced a line around his mouth and the words he longed to hear caressed his soul.

"Kiss me." She leaned forward and brushed her lips against his. "Hold me. Give me something good to remember this day by. Something magical to hold on to when the past tries to take control."

His racing pulse echoed in his head as he fought to calm the urge to give her more than she asked for. Years had passed by since he'd genuinely appreciated a woman's company. His reputation portrayed him as a cold fish in the bikie circle, not that anyone would reproach him about that. Many a groupie had tried to flirt and tempt him to their beds. He'd stood firm and remained choosy. It came with the persona of Reaper. Oh, he hadn't abstained altogether. He still enjoyed basic human needs, but he had chosen with care. Kept his liaisons fun and light hearted with no attachment. Now this woman wanted him to hold her, kiss her. She did things to his libido no other woman had come close to achieving. Hell, she did things to his heart even he didn't know were possible.

"If I kiss you, I don't know if I'll be able to stop at just that."

"I thought you didn't question things, just went with your gut."

He chuckled as she gently threw his words back at him, and he could hear the smile in her voice as she said. "Look, this is out of character for me, then again, so is this situation. I don't know why I should, but I want the magic of your lips on mine."

"Magic hey." He shifted his upper body, so his hand rested on his chin, and his elbow on the mattress, so he could look down at her. "Somehow darlin', I think the magic is coming from you." Their eyes connected. He studied her for a while, staring into the soul laid bare for him to see. Every nerve ending felt like molten lava, his body rock hard with the desire for action. It took all his will power to keep things light. Most of all he wanted to be able to stop when she asked.

His muscles tensed as he lowered his mouth towards hers, and for a fleeting moment he felt her stiffen. He paused, asked a question with his eye; she relaxed, raised her arms to pull him closer. Her eyes fluttered closed, and her lips opened to meet his.

CHAPTER TWENTY

From the first moment of contact with Matt, Kellee knew her thoughts were flowing from her heart and not her head. The physical need for him overpowered her rational side. Drawn undeniably to his charm with such an intensity, she craved to make a memory with him, one to wipe away the past for good. She recognised in him his kind and gentle side. He may keep it well hidden, but she believed if he could get her out of this mess, he would. Until then, she desperately needed something wonderful to hold on to.

In the dim light she couldn't see the colour of his eyes as he stared down at her, but she could feel the heat radiating from within their depths. She delighted in their sexy glow and welcomed the rich seductive vibe as he poured out his desire for her.

She remembered the gentle passion in his kiss before, and a desperate need clawed at her heart, as if nothing else on earth mattered. For a moment, her head took charge. Was she doing the wrong thing and falling for the bad guy?

All her uncertainty vanished as he hesitated, allowing her time to withdraw. His actions and her fear intertwined, forming a mutual base for her heart to feel secure. She needed this. To see him towering above her now, with that addictive smouldering look, made her feel one hundred percent woman.

Her hands reached up and embraced his shoulders, admiring his ability to make her feel desired. His muscles rippled under her touch as she pulled him closer, wanting his mouth on hers.

His lips when they finally met, playfully encouraged her to join him in a sensual game of nibble, suck, and kiss. His magic tongue wove a web of delight so deep she momentarily surrendered to a flood of sensation before remembering to pay attention to what he needed from her.

She concentrated on the kiss, taking the things that gave her so much pleasure, and mimicked them back at him. Pushing aside her own feelings, she could zero in on what she thought he would like. He pulled back, flashing his lopsided grin and she melted again. No one should look that sexy.

"Stop over thinking and relax. Do whatever makes you feel good."

The soft humour in his voice almost made her panic. Did he require her to speak? She never talked during sex. Simon had detested it. The thought of her treacherous partner sent a cold arrow of dread shooting into her mind, and she pulled out of the embrace with a firm. "NO!"

Matt sprung away and she immediately felt his loss as they lay on their own sides of the bed, not touching. She didn't know how to get herself back in his arms. After a while he responded with a voice thick with suppressed need.

"It's ok. We can sleep."

Kellee craved his kiss, wanting him with a fierce desperation. She justified it by telling herself she needed to make new memories, not quite ready to admit she found him irresistibly attractive. She summoned her courage, sat up and faced him, removing the protective baggy shirt and spoke in a sure voice.

"I didn't intend that *no* for you. I said it to the invading thoughts in my head."

He turned and propped himself on one elbow and looked at her half naked body in a way that made her blood sing.

"Are you sure? I think we both know we won't be just kissing. Once I start, I honestly don't know if I can stop on command."

His head cocked to one side and smiled, her heart picking up pace at how the action softened his face.

"To be truthful, I don't think I will be able to stop either." She laughed, unresisting as he reached out and rolled her on top of him. He held the same humour in his tone that seemed to dance in his voice whenever he found himself alone with her.

"Good, I thought another hot shower would be in order."

She pushed up on her arms, so she could look directly into his face. "I thought a cold shower did the trick?"

He chuckled, cheeky and mischievous. "Not in my case, I needed the opposite reaction."

It took a moment for his meaning to sink in. "Oh....oh!" She sat bolt upright, tucking her knees under her so she straddled his waist. Her face turned to fire, and she felt the flush right down to her groin when he touched her hips, pushing her back slightly.

"A little lower darlin'."

He felt tantalisingly hard, pulsing and nudging at her bikini bottoms. She squirmed and nestled herself against him, stifling a moan as she went into sensory overload. He groaned long and deep, exciting her as she looked down at the sexual desire on his face. A first for her, being in this position, looking down on the man she wanted to make love to. She'd never been encouraged to use her sexuality before and her genuine shyness took hold. Not so much about her body, but about sex. No talk, no noise, had been drummed into her over and over and she found herself a little unsure of her next move.

Confident caressing hands spanned her waist running a sensual path underneath her breasts. Breath caught in her throat as he traced the outline of her bikini. His hand slid up to the shoestring strap behind the back of her neck, the fabric fell hanging below the flesh left exposed.

Her eyes were fixed on his hands. His gaze fixed on her breasts. The sensation when the two came together caused her to bite her lip trying not to cry out her pleasure. Nipples puckered under his meandering fingers, and she automatically went to cover them.

He caught her wrists and tugged her forward. She fell, her hands landing on either side of his head, immediately releasing the pressure between their lower bodies.

"So much better darlin'. Any more squirming would see this end all too soon." She gave a shy smile, liking the way he talked, his words deep and rich, laced with honey. The vibrations from his voice added another element to her over sensitised body. He released her, leaving her towering over him, her breast dangling above his face.

She knew what he wanted her to do, and she felt encouraged by the passion in his eyes as they looked up at her. Memories were being created and she revelled in the power he was giving her. Ever so slowly, she lowered her breasts so one dangled a fraction over his open mouth. Her body jerked back a little as his tongue flickered out across her nipple. She watched it pucker, become elongated and strain towards him as though it held a life of its own.

"Oh yes darlin', tease me." He followed the words with a deep sexy sigh.

She chuckled softly, loving the way he made her feel. Everything about him evoked relaxation and comfort. Like a magnet drawn to its counterpart, she lowered her nipple into his mouth, intending to pull it straight back out. His lips closed around it and he suckled deeply, causing a million fragments of pleasure to shoot to her groin. She clamped her teeth tight, trying to suppress the moan she felt building. In the end it came out as a tiny 'oh', as he released and began feasting on the other side.

She tensed as his hands snaked around her back, causing a moment of panic in case he investigated her scars. He hesitated before sliding his hands towards her hips, making and holding eye contact with her. Fingers glided softly over the curve of her waist as he searched her eyes in the dim light. His hands lingered a little, giving her time to feel comfortable, then he gave her a brazen wink. He continued until they pushed gently against the side of her hips, nudging her backwards slightly.

Thinking he wanted her to lower herself again, she faltered when he spoke.

"Uh uh... Too dangerous if you do that."

What in the heck should she do?

"Kiss me." He encouraged softly.

She smiled, surprising him with a brazen wink of her own, revelling in his understanding. Their lips met and she felt like she had known their touch and taste for a lifetime. They opened under her probing, and the sensation of her being on top and being in control encouraged her to be bold. She explored his mouth with a new-found freedom, deepening the kiss with all the long-suppressed passion she possessed.

He sighed, his breath mingling with hers and kissed her back with an excitement that matched her own. His hands still resting on her hips started to move. She gasped and bucked as he moved one hand between her legs and down the length of her crutch, squeezing on her buttocks as it reached the other end. Her breathing became erratic as he slid his fingers back, letting them dance lightly on the fabric. The strings on both sides of her bikini fell away as he pulled at the bows.

"Can't wait to explore your beautiful body." He did the same again, this time running his hand through the heat of her arousal. He squeezed her buttocks, slipping a finger between the cheeks before dragging it back to play at the entrance to her vagina. "You feel so good."

Kellee forgot to breathe until she felt her face overheat. It did feel good. Too good, and if he didn't stop, she would come right in his hand. A strangled sound escaped the back of her throat, turning into a squeal as he flipped her over onto her back in one swift move. His kiss deep, and sensual sent her passion soaring. A kiss to end all kisses and she responded with an eagerness that surprised herself. This man sent her wild.

Panting hard, he broke away and pushed back, jumping on the bed, shook it a little as he ripped off his shirt and disposed of his track pants in record time. His penis, in all its glory, stood to attention, potent and strong against his washboard stomach.

She delighted in seeing him naked like this, and she wanted to run her hand all over his magnificent physique. She knew what to do with a man's body. It was his charging her body with feelings and emotions, that she didn't know how to react to. She rose, reaching up for him.

He laughed and sprung away, wobbling before he plonked himself down on the side of the bed. He turned back and looked at her. "Danger zone. I wanted this to be prolonged and thorough, but that's never going to happen, not with the way you make me feel." He opened his bedside drawer.

Lured by the muscles on his back and the tattoos blazing across his shoulders, she came up behind him as he slid on the condom. Rising to her knees, she ran her hands over sun bronzed skin, around his waist and up over his chest, resting her head on his back. His sexy growl rumbled inside her as she kissed the side of his neck, tracing with her tongue the muscles on his shoulders, bringing her hands up to caress his nipples, surprised when she discovered one pierced. Tentatively she tugged on it. It fascinated her, she felt compelled to suck on it.

Matt growled again, low and sexy. "Hell woman," he lifted her into the middle of the bed, "what you do to me." He pushed her knees apart, kneeling between them.

Placing one hand on either side of her shoulders he held himself poised over her. Strong and handsome above her, she couldn't resist staring at him for a while before she lifted her arms to wrap them around his shoulder, bringing him closer to her. She kissed him long and hard.

His cock inched its way to its destination, rubbing hungrily against her, encouraging her to open her legs wider. She lifted her hips in anticipation, tensing and almost pulling back, feeling like she needed to say something sexy, but not knowing what.

Once again Matt made her feel instantly secure with his lopsided smile and the deep sensual voice that drove her wild, "You are not about to say no are you?"

She opened her mouth but didn't know what to say, so she shook her head and smiled.

"Hell woman, you are so sexy and beautiful, I don't think I could stop even if you begged me." He pushed himself a short way into the warm haven he sought. "This is what you do to me, I am rock hard and wanting you so bad it hurts." He plunged in as deep as he could, smiling when she let out a tiny gasp of pleasure. "Somehow darlin', I think I am only seeing the surface of what's hidden inside of you."

His mouth met hers as they began the dance of fulfilment. Kellee couldn't stop running her hands over his back and shoulders. His heated skin felt both soft and firm, muscles rippling and bulging as he seductively kept an even tempo. Thrust and retreat, thrust and retreat. A mouth of magic nuzzled its way under her chin to the base of her neck and she let another small moan slip through her lips.

The size of his body matched hers perfectly and they were able to gain easy access to the places they wanted to explore. She ran her hands down to his buttocks and grasped tightly, urging him deeper and faster. Release felt close, oh so close. She tucked her knees, placing her feet next to her own backside, spreading legs wider and giving her the perfect leverage to lift as he thrust. She clenched her lower abdomen muscles, drawing him into her depths, raised her butt and ground into his pelvis. A little more, just a little more.

His growl of delight at her movement, sent her spinning towards climax as he pumped harder and faster, coaxing her on with soft sexy words whispered against her ear. Sweat formed on her brow and she could feel his skin slick with moisture as he moved against her. Sounds of his pleasure surrounded her, excited her. Sensation upon sensation built to a crescendo. His breath came in short gasps, mingling with hers and when he thrust again, he pushed against her clitoris, sending her spinning over into a land of astounding rapture.

Shuddering and shaking beneath him, Kellee threw her head back, mouth open wide and rode out her orgasm almost in silence. A couple more thrusts and he followed on the waves of his release, with a vocal symphony that sent her quivering anew with desire for him.

As the last of the spasms left his body, he rolled off her, his breathing erratic. Kellee's heart raced, and she appreciated the space to gather her own breath and thoughts. Her mind was reeling with the intensity of what had occurred between them. She'd never experienced anything like that before, ever, and she knew, regardless of what lay ahead, she held a memory that would last a lifetime.

Slowly the world stopped spinning and her heart settled into its normal rhythm. She turned her head in his direction, to find him propped on his side, elbow on the bed and his hand resting on his cheek looking at her. The sexiest, cheekiest grin plastered across his face. He looked like a little boy pleased with the best Christmas present of his life.

"Holy smoke woman, I am never going to want to let you go."

Her smile faltered as the double meaning in his words hit home. She watched the happiness fall from his face when he realised the implication. And she instantly wanted it to return. She not only found him incredibly handsome, with his brown unruly hair, curling and sticking out at odd angles, but when he did smile, she felt a connection to the personality hidden deep inside. It changed his face. The harsh, tough lines were replaced by an engaging boyish charm.

She kissed him long and sweet before she spoke.

"I hope you never let me go." A half smile returned as she pushed him back and straddled him like earlier, this time pinning his arms to either side of his head. "You're my best bet at survival, remember. I am depending on you."

Bending her head forward to kiss him again, she let out a squeal as strong muscles flipped her and she found herself effectively pinned to the soft mattress, their faces inches apart.

Her hazel eyes locked with his and it pleased her to see some of the light heartedness creep back into his expression, but his tone still held an underlying seriousness as he said:

"I promise, I won't let you down."

"I know." she replied, and as his mouth closed over hers, she understood it for the truth it was. For some inexplicable reason, she believed in this man's ability to see her safely through this. There was more to him than he showed, and for now, she felt secure enough to follow his lead, and she would back him up wherever possible. Then, everything else in her mind fled as she again became lost in a world of exquisite sensation.

CHAPTER TWENTY ONE

Although the mattress was designed for luxurious comfort, sleep evaded him. Restless, Matt turned onto his side and glanced at Kellee, who appeared relaxed, and snug, curled up, facing away from him. Her breathing, soft and even, indicated she was asleep. A twinge of awareness stirred as he studied the curvy outline of her body. He did his best to push his softer feelings away. After they had made love the second time, they'd kissed, cuddled, and talked. Not about the situation they were in, but small chatter about mundane things.

They kept the tone light. Kellee chatted, he listened, adding fragments about himself every so often. He learnt she liked to wake up with a cup of strong black coffee in the mornings and that she would do anything for a bowl of cookies and cream ice-cream.

Matt didn't consider himself to be a highly sexed person. He enjoyed a woman's company, but not so much on a casual level. Generally, he liked to have a connection happening, so it meant something. In his line of work, such connections were rare. He remembered Jess and still found trouble thinking about her without the attached sadness. Young and full of life, she joined the Gang, ready for the adventure of being a Club Member. Within weeks, she realised she didn't belong in the slot naturally designated for the gang's sluts. On a particular night, she suffered a rough time from some members. She attempted to leave and had been stopped in a very crude and cruel manner. Matt had stepped in and claimed her. No one dared mess with the Reaper. She had stayed with him for almost a year in the Brisbane chapter. Thrived on the status of being an untouchable. Matt genuinely liked the woman and enjoyed the attention she bestowed on him. A mutually agreeable arrangement had been formed, her safety and status assured, and she had given him the perfect excuse for not sleeping around.

Kellee promised to be an entirely different matter. She activated something deep and dormant within him. He already felt possessive and protective towards her, and he knew he would have to be careful to keep his true feelings hidden. For both their sakes.

As if she knew his thoughts were about her, she stirred and turned to face him. He couldn't help but smile at her sleepy expression and tousled hair. "Nowhere near morning yet, so there's no coffee." he teased.

She sat up, pulling the sheet under her chin. His fingers twitched, tempted to pull the thin fabric down and expose her beautiful breasts.

"Not coffee. " She stretched and yawned. "More sleep, but I need to go to the bathroom."

Matt rolled onto his back and tucked his restless hands safely under his head. "You don't need to ask me. If you gotta go, you gotta go." Immediately contrite at the shitty sound of his voice, he sat up, "I trust you Kells, just go."

"My name is Kellee." she stood, trying hard to smother a smile as she secured her sarong.

"Hells Bells Kells, I'll try to remember that."

He caught the pillow before it clobbered his face. "Perfect throw, excellent aim, great for family cricket matches." He stunned not only himself, but her with his spontaneous outburst. She turned back, her astute stare on him, brows furrowing together, then lifting as she replied. "I'd bowl you out before you could even move the bat."

At a loss for words, he followed the sexy sway of her hips and the seductive length of her legs until she shut the door behind her. Immediately he missed her warmth and that started the alarm bells ringing. Trying to stay detached, he set his mind to thinking about the Compound and what he would find there. Wherever the place might be. Top priority, in the next twenty-four hours he must get in contact with MICO.

This part of the gang or organisation - he wasn't quite sure what they were any more - certainly kept things close to their chest. He desperately needed to warn his team, each passing moment filled him with dread. This undercover operation was proving to be far bigger than they had anticipated. Human trafficking. His heart went cold at the thought. There was no doubt in his mind that they planned to sell Kellee to the highest bidder. The thought filled him with dread. Over his dead body. He needed to get her to safety before the Compound.

Next Priority. Find out what happened to his brother. Though, if he were honest, that would always sit at the top of his list. He always had questioned his brother's death. Out of his five siblings, Patrick, the one with whom he shared a room and enjoyed childhood escapades with. His twin. Not identical, but twin, nonetheless. His older brothers, Robert Jr and Steven were total neat freaks, both adhering to the strict military upbringing demanded by their Father. His two younger siblings Kevin and his only sister, Jo, having never experiencing the stabilising influence of their mother, always searched for and found mischief. Both were absolute daredevils on bikes, especially Jo, who, being the youngest, and the only girl in a male dominated household, wore a chip on her shoulder that made her a tough adversary at the best of times. He wondered how Jo would react to Kellee.

A full circle, his thoughts revolved back to Kellee. Gees how long did a pee take. He needed to go himself. He jumped off the bed and walked stark naked to the door.

He scratched at his butt cheek and raised his hand to knock when he cocked his head and listened. Rapping three times with his knuckles, he called out "Are you talking to someone?" Did she have her phone? He racked his brain. He'd left it in her pack, but kept the battery. The temptation to barge straight in almost won, but he stopped with his fingers on the handle.

Her voice floated through the wood, " Err, to myself, won't be a minute."

Patiently he leaned on the door frame, 'a minute' dragging into five.

"Sorry, giving myself a pep talk really helped." The smell of peppermint toothpaste was on her breath and tickled his nose as she leaned in, giving him a quick kiss. He forgot to be annoyed as he wrapped his arms around her waist and pulled her in close.

"A pep talk, huh."

"Yea. Well, life's not easy right now."

He glanced at the pack dangling loosely by her side, trying to remember whether or not had she carried it in with her. "What's with the bag Kell's? Going somewhere?"

"Kellee, remember."

"I wouldn't mind taking a peek inside."

She executed a barely visible nervous hop from foot to foot, opening and holding out the bag so he could see the contents. "I took some shampoo and conditioner. Better to be prepared, who knows what the next place will have."

Matt automatically lent forward to check the outstretched bag, then stepped aside to let her pass. "Smart thinking Kell's."

The breath of relief she tried hard to conceal, raised a hint of suspicion in him. The fact she didn't correct his 'Kells" again had him thinking. He headed into the room and scanned around. Nothing seemed misplaced. Glancing over his shoulder, he could see her still watching him. Purposefully, he leaned back and closed the door. Two could play that game.

He checked the cupboard. Only hair products seemed to be missing. He must be too on edge, reading more into things than he should. After relieving himself, he washed his hands, grabbed a tub of moisturiser from the ladies' side of the cabinet and some shaving gear from his. Her instinct could ring true, nothing like being prepared.

"You left something behind." She still seemed anxious and jumpy. He tossed the moisturiser across the bed, she caught it with a quizzical look, then relaxed and smiled, turning her attention to his naked physique. His prick stirred as she moistened her lips, dragging her eyes on a slow journey up his torso to his face.

"If you keep looking at me like that there'll be no sleep at all tonight."

"What time is it?"

Matt checked his watch, "Almost ten past three." Familiar now with standard time telling, instead of the twenty-four-hour military clock. It had taken him quite a while to avoid military time, after a lifetime of use. It was second nature now to revert to standard time telling.

"We need to sleep."

"Yea." He agreed as he climbed in bed next to her. "Hope you don't mind if I don't snuggle close."

The warmness in Kellee's voice settled over him like a blanket, and he felt himself relax.

"Goodnight Matt, sleep well."

"Hmm, ditto." As he drifted off, his thoughts fixed on Kellee. He believed one hundred percent, if he hadn't made the show of cutting off Kellee's finger, Granny would either have done it herself or got Ed to do it. Heavy with guilt, he once again went backwards through the day's events, searching for different angles on situations. He examined each opportunity, and every time, scenarios led to her being in deeper trouble, if not dead. His last thoughts, as he encouraged his body to relax and drift off into sleep, were number one, how to safely extract her from this mess, and two, how to manage some free time to contact his Team.

The sound of a metallic click shot through every nerve in his body. He jumped instantly awake and was reaching for his gun, when he felt a warm steadying hand on his arm, and a soft shhh sound. Kellee held a finger to her lips and pointed to the door. Some strange sounds came from the corridor. She held up the handcuff to indicate she'd re-attached herself to the bed, then lay back down, pretending to sleep.

The noise didn't sound threatening, more like muffled grumbling, but he wasn't taking any chances. At the first rattle of the door handle, Matt exploded out of bed, dive rolled across the floor, stopping in a crouched position of advantage. His aim steady as the door opened.

"What the fuck Granny, Ed?" Matt lowered the gun and stood, squinting as the light by the door flickered into brightness. "You almost got yourselves killed."

"Cuss word forgiven Pretty Boy. Greet me in that state, and I will forgive you anything."

Matt realised he stood butt naked and not able to do a damn thing about it, except walk back to the bed and pull on his jeans.

"Don't dress on my account." Granny cackled.

"What's up?" He turned to face her as he threw on his t-shirt.

Granny and Ed stepped further into the room. "Acceptable reactions Matt, not like Jimmy, groaning and grumbling like a bear with a sore head. Took forever for him to wake up."

Matt was doing his best to hide the panic he felt from showing on his face Had they come to check on him or what? Thank goodness for Kellee's initiative in acting so quickly. He could see Granny assessing the woman on the bed.

"Good to see you obeying orders. You keep a close eye on her now, always attached to you or something solid. While we are en route, she is your responsibility." She turned her back and walked out of the room with a final, "Ed will fill you in."

"The fault's hers." Ed took a few menacing steps in Kellee's direction. When Matt ignored the movement, he stopped and spat. "She's a pig, and somehow MICO got wind we are here and are planning a raid."

Matt assumed a slightly confused expression. "Yeah, Granny told me before about her being a grunter, but who or what is MICO?"

"Fuckin' interfering ass-holes." Ed shot a worried look over his shoulder.

"Granny's gone, Mate. Who the fuck are they?"

"Military Intelligence Covert Operations. They fucked up my last job, planted two agents right in the gang I was checking out."

"Not very covert if you have Intel on what they are up to." Matt lightened his tone, framing his answer to draw out some information, while his mind whirled in turmoil.

"Yea, well, we got friends in the right places," Ed puffed out his chest, full of his own importance, "with a bit of luck, the surprise we leave them might reduce their numbers, fuck wits."

Matt laughed along with Ed, covering up his urge to panic about a possible mole in his organisation. He needed to contact the Base urgently. Not wanting to raise any suspicions with more questions, he chose to make Ed feel secure and in charge. "So, what now boss?"

"You got five minutes to be ready and waiting in the kitchen. We're leaving early."

"Right."

"Memorise this address. Tree Fern Lodge, Kuranda. Cabin 4. Cassowary Drive. About a kilometre down on the left. No writing it down. If you're nabbed on the way, forget it and keep your cool."

"Got it boss. We're not going straight to the Compound?" He risked the question.

Ed threw his arms in a wide sweep. "This house is now a target. We need to protect the Compound, so evasive actions must be implemented. If you're caught, don't say a word. Our lawyer will do what he can."

"Understood." Matt's mind raced. How to get a message out? This was big trouble. With this interruption, came perhaps an opportunity to let Kellee escape.

"Granny's got some stuff for you in the kitchen. She'll let you know the next step." Ed clapped Matt on the shoulder. "Jimmy moaned and groaned about being disturbed. You, man, take it as it comes, obey orders without question. I could do with a few more of your calibre. I look after those who are loyal." He walked to the door, grabbed a bag he'd dropped when he came into the room, and threw it on the floor at Matt's feet. "Disguise for the bitch. Five minutes."

"Yo boss. I got one question?"

Ed turned and looked back, raising his eyebrows.

"That surprise for MICO, Hope it's a fuckin beauty?"

"Granny intends to send them flying," Ed accompanied his sneer with a wicked laugh, "into a thousand little pieces."

Matt laughed with him. Walked him to the door, then shut it behind him with a click. Kellee went to speak. He made a stop sign with his hand. Dive rolled over the bed, came up and gave her a quick kiss on the lips and whispered in her ear, "Smart move darlin'. Time for questions later." He unlocked her cuffs, tipping the contents of the bag on the bed. "Be ready, quick as you can. I'll use the bathroom first."

Not wasting any time, Matt returned within the minute, pleased to see Kellee had made fast progress in donning the clothing provided. She pulled a face at him. The dress, a little loose and short on her long frame, still looked good. Normal and nondescript. He smiled at the wig she held up dangling over her fingers.

She rolled her eyes and hurried into the bathroom. When she emerged, she looked totally different with her soft auburn hair hidden under the long wavy blonde wig.

"Don't you dare say anything about blondes having more fun..."

Her attempt at humour trailed off mid-sentence as she stood uncertain in the middle of the room. Apprehension and maybe a little fear showed in her expression, and he took a few precious moments to pull her close and stare deep into her eyes. "Believe in me. It may not seem like it at times, but I will do everything I can to keep you alive and protected."

"I have faith in you." her simple words bled into his heart like a poison tipped arrow. Could he keep her safe? Self-doubt raised its ugly head. He slammed it straight back down again. Things may have been easier with only himself to worry about, but hells, he would give it his best shot. He needed to detach, yet the desire to hold and comfort her almost overpowered him.

She reacted first, pulling away, stuffing the bathers and sarong into her pack. Hoisting it on her shoulders, she said, "Come on let's move." Little did she realise by her actions his heart bled a little more.

One thing she'd forgotten. He saw it in her eyes, that momentary panic as he snapped the cuffs on her wrist then his. Not quite as composed as she would have him think. Well, him neither. He gave her a wink and a reassuring smile, picked up his own pack and they headed out the door.

CHAPTER TWENTY TWO

Terror squeezed her heart. What if they discovered what she had done? The soft tug on the handcuff propelled her forward. She shot a last look over her shoulder towards the bathroom, pulled herself together and followed a fraction behind Matt, using him as a shield as they rounded the corner and walked towards the kitchen and a room full of people. Jules, Jimmy, Ed and Granny plus three other strange men, did nothing for her confidence as their eyes focused on them.

"Hey Fuzz." Matt almost knocked her off her feet, as he greeted a buff, heavily tattooed, bald headed man with an animated clap on the shoulders, with what appeared to be a genuine smile plastered across his face. Matt's ability to change personality astounded her. She tried to push away the doubts beginning to gnaw at her resolve.

"Reaper, ya mangy dog. Killed anyone lately." It was a statement more than a question as Fuzz enthusiastically returned the greeting. "Haven't seen ya since that rave in Brissy."

Kellee hung back, not wanting to attract any attention. A near impossible task as her height put her amongst the tallest in the room. Slouching wasn't in her nature, so she stood naturally tall with her eyes downcast, hoping they ignored her. Fuzz apparently wanted to play.

"You got yourself an avatar, wrong colour, but man look at those legs." Fuzz grabbed the cuffs lifting them in salute before pulling her towards him. She expected Matt to be firm and take control, but he stayed relaxed and stepped forward, allowing his friend to wave her arm in the air. Kellee lifted her head and made eye contact with the man. She was slightly taller, and, although short-lived, she welcomed the pleasure of having made him raise his eyes a fraction to hold her glare.

"Feisty mumma," he made revolting lapping motions with his tongue.

Kellee shrank internally. She couldn't do this. Yet the intensity of the eyes on her and all that was happening forced her to stand her ground. Options were limited. She held firm, only to have Fuzz yank harder this time towards his groin.

Inches from the prize, Matt intervened. "My hand's not going anywhere near your fuzzy dangler." Kellee winced as the steel dug into her wrists, and she let out a small squeal as she was propelled backwards to Matt's side. Instinctively, she went to pull away.

One swift tug and she catapulted back, almost bumping into him. "Heel darlin'."

"Pretty Boy, Fuzz. Behave. We are on a deadline here."

Fuzz burst into a beefy, robust laugh, then sobered instantly as the old woman stomped her cane on the ground, not amused. "Sorry Granny, but this boy is anything but pretty."

Understanding flashed through Kellee's mind as Matt's fingers lightly brushed against hers, the repeated light contact reinforcing her feeling that he reacted on purpose. Was this Matt's way of protecting her, letting the external happenings give him a reason to keep her at his side?

Furtively, she watched him work his charm. Not only did he fit in; he blended perfectly and with complete confidence. Respect from them, including Granny, was automatic without his even trying to earn it. And that surprised her.

Bang, the wooden cane rapped on the floor. "Right listen up, we need to be out of here pronto. This is what's happening. I want your phones and weapons on the table."

Ed sneered as Jimmy grumbled the loudest. Matt stepped forward placing his phone, gun and knife in front of Granny, then patted down his pockets, and added Kellee's phone battery to the pile.

"Fuzz, take one of the boys and check the bedroom and bathroom the bitch used. Make sure she didn't leave anything behind." Ed's words sent spikes of fear racing through her. On TV these things played out so simply. You never considered the absolute terror shooting through your body at the thought of being caught. If they found it, she didn't think she would like what the old crone would do to her.

She must have pulled on the cuffs or did something unawares that alerted Matt. He glanced at her strangely, then covered it up by tugging her pack off her shoulder, almost making her stumble, and held it out towards Granny.

"You want to go through this?"

"Has she or the bag been out of your sight?"

"Nope."

Kellee was amazed at how easy the lie slid from his lips.

"No need then, stay alert though, she has been known to stash things down the side of chairs."

Kellee's heart leapt in her chest as Granny banged her cane on the table. "I want nothing left behind, not that any evidence will really matter. This place is set to blow sky-high, timed for just after MICO's arrival."

Her hopes withered a little more. The spark of hope she harboured fled when Matt failed to react at all to the words. He stood there like a drone, waiting to be activated. The tiny flicker of a thought that he really worked for the police, or a secret agency evaporated, an unlikely dream from a desperate woman. All the 'trust me, have faith in me' stuff didn't mean a thing. Keeping her safe may be in his best interest but for what ultimate goal?

Time for thought vanished as Fuzz and the other man came striding back towards them. Kellee's nerves kicked into overdrive. Had they found it? Her breathing shallowed to the point her head started to spin.

"All clear, Granny." The voice floated through her sea of apprehension and a wave of relief rolled over her. Head bowed, but remaining alert, became her preferred stance. She could hear Jimmy and Jules grumbling about being patted down, especially Jules who didn't like the roaming hands of the man who did the job.

"Quit your whining girl. Your belongings will be returned once you are at the Compound." Granny opened the lift. "You two boys first, then Fuzz - you take down these two whiners. I want to talk to Pretty Boy. Once I am done, I will send them down and you can take it from there."

The first two went down. Fuzz stood before Granny and said hesitantly. "Aren't you coming? I got my orders, you're to travel with me."

"Orders from whom Sonny?" A weary age crept into the old woman's voice.

"Mantis."

Granny sighed, her whole body crumpling to a wearied stoop. "Fine. Mantis and I go back a long time We started this business together," reaching up she patted his cheek with a frail hand. "I am going to request one thing. Leave me alone for a while up here after they have gone. Wait for me in the bunker. I have lived here most of my life and I need to say my goodbyes."

The emotional hitch in her voice convinced Fuzz, who held her hand saying, "take as long as you need." Kellee almost snorted, not convinced at all. She camouflaged the sound by a cough and kept her head bowed, knowing the old crone was up to no good. She had seen this transformation in reverse. Matt's squeeze on her hand annoyed her. She pulled away with a noisy clank of the cuffs. Did he really think she would say something?

"Darlin', if I want to play with your butt, I will." With a sharp tug, he pulled her in so close she crashed into the solid wall of his chest. "Be nice now." His words were light and playful, but his eyes briefly flashed a warning. She hung her head, remaining alert and watchful out of her peripheral vision.

Granny turned to them once the lift doors closed behind Fuzz, Ed and Jules. "Are you sure you can manage her?" A sharpness rode her tone.

"She's a handful, but not a problem."

"Excellent. From now on if she plays up, she is dispensable. We can't afford trouble."

"Understood." He yanked on the cuff and Kellee resisted the urge to slog him one. He didn't have to be so cruel.

"Should she die, the world won't stop spinning. They might give you a hard time at the Compound, but I reckon you can sweet talk your way around it. Her loss would be a small speck in the scheme of things."

"You're not coming?"

"Don't spoil my trust by asking questions. Take back your gun and your knife."

Kellee cringed at the interaction between the two. Her arm jerked as Matt quickly stashed his returned belongings in his pack, blatantly disregarding the fact they were cuffed together.

"Here is a phone, receivable only. This has been organised by Mantis, so regardless of what I do, you follow through with his orders and you will be looked after. Rich beyond your dreams."

"Music to my soul Granny."

"Also, if the opportunity arises, waste Jimmy. Jules as well if she gets in the way, curse the whining bitch. Although, she is worth money, so it will stand you in better stead if you arrive with both women. When it is deemed safe someone will call and relay further instructions on how to find the Compound. I tell you this, things are clamping down, the Law is hot on our trail..." Granny's cackle set Kellee's teeth on edge and fear raced down her spine..."but we are a couple of moves ahead. Tie up these loose ends and you will be fine. Your life from now on will be full of safeguards like this, so obey orders to the letter. Once we ascertain MICO is no longer a threat, everything will move along quickly."

"What about Ed?"

"You and your questions boy. Don't you worry about him, he has his own agenda. Precautions boy precautions."

"One last question...will you be ok Granny?" Matt's grin was as cheeky as all hell and there was a genuine concern in his voice that Kellee couldn't fathom. Surely he was not taken in by her demure façade.

"Such a handsome man, aahhh, to be young again..."Back in old woman mode, she let the words trail away and Kellee resisted the urge to scream 'fraud' at the top of her lungs.

Granny reached a shaky old hand and patted Matt on the arm, "Of course I will be fine, just do as I have asked. I want to enjoy the sunrise from this house one more time, then I will go down to the bunker."

Kellee watched in horror as she placed something in Matt's free hand. His expression turned greedy as he put it in his pocket.

"Take care Granny. I'll tell Fuzz you'll be down within...say - an hour?"" Perfect. You can add mind reading to your skills. Take care of yourself Pretty Boy."

Kellee glanced back at the old woman as Matt propelled her to the lift. Granny's smile mutated into pure evil. She almost couldn't believe her eyes. Once inside the lift, Matt turned to hold his hand in a goodbye salute, Granny's face was sweet, simple and frail.

Once the door shut, Kellee let fly, wrenching hard on the cuff, so he copped a taste of how it felt. "She is up to something. We can't let her kill innocent people."

"Let me do what I have to." He moved closer, placing a quick kiss on her lips, "Keep your mouth closed and stay alert. I work best alone, remember. I will protect you. It may not feel like it, but I will."

There wasn't time for anything else as the door whooshed open, and they stepped into the bunker.

It wasn't only Kellee's jaw that dropped, Matt stopped stock still taking in his surroundings. The vast room, almost empty, echoed back every sound. A few bits of paper, dirt and dust littered the expanse of dirty concrete. In the far corner stood a wire cage with its door ajar. In an instant, Kellee confirmed her hearing hadn't failed her. She must have heard soft crying. Cold fear crept up her spine. How could they have moved out so quickly and quietly?

"How?" She muttered the word aloud as Matt pointed to a moderately sized tunnel entrance halfway along the back wall. How could she have missed it?

"Holy smoke." Her confidence evaporated. This operation shouted big money, organisation, and success. Her knees went weak, and her chest became so constricted, panic started to rise. How could she possibly get out of this alive? "This was so....so..."

Matt pulled her close. "Easy darlin', you got me remember." The words brushed against her ear, his breath tickled her neck and for a moment a tingling awareness raced through her body. She thought he was going to kiss her. "Keep calm." He walked over to where Ed, Fuzz and the others were.

"I'm impressed." Matt swept his free arm in a wide ark.

Fuzz looked around, "'bout time you showed up. Where's Granny?"

"The old duck asked for a bit of time. Think she is going to miss this place."

Fuzz's laugh bounced around the empty room and came back tenfold, causing Kellee to step back a pace. "Don't let her catch you callin' her that, she'll have ya guts for garters."

Matt roared with laughter, clapping his mate on the back. "After she beats me half to death with her cane."

Fuzz laughed with him, and Kellee found herself again annoyed as he arrogantly disregarded the fact he wrenched her this way and that when he moved his hands.

Kellee didn't think it was that funny. Finally, when the laughter subsided, Matt continued in a more sober tone. "Said she would be down within the hour. Wants to enjoy the sunrise one last time."

"Fuckin inconvenient is what it is. I want to start moving, don't like hanging around a place when I know a raid's comin'." The ferocious expression across his face did nothing to ease her panic.

"What's going on with that? Security's impeccable. How did they find out about this place?"

"Mantis has eyes in all the right places. Must be high up in the government circles; maybe even a member of MICO himself." Words became almost illegible as he mixed them with a heavy dose of laughter. "They got no idea he reports their every move. Even got one of them wasted last year, words out he's itching to find another."

She couldn't see it, he hid it well, but she felt it in every part of his body. Matt struggled for control, his arm went stiff as he clenched his fist. Instinctively and subtly, she reached out with her fingers, rubbing them gently across this hand until it relaxed, and when he spoke you wouldn't have guessed there had been anything wrong.

"How do you know so much? What are you, his right-hand man?" Matt thumped him on his shoulder.

"Gettin' close." Fuzz puffed up with importance. "I shouldn't be telling you this, but you and me go way back. Hey Bro?"

"Owe you my life Bro."

"And I owe you mine."

They did a private macho hand punch, ending in a chest slap with a tight fist thump. Inwardly Kellee rolled her eyes. She had to give him credit, Matt excelled at casual. She had seen so many sides to him, it was hard to tell which one was real.

Fuzz continued, "He knows there were two Brennan boys undercover. His feelers stretch all over Australia. Got rid of one, can't find the other."

"I thought we were dealing with MICO?"

"The Organisation is government assisted but run by the Brennan family. The Father, a military man through and through, started it years ago. Popped out five sons and a daughter, the bitch. She fouled up Ed's last mission. Fuck, I've never seen him so pissed. He almost caught her. She slipped through his fingers, bringing a small section to its knees at the same time. Left them with no choice other than to disband two gangs. Mind you, they were minor players compared to all this." He threw his hand in a general sweep of the bunker.

"No wonder Ed's being a fucking shit."

"We better haul out."

Fuzz started towards the tunnel. Matt tugged on Kellee's wrist, urging her to keep up, completely ignoring her reluctance to step any closer to the black gaping hole. She took in everything they were saying. Determined more than ever to escape, find the authorities, and let them know.

They stopped at the entrance. To Kellee it resembled a beast ready to swallow them whole, and once again she steeled herself to hide her fear. She didn't want to distract Matt from getting any more information. And the more she heard the better.

"Transport should be here any minute."

Matt remained silent and Kellee moved restlessly from foot to foot, wondering why he didn't ask another question, when Fuzz spoke again.

"Best advice I can give you is stay quiet, be invisible and you will be surprised at what the bosses will say in front of you." Fuzz looked down into the yawning black hole, and then behind him as if to make sure no one listened. "I heard Mantis has managed to infiltrate one of his own, right into the heart of MICO headquarters. The second oldest Brennan boy, Stephen, is the

genius behind the clandestine work they do. Mantis is after him."
He lowered his voice in conspiracy, "I reckon his plan is to knock
them off one by one and leave the father left with nothing. Been
fucking with his head ever since old man Brennan's wife died. Car
crash. Some say it wasn't an accident, who knows?"

Again, Kellee sensed Matt was experiencing deep emotion. His
body went rigid, his fist tightened, and his breathing indicated he
was not quite as controlled as he had been a moment before. Fuzz
continued to yabber, oblivious to Matt's tension. Why she decided
to react the way she did, she had no idea; a weird impulse to help
him and something she would have to examine later.

Pulling back hard on her bonds, she injected a generous dose of
fear into her voice, "I can't go in there... that tunnel. I just can't."
She started gulping in gusts of air as if beginning to hyperventilate.
"Way too dark, I can't breathe..."With a dramatic drop to the floor
she almost brought Matt down, and when he went to steady her,
she squeezed his hand as tight as she could.

He wrenched her to her feet, giving her a quick appreciative
glance. "Stupid bitch. Shut up, or I'll do it for you."

One last dramatic sob escaped, before she made a concerted
effort to calm down. The scenario hadn't been hard to act. The fear
felt real and being close to hysteria was genuine. She did not want
to go into the tunnel.

"What the fuck was that all about?" Fuzz exclaimed.

"Claustrophobia." Matt rolled his eyes, "Should have seen her in
the back of the Ute when they pulled the cover over her. Major
freak out."

Fuzz let out a cold chuckle, "She's gunna love the Compound
then."

Kellee was glad to find Matt back to his normal self. He started
joking around with Fuzz before he turned serious again. "Hey
bro. Thanks for the insider info, I owe you one." He gave him a
brotherly punch on the arm.

"You'd do the same for me. Remember to keep your head down and your ears open, follow orders and you'll be back to working with me in no time. I'm with security. Next time I see the boss, I'll put in a positive word."

"So, what's with the tunnel. Fucking impressive; must have taken years and a heck of a lot of money to build?"

Keeping still and quiet, Kellee wanted them relaxed and talking. The more she heard the better chance of the law finding them when she escaped.

"Never bothered to ask. Think this is impressive? the Compound will blow your mind."

"You cleared the bunk..." The words faltered on Matt's lips as Fuzz held up a hand, listening and cocking his head to one side. He reached into his pocket and flashed a torch on and off. Out of the darkness an electric buggy hummed into view, and he jumped straight into action. The driver cracked a u-turn and pulled up close to them, uncoupling the second vehicle that rode empty behind the first.

"Where's Granny?" The new guy asked, looking around.

"I'll bring her over in a while." said Fuzz

"The plan was for the four of you to ride with me and this car stays here, like always. We leave one behind for the house in case it's needed." He sounded tired, grumpy, and irritable. Perfect, thought Kellee. Tired people made mistakes.

"This is not like other times, Pete." He signalled for Matt and Kellee to climb in the back of the open framed vehicle. "Feel free to step on Granny's toes. Go ahead and drag her down here before she is ready. Count me out. If she's asked for a bit of time before she leaves, as far as I am concerned, she can have it."

Pete grunted, then said, "Well fuckin' hurry up. After we set these guys up, you and me and Granny are meant to go back to the Compound together with the last load. I'm beat, it's been a long night."

Fuzz stretched and leaned both hands on the roll bars above Matt's head, grinning down at him. "You were asking how we cleared the bunker so fast." He nodded in the direction of the tunnel entrance. "You'll spot 'em, local scum, cheap labour. Not far inside, in an alcove on ya right. You'll appreciate it, Reaper." He pushed back, so he and Matt had room for their private salute. "Be seeing ya soon, bro."

"Hey Pete. This is my mate from Brisbane. Matt, aka the Reaper. The lanky bitch is a pig. Keep her safe, Granny intends to paint her like an Avatar for the sales." His words and laugh turned Kellee's stomach sick.

The engine hummed into life. A soft almost welcoming sound and before Kellee could blink, they were through the yawning mouth of darkness. Matt's warm fingers wrapped around hers, offering comfort and support. She found it soothing, the panic she expected to feel didn't overwhelm her. The open frame helped. A stale but welcome airflow hit her face and sensory lights offered a subtle sense of visibility.

Kellee almost gagged as the overpowering stench of rotting blood hit her nose. Matt pulled her hand into his lap and rubbed her arm with his free hand and for the first time since her shooting, she dissociated the metallic tang with her own experience. As the buggy approached the entrance to the alcove, it slowed. Her only emotion was horror and sadness for the pile of twisted bodies lying on the rough stone floor.

Pete was grinning like a Cheshire cat into the rear vision mirror. He half turned and gave a thumbs up. Kellee fought back the urge to vomit. She closed her eyes and placed her free arm over her forehead, tugging her other hand away in a bid to gain some space. Matt held firm, possessively clutching her hand, as they picked up speed again, leaned towards her and whispered, "remember my promise, no matter what... remember."

Kellee drew on all her inner strength, determined not to let the sight of the dead bodies, and the predicament she found herself in, take control. Stiffening her back she endured the journey, taking in every detail she could.

The tunnel was surprisingly well-built, and the wear on the ground showed frequent use, providing them with a smooth ride. The side jutted out unevenly with rock formations. Sensor lights blinked on as they approached and vanished once they were no longer in range. With the headlights shining bright, it gave a clear vision of the road ahead.

Every so often you could see where the stone had crumbled away, and it had been concreted solid again. Sometimes moisture flooded the sides and formed small pools, which the vehicle splashed through without changing speed. They must be going through hills behind the house. Kellee racked her brain trying to visualise the google maps she had studied.

She remembered thinking at first a river ran through the hilly range separating the southern end of Cairns to Redlynch. Further investigation of the map led to the discovery of Old Morris Road. It ended at Lake Morris, also known as Copperlode Dam, Cairn's water supply. This winding forest clad road intrigued her it ran the length of Cairns, but deep within the hills. She had planned to drive it and picnic at the lake. They had to be travelling under them. So far they had been going straight, now the tunnel started a downward descent, the temperature dropping from cool to a frigid chill.

Kellee shivered and tried not to think about the tons of rock and dirt above her head, concentrating on keeping her breathing steady and even. To lose control now would only make her situation worse. She suppressed the panic sitting close to the surface, and let her stubborn streak take over. Her palms were sweaty, and she wanted to wipe them on her dress, but it was impossible with the firm grip Matt had on her hand. A couple of times she tried to pull away. It only made him hold on tighter, and she silently acknowledged the comfort and strength it gave her. Hopefully, this ride wouldn't be too much longer.

"What's up?" Matt reached forward to touch Pete on the shoulder as he slowed to stop at an intersection. He turned off the engine, creating an eerie silence punctuated only by their breathing.

'Standard procedure Mate. There are a few different ways we can go from here, depending on our destination."

"Hope you know which way to go." Matt teased, squeezing her hand again as if he realised her heart rate had skyrocketed. Without the cool air created from the forward momentum, the walls and roof felt compressed and suffocating. The wig didn't help her either, it was irritating and for the tenth time she brushed strands of hair away from her face as she breathed calming breaths out through her mouth.

Pete laughed. "Must confirm before we continue, otherwise the welcoming committee will shoot first, ask questions later. Standard security protocol, for us and for them." He looped his arm over the back of his seat, swivelling to face them. His grin enhancing the handsome lines of his clean-shaven face. "You better get used to it. It's how we keep safe. For example, if they don't answer the right way, I'll know something is up. Report it and try a different destination. By the same token, if we don't check in it will be assumed we are hostile and...kaboom." He emphasised the last word by throwing his hand in the air, making a blowing up sound that ricocheted around the enclosed space.

Kellee jumped, stifled a cry and sank back against the seat, successfully pulling her hand from Matt's lap. How could she have thought Pete's face was handsome? His piercing sneer turned it into something cruel and it made her even more uncomfortable. Finally, he turned to the front and spoke quietly into a handset. She couldn't quite determine what he said, but it sounded like a code. He must have been satisfied with the reply, because he stuffed the device back into his pocket.

"All's clear." He called over his shoulder as the engine kicked over and the vehicle continued, humming quietly.

They travelled over level ground for a while, Kellee feeling a little better once the air movement returned. She counted two more tunnels going off in different directions, but they drove straight ahead until the road started to climb steadily. Pete veered sharply right, almost unbalancing Matt as he bumped into her. He leaned forward raising his voice loud enough for her to hear.

"Much further?"

"Nah. Once we level off again, a couple of minutes max. Underground getting to you?"

"Not really, but I'll be glad to breathe fresh air."

"Know the feeling. Been working through the night, shifting the goods. Ready for grub and some shut-eye."

"I was impressed with the speed you guys must have worked, that place was chockas."

The ride turned rougher, and Pete stopped turning his head toward them, shouting over his shoulder instead.

"Teamwork. Three houses chipped in, hired some local suckers. Done in no time."

Stunned, Kellee closed her eyes. At least three other houses, holy heck. This was a huge operation. She thought she had a handle on Matt's tactics now. He was fishing for information and with the bait dangling, he waited. He remained silent, leaning towards the front. She reckoned he was waiting to see if Pete would say anything else. It paid off.

"We are a smooth, well-run operation. There are four houses around Cairns. Granny's is the biggest one though, the others are tiny in comparison. Border security is tough in the Far North, works to our advantage." He chuckled. "Especially when some of them are on the payroll."

Matt laughed with him.

The road levelled off and the vehicle picked up speed. Kellee breathed a sigh of relief and inhaled deeply. She was rather pleased with the way she was handling the whole situation. Her nose twitched at the thought of fresh air and the fact the tunnel grew a bit warmer indicated they must be getting close to the end.

They travelled along in silence for a while. Kellee's arm was starting to ache, with Matt leaning forward, resting comfortably on the passenger seat in front. It left her with no choice but to lean forward as well. Mind you, this put her in a better position visually and hearing wise, but now her fingers were tingling as the blood flow was restricted and the cut on her little finger pulsed to the beat of her racing heart.

Nerves jumped wildly; her body filling with apprehension as they slowed to a crawl. She wanted out, not to be standing idle with tons of rock hanging over her head.

Pete stopped the buggy and looked back at Matt. "You seem like a good bloke. Any friend of Fuzz's is okay with me. At the Compound I'll put in a word. No doubt Fuzz'll do the same. Our boss is second in charge of security. Be good if you were assigned to us. Security's the best and it has the most perks. Think you, me and Fuzz will work good together."

"Sounds great, look forward to meeting him."

"I tell ya, he's a smart bastard, bet he will have his boss's job before long. Then it is one more step to the top. I wouldn't cross him though. Ruthless."

Kellee thought of the dead bodies in the alcove. This security boss was not the only ruthless bastard around here.

"One more thing." Pete continued. "Follow orders and the protocols, even if it seems excessive. Once you accept it, you'll realise how safe it makes you. Able to rely on your fellow mates and know they always have your back."

"Thanks Pete. Appreciate the heads up."

"We got the go. Lights off from here. In the event of anything being wrong, I would leave them on, and they would be alert and ready. You understand."

"Got it. Smart moves, a good way to keep alive."

"Any second now they will flash me to say all clear. Might seem a lot of checks, but at least we know when we arrive, we are amongst friends. Here put these on and stay seated until you are told to get out." He passed Matt a pair of sunglasses and soon Kellee realised why.

They burst out from the dark into the glaring light of a smaller, well-lit version of the bunker they had left. Kellee squinted against the pain of the blinding brightness.

From what she could see, the scene could have come straight out of a movie. Men milling around. Boxes piled high on the floor. It looked as though these were being loaded into small vans with some sort of logo on the side. All work stopped as the men looked towards the new arrivals.

Pete alighted first, asserting his authority, "Stay alert men, Fuzz will be coming through with Granny shortly."

"What the fuck! We need to get moving now! You were all meant to come together."

Pete might be small, but he had a wicked snarl, and obviously wielded more power. "Do as you're told. Same security procedure. Take it up with Fuzz and Granny if you have any complaints."

At the mention of the old woman's name, the man ceased grumbling and resigned himself to waiting.

"Guys." He waved the small group of men to come over, firing off their names one by one. Then he introduced Matt. "Meet the Reaper, a friend of Fuzz's. He's joining the team."

Kellee scrambled to keep up as Matt leapt out of the buggy, her eyes finally adjusting to the light. He took off his glasses and tossed them onto the front seat. When he turned to face them, his cold expression and the ice in his tone made her shiver. "Call me Matt." He shook hands and made small talk, doing nothing to stop lecherous eyes looking her over like a prize cow on a stud farm.

Now on her feet, she towered above Pete by a good half a metre and stood taller than most of the men. A couple were her height, but they all looked intimidating. One of them, a rugged looking man in trousers and a singlet, blazing tattoos across his arms and barrel chest, stepped so far into her personal space, the reek of dried sweat mixed with the stale food on his breath almost made her gag.

"I'll take her from here." His voice rough and callous faded into insignificance as his cold, narrow eyes glared at her.

CHAPTER TWENTY THREE

Matt didn't move or react, although he went on high alert. He sensed Kellee's panic and relaxed his arm, allowing her to step back a pace. Letting something happen to her was not going to be an option. He weighed up his choices as the man in front of them spoke again.

"As I said, I can take her from here."

"I got orders. She stays with me." Matt altered his stance, taking in the other man's height and weight, having no doubt he could take him in a fair fight. He clenched his fists, causing the cuffs to rattle. He groaned internally. This was going to be tough.

For the second time tonight, he became aware of the woman next to him silently backing him. She moved in closer, still behind him slightly, but he found movement in their joined wrist. She lightly touched the palm of his hand, and he understood she was ready to move with him should it come down to blows. Such a strange and alien sensation, given he worked alone, always.

Realising he had been standing for far too long, he added steel to his voice. "Not throwing the first punch, man. If you want her, you take her." He lifted his cuffed wrist, "you'll have to fucking cut the hand off man, hers or mine."

His opponent struck with predictable speed, aiming a violent fist at his head. Matt thrived in this environment, only one man ever bested him in a straight fight, his twin brother Patrick. He ducked his head to the left and followed through with a lightning jab, pulling back at impact, so it connected but didn't knock him out. The man staggered backwards, trying to steady himself before he poised to retaliate.

Matt held his fists rock solid, the ferocity in his voice forcing the onlookers take a step away. "The next one, I won't hold back."

"Fuck." The man spat blood and swiped at his lip. "You punch like the boss, didn't see that coming." He moved his jaw back and forth. "Next time Fuzz can do the fucking testing." He straightened and gave a split lipped grin " Well done, you didn't break your orders. I am all for you joining us in security. We'll be short-handed soon, the boss being on the verge of a promotion any day now, and Fuzz will take his spot." He held out a welcoming hand to Matt. "The name's Alf."

Inwardly Matt sighed with relief, but something shifted within his core. His mission came in at top priority, but now he realised, there was no way he would be able to continue at the expense of the woman standing by his side.

"Chill bro." Pete clapped him on the shoulder. "Expect the boss will test you too." He laughed at Alf, "Gotta be around to see that one."

Matt clasped Alf's hand and pumped it up and down a few times. "Had me going there for a minute mate."

"Given worse, taken worse," said Alf, still rubbing his jaw. "Where'd you learn to be so fast?"

"The quick or the dead is how I grew up. I refused to let death win."

He joined their hearty laughter, aware of how uncomfortable the woman next to him must be feeling. Not a great deal could be done to relieve that, except reinforce, whenever possible, he had her back.

"Got any food? Man, I am hungry." Matt took the opportunity to look about him. "Where are the others?" This place certainly didn't have the finesse of Granny's bunker. It felt more like a small warehouse to him.

Alf snorted, "The cranky bitch and Jimmy are waiting by one of the vans." He checked his watch. "You will be joining them in ten minutes, give or take. Your exit is timed for one of the usual runs so everything seems normal."

"Smart. So, where are we?" Matt leaned causally back against the buggy, arms resting on the framework, noticing Kellee did the same. He glanced across at her, "Good girl." He blew her a mocking kiss. "Be glad to remove these cuffs.'" He jiggled his uplifted hand, so they rattled.

Pete joined in with a jovial laugh. "Having a bit of skirt to play with can't be all bad."

"I'll give you that. We certainly didn't get much sleep last night." Matt grinned at Kellee, hoping she would understand his need to act this way. She blushed and lowered her face, a perfect reaction. He wanted to put his arms around her, reassure her all would be OK. He looked back at Alf who continued.

"This ain't our place. Works as a dispersal centre under a front as...wait for it...a flower warehouse." He snorted a laugh and a man waiting by the tunnel entrance glared at him. Alf gave him the finger.

"He's not too happy. We took charge while things were being sorted out. Security's number one. As far as we know, MICO has no idea about the other houses. Not that we have been told anyway. If higher up has even an inkling they have that Intel, we'd be warned and shut down."

"Sounds like security is the place to be."

"You bet her sweet ass." Alf waved his hand at Kellee, who continued to keep her eyes lowered. "We're above most of the departments, Distribution, Acquisitions, Distractions and maybe IT. They're kinda level with us. Stick to themselves, stuffy little nerds."

Matt wanted to ask what Distractions entailed. The Organisation seemed astronomically bigger than they envisioned. Very well-organised, which made him all the more determined to get to the top. He was sure to find out more as they got to the Compound, so he asked the next question he wanted an answer for.

"What about Ed?' Matt peered around looking for him. "Is he in Security with you guys?" He let the query hang in the air by relaxing his stance and reaching across to play with Kellee's hair. The wig felt soft and real, although he much preferred her natural colour. Being close to her, even under these circumstances, turned him on big time. He intended turning back to Alf when he saw her nipples respond to his touch and her cute tongue flickered across her lips. She peeped up at him from under hooded eyes and bit her bottom lip. And in an instant, he understood what she was doing: making the boys relax even more. Clever and smart as well as beautiful. His heart swelled.

Alf's eyes boggled as she slowly crossed and then uncrossed her shapely legs. Matt wanted to smash his face to a pulp. He was debating whether to repeat his question when Alf shook his head, and returned his attention back to Matt. "Nar, not security. Don't know Ed that well. Ruthless fucker. He got a genuine kick out of slashing those dope head losers' throats. Like a mad man. The grapevine says that's why Mantis likes him."

"Mantis?" Matt hated to interrupt, but years of relying on his own instinct guided his actions. "Who is he? I keep hearing that name?"

"No-one knows. He's the head honcho. Don't think anyone has ever seen him." Alf's tone was edged in sarcasm. "Apparently, he phones Ed personally. Rang him as he pulled in, gave him a private job to do. Unfinished business. After the call all Ed said was," I'm outta here, give me a car, Mantis' orders. Have a lead on Mouse and when I find her, she's dead meat."

Pete added his opinion. "We think he's Mantis's Hit Man. The talk in the ranks is, he slit the throats of half the gangs of low-level bikers on his last job. His name was Thumper then. Call him that now, and you'll likely lose all your blood to a gaping throat smile. Been constantly muttering under this breath about how things got messed up big time. Grumbles about agents infiltrating and swears he's gunna repay this chick, Mouse. Ha ha ha, her life is about to take a turn for the worse."

"He sure sounds like a bloke you don't want to find yourself on the wrong side of." Matt moved away from the buggy, stretched, then straightened ready to move. "Time to go yet?"

"Gotta wait until the van pulls in. Should be any...what the fuck was that?"

Alf spun in the direction of the tunnel. Pete, already half-way there, shouted, "It doesn't seem close, but you can clearly feel rumbling coming closer." A second blast stopped him in his tracks. A huge thunderclap which appeared to be coming from a fair distance away could be heard and felt.

The noise from deep within the earth grew louder as the sound travelled through the hollow passage. Matt was the first to spring into action. He raced towards the man who had been waiting by the entrance of the tunnel. As the man turned to flee, Matt grabbed him by the shoulders and took the radio he was still clutching out of his hand. "Go outside, check things out, and then hightail back in here to report. Take a couple of the workers with you. Find out what's going on."

Flicking the 'send' switch Matt spoke clearly and totally in control. "Hey Fuzz, bit of disturbance your way. What's happening bro?"

Nothing but static.

"Try again."

The soft voice at his side startled him. She had reacted faultlessly, followed his lead, keeping pace with him, so he had momentarily forgotten they were still attached. God she was beautiful. Staring at her, only having to look down slightly to hold eye contact, proved to be a huge turn-on. If he ever needed a partner, he wanted it to be her. Stunned, and shocked by the thought, he turned away and spoke again into the radio.

"Fuzz...you old bastard, what are you playing at down there?"

This time a voice came back loud and clear. "Fucking Granny. Think she's blown the place up. I'm driving bat shit crazy. Tunnel's collapsed behind me, but I think it has stopped."

"Damn you're alive. Thought I was going to jump straight into your job."

Violent coughing erupted from the handset. "Fuck off. Breathing so much dust, I can hardly talk. The light systems gone out and one of my headlights burst."

Silence reigned for a while. Matt searched his jeans for the key, unlocked the cuffs and put them in his pocket. "Stay by my side." Kellee gave him a surprised and grateful look, nodding as she rubbed at her wrist.

"Sure that's wise?" Pete and Alf stood beside him. Matt reluctantly dragged his gaze away from Kellee. Maybe an opportunity might surface to aid her escape. Something strange stabbed at his heart. He squashed the emotion, no time to analyse his feelings now.

"I can deal with her and this. Don't want to be cuffed if I have to kill her and run. She knows if she moves from my side my knife can outrun her feet."

The handset crackled to life. "The tunnel is a bit clearer now. Think your end will be fine. I am not half-way yet, but fuck man, finding things scary as shit down here. If I bust the other headlight..."

His words trailed off...

"Take more than a dark tunnel to stop you bro. Keep the radio handy, we'll find you if that happens."

The men who had been sent outside burst back in through a side door and came racing over. Matt held the handset up so Fuzz was kept informed.

"Huge explosion over Cairns' way. Dawns breaking, and you can see clouds of smoke coming up over the hills. Most of the street is out looking."

"You hear that Fuzz? Sounds like you're right."

"Stupid old bitch. Hope she blew herself up as well." The grumble in his voice sounded like the old Fuzz. "The dust's clearing. Now it's as creepy as hell down here. Hang on and let me think for a minute."

Pete snatched the handset from Matt, scowling. "Not only do you punch like the boss, you act like him as well. " He scowled deeper. "And I don't like her being loose either. She's a cop, remember."

"I'm with you on that Pete, about the cop that is, but I don't mind your quick reactions Matt." Alf clapped him on the shoulder and took the handset from him. "Good to have you on our team."

"He's not on our team yet. Gotta go past the boss. I don't fancy it being on my head if she gets away on our shift. Not particularly keen to do a dance with the boss's fists."

Matt wanted to smash his scrawny face. He also recognised it was time to give a bit of ground. Kellee stayed by his side, and she nudged closer as Pete and Alf approached. He grabbed her arm, "Come here my little Avatar, you're scaring the locals." He clamped the cuff back on her wrist, then his. The steel, warm from his pocket, didn't feel out of place. In fact it warmed his heart being attached to her again. Made him possessive and curse his testosterone... horny. She quickly averted her eyes as he grabbed her arm, but not before he saw amusement dancing in the hazel depths. Obviously, his words amused her. The warmth spreading through his body turned into anger as Pete opened his annoying mouth. "She's too lanky for me. Although..." he stepped right into her personal space, brave now the restraints were back on her

wrists. "When I fuck her, I'll enjoy a feast of titty at the same time."
He roared with laughter at his own joke.

The handset buzzed back to life. Matt's temper was barely in
check. Kellee's soft hand rubbed against his, relieving his tension.
The urge to smash Pete's face in subsided.

"You there Alf?"

"Yep."

"This is what's going to happen. First... is Ed there?"

"Nope, off on a job for Mantis."

"Good. That makes life easier. He was too chummy with
Granny. After this I trust him even less. I am past the half-way
mark. We are going to have to take things into our own hands.
Pete?"

"Yo."

"Send a message to the boss. Tell him we are handling the
situation, but need to talk. Hopefully, I will be back by the time
he calls. If not, tell him what we are doing. Put Alf on."

"Righto boss." Pete tossed the handset to Alf and walked over to
a box on the wall. He punched in a code, took out a phone and
tapped away.

"Alf, send the four of them off, tell them to lie low as planned
until they are contacted. Then, I want the flower-house cleaned of
any incriminating evidence, move whatever you need to the gigs in
Babinda. I'm sure that's what the boss would want us to do. I don't
know how concealed the tunnel will be. If it's found, they'll find
the warehouse and possibly the other houses. We may have to clear
them as well. Now move."

The handset clicked off, then clicked back to life. "And I am
not doing the security procedure as I arrive. Expect me to come
out skidding sideways, this tunnel is creaking man. Catch ya later
Matt, thanks for before, the love in ya voice was just what I needed.
But you ain't having my fucking job ya bastard, at least not until
the boss moves up and I take his place." His laugh turned into
coughing as the handset once again clicked off.

Alf jumped into action. "Matt, come with me. Bring the pretty Avatar." He chuckled at his own joke. "Pete, find the Foreman. Let's pick up the pace and move all this stuff to the other houses. I want to be done, pronto. Then we are out of here." He threw out orders as he walked. Matt followed him to the box on the wall where Pete had retrieved the phone. "This is all you will need. The key to your motel room. You remember the address?"

"Yes boss." Matt shoved the key into his pocket and started to repeat it.

Alf held up a silencing hand. "I don't want to know. Something you'll get the knack of. Tight Security. You're only told what's necessary. I have no idea where you are going, I don't care. The less I'm told the better for us both. You follow the orders you got; someone will be in touch."

Alf talked a lot with his hands. Finally, the hands stopped moving, and Alf tossed him another set of keys. "For the car. Orders are to have you dropped off. Just press the remote button and you'll find the car. You drive to your destination, no stops. It's GPS tracked and you are under surveillance, so you'd better stick to the plan, or you will be pushing up daisies. You won't need money; everything is paid for, and the room is stocked with supplies. Any questions?"

A million questions formed in Matt's mind, none that Alf would be likely, or able to answer. He shook his head.

"Right, you're set. That van over there and for the record, I am not your boss - yet." He grinned as they clasped hands. "I'll be seein' ya."

Matt's smile was genuine and relaxed as he returned the hearty handshake. The answers would have to wait. Patience was a virtue. "Thanks. Tell Fuzz I look forward to seeing his ugly mug again soon."

CHAPTER TWENTY FOUR

I n the confined space of the van, an aroma of roses dominated the air with its sickly sweetness. Sitting squashed next to Matt on the floor in the back, Jules lifted the lid off one of the boxes and the perfume intensified.

"Quit making the stink worse." Jimmy turned and leant on the back of his front passenger seat next to the driver.

"Aww but I like the smell." she pouted. "Never been given flowers before."

"Well no one is giving you them now, so leave 'em be."

"I can do what I want," Jules reached out again for the box closest to her.

"No roses and no talking." Matt injected enough authority into his voice for the young, misguided woman to pull her hand away with a sulky challenge.

"Who put you in charge?"

Matt glared, saying a prayer of thanks when she turned away and fell silent. The last thing he needed was to be saddled with Jimmy and Jules. Their presence would make it so much harder to help Kellee escape. He internalised his thoughts, using the spare time to think about and process recent conversations.

Mantis. He held the name in his mind for a moment, before filing it away and pulled out the next piece of information. The mole and the risk to Stephen were scary prospects, but nothing could be done about them until he was able to contact his Team. Next, he considered the possibility they already knew about him. They might know *of* him, but not his identity. He would have to be extra careful.

Finally, the last piece. Reluctantly he allowed his mind to focus on the unthinkable. His mother's death may not have been an accident. That thought shocked him to the core. She had been killed in a car crash when she was eight months pregnant with his sister Jo who, protected inside the womb, survived. Aged five at the time of her death, he held vague memories of his mother's love. These were enhanced by the stories of her told by his two older brothers. And the scent of frankincense. It had taken him years to work out what the unique fragrance was that surrounded his memory. Could this have been murder? He needed to discuss this with his family. Did his father have any idea? He left thoughts about Patrick alone, not wanting to bring that out into the open yet.

The van lurched to a sudden stop, and they all grappled for stability as they banged and slid into each other. Matt took the opportunity to pull Kellee closer, throwing a steadying arm around her.

"Sorry." The driver spoke over his shoulder, as they started off again, "Bloody traffic, congestion even this early. Once we hit the highway, it should clear."

Kellee was wedged nicely between him and some boxes. He reached out, motioning Jules to move closer. "Tuck in here, stop yourself being from thrown around so much."

"Thanks." He didn't like the way she snuggled extra close, nor the hand she placed high up on his leg, and he tried hard to suppress a smile when Kellee muttered a barely audible 'good grief' against his ear. Turning his head, he gave her a broad wink. He needed to find a way to let her escape. He couldn't let her be taken to the Compound. If that happened, he feared she would never leave the place alive.

The van slowed again, travelled on a bit further, and then took a left turn. Matt switched his attention towards the front trying to see where they were going. There were no windows in the back of the van, but the bright morning sunlight flooded through the front. By his reckoning, they should be heading along the highway with the northern beaches on their right. The driver turned left, past the Smithfield shopping centre and started the twisting climb up the Kennedy highway towards Kuranda, leaving the sea far behind them.

"What ya doin' that for?" Jules twisted away and scowled as Matt secured his handcuff onto her wrist.

He grinned at the woman, determined to keep things relaxed. "Chill, just giving my hand a bit of a spell. You try being cuffed all night, bloody uncomfortable." He rubbed his wrist to emphasise his point.

Jules pouted. "Don't let her escape. She's seen me face, all our faces."

"Stop panicking Princess." He gave her a wink, watching the way her face flushed pink as he turned his lopsided grin on her. "I'll be slitting her throat if she tries to take off." He pulled out his knife and tucked it next to him. "I'll cuff her again before we get out."

" How come ya have your knife? Granny took all our stuff." Jimmy asked, bracing himself as the van slowed for the hairpin curve that started the winding climb up the Kennedy Highway.

"Thought she gave everyone's gear back. Don't ask me why she singled me out."

"I want mine. " Jimmy's scowl deepened. "Don't like what's happening. Do you think that was Granny's house back there? Reckon she got blown up? Man, imagine being in the tunnel."

The van slowed down behind a caravan as it crawled up the steep incline.

"Yea, No doubt." The explosion fit in with the way she behaved when she asked him to stay back. But he doubted Granny perished; far too smart for that. "And before you ask, I don't have any more info than you. We will all have to wait till someone tells us." Matt fell silent, concentrating on keeping the two women secure as the road twisted and turned. Overtaking lanes were fair enough, but this twisting, hairpin route needed to be a dual highway. The amount of traffic on it so early was incredible. In front of them, the caravan plodded along, and Matt appreciated the way their driver relaxed, bid his time and overtook on one of the overtaking lanes.

He looked across at Kellee. She seemed pale, but still gave him a slight smile. Resisting the urge to hold her hand, he looked out of the front windscreen as the rainforest flashed past in a blur of multi toned greens. A brush turkey played daredevil on the side of the road and a few birds fluttered with flashes of colour as the car sped by.

Matt's mind was constantly searching for a way to let Kellee escape. He could pull his gun, hold it to the driver's head; Jimmy and Jules were unarmed. Then what? He had no means of contact since Granny took his and Kellee's phone.

Jules rubbed her hand further up his leg. Matt gritted his teeth, wishing she would realise she was being used, and that one day soon she would be disposable. What would she be like if taken out of this environment and provided with some stable and positive influence? Teach her she had self-worth and not let men walk all over her. He had seen it time and time again. What made young women do this to themselves?

Where Jules was clingy, Kellee moved slightly away from him. She seemed thoughtful as she fiddled with the cuff dangling from her wrist. What she must be feeling cut deep into his mind. She had stayed withdrawn and huddled against the flower boxes and it made him feel more determined to bring this Gang to its knees. The human trafficking side of things coming to light was horrific.

Kellee stirred, shifting her position, stretching out her legs. She looked stressed and exhausted, and he just wanted to pull her into his arms and chase all that anxiety away. He knew that even at the expense of the mission, he couldn't risk her being taken to the Compound. As much as he would like to see it through to the end, he couldn't see that happening. Now his priority was to save Kellee. At least his Team would still have gained a lot of valuable information. Options could be kept open. Free Kellee first, and should a path arise for him to continue, he'd take it. A new question arose. Should he wait until he contacted his Team or make a move at the next available opportunity? He would follow what he always did... his gut.

As he considered a way to warn Kellee he was planning to act, the vehicle shot forward in a burst of speed, veering sharply to the left and before he could brace himself, Kellee's scream over overrode the squeal of the tyres as she was flung onto Matt's lap and, as the momentum tossed him sideways, Jules landed on top of them both with a loud grunt. A screech of metal on metal and the rear of the van jumped and slid to the left, swaying as the back tyre fought for traction on the loose gravel. The driver wrestled with the steering wheel, finding the road surface again and this time they were all thrown to the right. Flower boxes continued to tumble around them, bursting open, the interior overpowered with a blend of rich, exotic fragrance.

"You two OK?" Matt extracted himself from a tangle of arms and legs, before unlocking the handcuff attached to Jules's wrist.

Kellee held her head, nodded affirmatively and gave him the universal thumbs up.

"Bloody hell. Watch ya driving." Jules scrambled upright. "You could'a killed us."

"All good back here. Bit of a mess. Anything I can do?" Matt knelt behind the two front seats, arms resting across the backs for support. He had a pretty good idea of what must have just happened, but not why. Their hostage? Not important enough for club rivalry. He complimented the driver.

"Epic recovery. Rival gang or cops?"

"Don't think it's cops." The driver tapped a button on his phone, placed a hand up to his ear and spoke. "Carrier four, got a bug in my blooms, are you on it?"

Matt watched the speedo as it dropped back to the legal limit, at the same time checking out what he could see in the rear vision mirror. There was no one behind them."Ok stay online." The driver addressed Jimmy and Matt. Although Matt felt it directed more at him.

"Rival gang behind. Shot out from the road on the right. Tried to ram the driver's door. Lucky this baby has some serious grunt under the bonnet. They just clipped the tail end."

Matt leant forward so the driver could hear him better, "they still after us?"

"Nope, our rear guard took care of them."

Matt clapped Jimmy on the shoulder. "You right mate?"

"You should have seen it man - came out of nowhere, huge bull bar on the front."

The driver listened to his phone again and said, "ring back when it's done." Then addressed Matt.

"Organise the sluts in the back. Tell them to find the four boxes with a double rose sticker on them. Chuck out the roses. You'll see the goods nicely packaged inside. Stash them into the bags you'll find there as well. Tell me when you're finished. Move fast."

Kellee refused to help and wouldn't look at Matt as he jumped to obey orders. He located the boxes and stuffed what he estimated to be ten to fifteen kilos of ICE into the first bag.

"Quit your whining Jules and pass me a couple more bags."

"Yea well, I keep falling over while the van is moving. Can't we pull over and do this?"

"Want a bullet in your head if they catch us? Just sit down and leave me to it."

Once he was finished, he moved the goods up to the front. "Sweet haul," he said to the driver.

"Just the dregs." The man laughed without humour. "Let's hope we live to reap the benefits. We got more bugs. See that car up ahead on the side of the road with its bonnet up? Didn't try to flag down our leader car. Should they attempt to flag us...shit hang on." He grabbed the phone and pressed the speed dial. "We picked up a bug. Come back and swat it. I'll activate the emergency plan."

Matt could see them in the rear vision mirror, scrambling to shut the bonnet and jump in the car. Glad there had been no time to activate any plan of his own – shit, a front, and a rear guard. They wouldn't have stood a chance. He mentally kicked himself for not realising they would be this organised. Then again, he had been ignorant about the drugs on board, and the enormity of their operation. The last thing he wanted now was to end up dead in a gang war.

"Our boys will intercept them. They're off to the left, you'll see them in a minute. They'll pull out behind us and slow them down. Take them out if necessary. Speed is the key here. We can't afford to lead them to where you were going to pick up your car, and we're not letting them get their filthy mitts on our stuff."

"What do we do?"

"Reaper, you'll be taking the women and the goods. We're dropping you off, while our boys are keeping them busy. Then we'll lead them into a trap, let them think we are going to the Compound. The old plan is aborted. Fuzz is organising another place for you to stay, at least 'till tomorrow. He said you can be trusted. He better be right."

"Call me Matt. Left Reaper behind in Brisbane."

"Yea. You were talked about as Reaper. It will take some time to remember."

"No probs man. Who are they and what am I expected to do?"

"Rival gang. Stupid enough, they call themselves, The Rivals. Been muscling in on, not just us, but other gangs up north. We gunna catch these bastards and send them back to their boss in pieces. Shame you'll miss the action. We're not leading them anywhere near the Compound. Can't risk it. Only a couple of people have the access route. Play your cards right and you will be one of them."

A different phone buzzed. The driver tapped receive on his steering wheel before touching his ear plug. "How's the bug situation?" It proved impossible to hear the voice on the other end, and his grunted answers didn't give much away. "Standby, I'll relay the info."

"Here's how it is going down. By the time we arrive in Mareeba, everything will be in place. I'll stop, drop you and the bitches off on a side street. Make it snappy. I'll be taking off quickly to draw these guys away. Me and Jimmy here, we'll be leading them into an ambush. Your job is to chill in the motel room till we come for you."

"Right."

"Hey, don't call me a..." Matt silenced Jules with a glare. He'd bet his bottom dollar she still didn't realise what a dangerous game she was involved in. One that wouldn't work out well for her at all.

"Speak to Fuzz. He'll tell you where, codes and a pick-up time. Only you and him are privy to that information." He grinned into the rear vision mirror, catching Matt's eyes. "Security at its best. Anyone else comes to your door without the code. Well, you're the Reaper, sure you can work it out."

Matt took the phone from the driver as he passed it over his shoulder. He put it to his ear. Yo." he listened intently for a while. "Got it. Catch ya Bro." He passed it back.

"There's a panel on the side, just behind the driver's seat under the window. Push it in and slide it back." The driver's voice sounded crisp and controlled. It made Matt wonder if he was cool-headed like himself or whether it could be an act. Maybe the whole thing was a test of his loyalty. The only thing to do was to go with the flow and bide his time.

The van cruised at a moderate pace, sticking to the speed limits. Matt waited for a straight stretch of road before he climbed over Kellee, nudging her into the middle so he could investigate the panel. It slid away when he applied the right amount of pressure.

"Awesome. Want it all taken out?"

"Just three and the black drawstring bag. Pass two over to Jimmy, keep one for yourself." Jimmy's hands shook as Matt slapped two compact handguns into his palm. Looking up at the rear vision mirror he knew the driver had noticed it as well, caught his eye and gave a slight shake of his head. Matt thought Jimmy was in deeper than he could handle, but then maybe not. The way he checked the weapon over, making sure the round was full and the safety on, seemed to give him a sense of power and security. His voice held strength when he said. "Want them kept out or in the glove box till we need them?"

"Keep them hidden, but handy. Matt, extra ammos in the bag for yours, plus some money and a burner phone. Fuzz has the number and will contact you before pickup. You can't call out, only receive, so if you find yourself in strife you are on your own. No info to give out. There are two codes on a piece of paper. Memorise and destroy. Answer only with the appropriate code. Understand."

"Yep." With no other alternative, Matt munched on the tiny slip of paper and swallowed.

"The most important thing. The packages. Worth more than the bitches."

"Got it."

"Stop lumping me the same as her. I am with you guys, remember."

The extra pout Jules added to her lips proved useless on the driver, who totally ignored her. He made eye contact with Matt again. "You going to be right with them two?"

Matt groaned. Didn't this woman ever learn? He gave Jules a decent warning nudge to stop her from protesting again, "She's cool. Hey babe. Maybe you and I will find a way to entertain ourselves."

The pout vanished. He didn't think it was possible for her lip to droop any further, but she proved him wrong, turning her attention towards him and adding a spoilt grumble to her tone.

"I offered before, but you were too busy." She rolled her eyes towards Kellee.

Leaning across and chucking her under the chin, he flashed her his sexiest grin. "Saving the best till last, babe." Her cheeks flushed bright red, as she fluttered her eyelashes at him. "I am trusting you to help me now." He gave her a wink, hating the deceit, then busied himself, putting what he needed into his pack and the rest stashed back behind the concealed panel. Kellee hindered his progress. She held a *good grief* look in her eyes and it took all of his self-control to keep a straight face as he manoeuvred past her, trying to get the job done. They were both tall and with the jostling of the van and her unwillingness to move out of his way he almost ended up on her lap.

"Shift your legs darlin'."

He loved the defiance from her as she attempted to fold them out of the way. Eventually she pulled them close to her chest and wrapped her arms around them, the empty cuff swinging, clinking softly with the movement of the van.

"OK. We're getting near the drop off point." The driver called over his shoulder. "Make it quick, they're not far behind. Get out, get moving and act casual."

"Got it." Matt took the cuff completely off and shoved it in his bag. "You play up, people around you will be hurt." He caught Kellee's eye and gave a soft concealed micro wink as he continued. "Kids or adults, makes no difference to me. Lots of little tackers on their way to school this morning."

"You ready Jules? Got your bag? You're out first."

"I'm fine."

His hand slipped from her arm as she slung the strap over her shoulder. "You're safe with me." He kept his voice soft, not knowing why he wanted to put her at ease. With a bit of luck, he would soon have the chance to contact his Team, and both women would be safe. He guessed he would have to call it quits as well, but his mind continued to work on various angles, trying to find a way for him to stay in the game. "Don't worry, I'll look after you."

Jules didn't speak again until the door of the van slammed shut behind them. She turned to him and glared. "How in the hell do you think you can protect me at the Compound? You ain't God you know. You heard him talk. He put me and her," she threw her arm wildly in Kellee's direction, "in the same fuckin' basket. I ain't nobody's property."

Matt clutched Kellee's hand tight and indicated that Jules move with him. "You just have to trust me. OK. When I make a promise, I keep it." He prayed that he could.

CHAPTER TWENTY FIVE

Kellee barely had time to blink before they were out on a narrow street, taillights winking as the vehicle drove away. She stumbled, slow and awkward, her legs stiff from sitting cramped for a prolonged period and they took a while to function properly.

Matt's hand in hers set her blood racing. She should be petrified, working out how to escape, but the need to feel his arms wrap around her and hold her tight, dominated her thoughts. Warm, fuzzy and safe, shouldn't be on her agenda. A lingering doubt still remained. Every so often her logical side shouted, telling herself to take charge of her emotions and to stop reacting to the bad boy. Memories of past relationships echoed in her head.

Her first, the teenage crush, naively falling for the cruel school hottie. The second, her partner. She had slotted perfectly into his rule breaking, make a difference, cop persona. She thought they were helping to make the streets a better place. How humiliatingly wrong that attitude proved to be. Should she allow those feelings now? Have faith in the man who offered so much strength and comfort just by the warmth of his hand?

Looking at him. She savoured his soft gentle grip as they walked shoulder to shoulder, his stride matching hers to perfection. Everything seemed dreamlike. This man couldn't be all bad.

Her persistent inner voice continued to scream. He fired at two policemen, killing one. Something you witnessed with your own eyes. Do not ignore the facts. Who cares how many times he has intervened in his unusually protective way. The fact remains, he shot the policemen. Sighing, she sneaked a sidewards glance in his direction. She had to admit to herself, he may be strong and rough, but if the chance to overpower him presented itself, she would take it. Things went way beyond the two of them, but for now, she let her hand slide into his, savouring the connection.

"You wouldn't really shoot a kid, would you?" Jules piped up from where she walked on the other side of Matt.

He remained silent, turning sharply into the motel entrance and propelled them towards a unit at the end of the row. With a quick assessment of their surroundings, he opened the door and ushered them inside. Removing the key from the lock, he closed the door with a loud click and stashed it away.

"Well, would you?" Gnawing like a terrier at a bone, she stood in the middle of the sparsely furnished room, hands on hips, her face devoid of colour and her lips drawn into a thin line.

"Shut up Jules!" Matt took out a few items from his pack, before throwing his and Kellee's on the bed. "Stash these bags in the wardrobe along with yours."

Kellee moved away slightly. Everything in his expression screamed danger. Out of the corner of her eye, she watched as Jules jumped at his command. And not for the first time, she understood why they called him The Reaper. He exuded authority that suggested he would snap your neck without a thought if you didn't comply. For a moment, a paralysis of dread inhibited her ability to move. What if her judgement turned out to be totally wrong? Confusion over which to trust, her heart or gut - both or neither - constantly switched and clashed.

"I said sit down."

Kellee jumped at the sound of his voice, flinching as he reached out to pull her closer to the inbuilt desk. His underlying gentleness came as a surprise when compared to the rough exterior projected. The cuff closed with a solid click around her wrist, and he had the audacity to give her a sly wink. Or could it be a murderous tick? Expressions and action were clashing. His hand fluttered over hers in a feathered caress, while his voice snapped with authority.

"I have things I need to do. Fuzz's orders." Retrieving a small wad of cash from the drawer of the bedside table, he flipped through the notes, then shrugged, shoving them deep into his pocket.

"Why don't we take off together?" Jules slithered towards him and went to place her arms around his neck. "A lot of money tied up in them packages. You and me? We could spend up big hey, buy us a real good time."

Matt sidestepped, grabbed the gun, checking the chamber and safety before shoving the weapon down the back of his jeans, pulling his shirt over the top.

"You said you were leaving the best till last."

Kellee didn't think Jules could pout any further and the accompanying expression of sulky annoyance did nothing to make her look alluring.

"Things to do first, sugar."

Matt's voice oozed charm, and Kellee tried to keep a grimace of frustration from her face. Did men really find that sort of thing appealing? She held no doubt in her mind that Jules thought she oozed sex-appeal as she added a slight tremble to her bottom lip.

"Well, what ya doin' and how long ya gunna be? A girl can't wait forever you know."

Matt studied Jules for a moment, then said. "Got orders to deliver this to a man at the servo up the road. You stay here and relax."

"You gunna leave me a gun? I can shoot."

"She ain't goin nowhere. She's cuffed to the desk."

Kellee realised Matt changed his speech pattern to match Jules. A very smart ploy to encourage her to be more relaxed.

"Ya got this sugar. I'll bring us back some grub. Too early for the pub, but we can pop out an' pick somethin' up later."

He chucked her under the chin. "I'll be fifteen, twenty minutes at the most, behave."

"I'll be your best time you eva'..." Jules called out as the door closed in her face.

"What are you looking at?" she snarled.

Kellee turned away, hoping Matt wouldn't be too long. She didn't like the manic glint in the other woman's eyes.

"Move ya fuckin' legs, bitch." Jules stomped, no-where near Kellee's legs, to open the mini fridge nestled under a bench next to the desk. The woman was clearly annoyed, first muttering under her breath, then cursing when she straightened, with, as she put it, 'an f'ing boring can of coke.'

"Tasteless without a splash of rum." She grumbled.

The can opened with a hiss and almost bubbled over as she poured the frothy liquid way too fast into a glass. Blaming the drink, she shook off the droplets covering her hands, then wiped them on her shirt.

Kellee licked her lips, acknowledging her own thirst. Jules took a few mouthfuls, then screwed up her face as she plonked the half-finished drink on the bench top. Perhaps she could use Jules' discontent to bring her to her senses.

"Jules?" The woman turned shrewd eyes on her at the first sound of her voice, giving her a different kind of pouty expression. The spoiled brat, get out of my face, pout.

"These men are not going to look after you. You do realise that don't you."

Jules' lip lifted in a half sneer, but she refrained from answering.

"I am a police officer and can help you. Stand by me, help me, and I will protect you when the authorities find us."

"The cops ain't gunna' find us. And I can look after meself." Her words rang with childlike defiance, but the uncertainty in her stance and actions showed them for the lie they were.

"How are you going to protect yourself against them?" Kellee genuinely wanted to help the young woman. Life circumstances had probably brought her to where she found herself now. If she woke up, helped Kellee, surely Matt would assist her too? And herein lay the conundrum. Her gut said trust him, hell, even her heart said trust him, but logically, should she?

"Don't need to."

Kellee watched in disbelief as Jules went to retrieve a bag. "Told ya, I can look after meself." She tossed the straps over her shoulder.

"Jules, I don't think that's a smart..."

"Fuckin shut ya trap. Ya think I'm stupid? Think I don't understand what's gunna happen." Spittle flew from her mouth. Sadness etched her features.

"Stealing their drugs will only..."

"I don't want ya advice."

Kellee spluttered as ice-cold coke hit her full in the face. The sticky liquid dripped down her hair, over her cheeks and into her lap. She flicked it out of her eyes with her free hand, pushing back her wet hair and wiping her hand on her clothes. Rage built. Being left defenceless and vulnerable was not something she appreciated. Lashing out at Jules with her legs proved fruitless.

"It's all your fault, gettin' tangled up in our heist. If it weren't for you, Reaper would be all over me. I seen the way he stares at me." Anger blazed across the young woman's face, a clear indication no help would come from her. With the bag clutched firmly to her side, Jules gave Kellee's legs a wide berth, opened the door and stepped through it without a backward glance. The firm click of the latch sounded final. Kellee found herself alone, covered in a sticky mess and totally frustrated.

CHAPTER TWENTY SIX

S tephen strode out of his office. "Everybody, stop what you are doing. Conference room, now!"

"What's up boss?" Bert asked as he dragged out a chair and sat at the round wooden table.

"Lift the chair, don't scrape," grumbled his co-worker Lucy. " Dragging grates on my teeth." She made an exaggerated show of lifting her own seat, only to have it repeat the same noise as she pulled herself towards the table. She rolled her eyes at him as he covered his ears with his hands, sporting a mocking expression of horror on his face.

Stephen ignored the banter. Both brilliant in their fields, he saw their need to goad each other. It eased stress and tensions within the whole office. Sometimes he wondered if they ever got together outside of work. If they did, they were keeping it quiet, and never brought any kind of romantic attachment into the office. Come crunch time, they pulled together, working as a swift efficient unit, which was what made his Team a powerful force to be reckoned with.

He stomped over to Amy's desk with a deep scowl and spun her chair around.

"Amy, that means you too. I don't care if you are half-way through..." He jumped back in surprise as she gasped and let out an oath.

"Oh shoot, you scared the bejeebers out of me."

"Bejeebers?"

"You gave me a fright. I didn't hear you coming. I sink into my own little world and zone out all outside noise."

"You did pass the 'alert and aware' components of advanced training, didn't you?"

Her brow crinkled. "I wouldn't be employed here without it." His eyes followed her as she walked over to join the rest of the crew. His question still hung unanswered. With all that was going on, maybe he should look deeper into the file on Amy Wilson-Jones.

"I'll cut straight to the chase." The six members that made up the core of his Team looked at him in anticipation. "I'm placing us in lock down." He glanced briefly at each of them, giving the notion of not seeming to pay them much individual attention. Jo and Axel, who had joined them at the table, would be scrutinising their reactions. Particularly Axel. He possessed quite a talent when it came to reading body language.

"One by one I want you to go with Jo and give her your belongings from the lockers and your desks. But before you do, I want any communication devices you own, phones, iPads, whatever you've got. Leave them on the table. Bert you're first."

Stephen couldn't explain why, but he wanted to leave Amy until last. He had noticed her momentary panic at his orders. "Team." His voice became solemn. "It is possible a traitor is hiding amongst us."

Stunned faces glanced around in disbelief for a few seconds, then Bert jumped up, tossing his phone on the table. "OK boss. Come on Jo, I'll grab my gear."

He was back in no time, and not even needing to be asked, plonked his jacket next to his phone on the table and asked. "Anything else you want me to do?"

"Just sit tight. Once this is done, I will explain where we are at."

One by one they did as they were bid. When Amy came back, she and Jo were laughing over some private joke. He didn't know why, but it bugged him. "Right, Amy. You're first. Bring your stuff. Jo, please stay with the others. Axel you are with me."

"Relax, these are just informal precautions." Axel said to Amy, as they entered Stephen's office.

"Thanks. I was beginning to think you had already judged me as guilty, being the newbie on the Team."

"All we need to do at this stage is to ask a few questions, check your gear and keep your electronics for a bit." Stephen ran his hand through short, cropped hair, pleased Axel had taken the initiative to put Amy at ease. He couldn't imagine any of his fellow workers conspiring against them. Everyone underwent intensive scrutiny to get to this level, but an unexpected breach of security on Kevin and Jo's mission had seen their lives put on the line. Leaked Intel had thrown them into intense danger. If not for Axel's mysterious connection with the anonymous Willow, things would have turned catastrophic for both his siblings and the operation.

"Right. Let's do this, so we can return to the task at hand. Mind if we check through your belongings as we speak?"

"No sir, nothing hidden in there, but be prepared. I pack for practicality, not for pleasure."

Stephen began to empty the contents of her bag, astounded at how much this small backpack could hold. She hadn't lied. The contents ranged from an inventive emergency kit, right down to an old compass and a small glow stick flare. "There's everything in here except for...I stand corrected." He laughed as he held up a single key, connected to a ring that supported a mini replica of a kitchen sink.

Amy chuckled. "A perfect gift from an extraordinary friend."

They went through a series of questions and Stephen found both relief and satisfaction in her answers. As an afterthought he asked, "You showed apprehension when I first mentioned lock down. Care to elaborate?"

She flushed as she looked up at him.

"My thoughts flew to my dogs sir. I own two energetic Papillons. They are contained in my house and will need attention, sir."

"This is only a temporary lock down. Everyone is allowed to contact someone outside, under supervision, to assist with personal affairs. You should know that. And you can drop the sir."

"Of course, I realised. I plan to attend a dog agility competition on the weekend, part of my private life. *sir*," she added pointedly. "We have trained hard for this. I will be very disappointed if I miss the event. I did put in an application for the days off, which you approved last month."

Naturally, she and everyone else enjoyed a life outside the office. He was the only one married to his job, and he couldn't remember the last time he had taken a day off. "Right, it's only Monday, so hopefully this will be sorted by the weekend." He went to dial, "what's the number you want to call?"

Amy sounded apologetic. "Can you use my phone sir? My neighbour Maggie is in her eighties, and lives alone. She has caller ID and won't answer unless she knows who it is. Can't stand telemarketers, upsets her greatly."

He picked up Amy's phone. The protective case was bright pink, and on the home screen showed a picture of two happy dogs. He shook his head and sighed, "What's the number and of course we want it on speaker."

"There is a shortcut." She leant across the table, activated the screen with her thumbprint and indicated a dog icon, "Just press that."

"Naturally." He tried without much success to keep the amusement out of his voice. In his line of work, you usually only saw the professional side of people. This was opening up a kaleidoscopic view into a personality he'd thought was black and white.

"Ok, that's all. Thanks Amy. You can go back and join the others." Stephen stood up and opened the door for Amy to leave.

"What do you think?" Stephen asked as he sat back down. He valued Axel's opinion and was impressed with the man his sister had paired up with. Axel had seemed almost invisible as he sat silent and still during Amy's interview. Even Stephen almost forgot his presence.

"She has a few secrets, but in my view, they seem more personal, not connected to the case. Concern for her dogs was genuine and she relaxed once she contacted the neighbour."

"OK, let's bring in the next one."

By the time the interviews were completed, nightfall cast long shadows against the windows. Walking back to the table he and Axel were greeted with a burst of laughter as Jo finished what he presumed to be a very funny joke. She laughed along with everyone else, looking up as they approached. Her smile as she looked at Axel said a thousand unspoken words. Quite frankly she radiated happiness.

"I've ordered Chinese. I don't know about you guys, but I'm starving." Winking at Stephen she said. "Hope that's alright. Seems like we are going to be here for a while."

"Perfect." He made an eye connection with each person before he continued. "Right, this is the situation. We thought our emergency extraction plan for Jo's mission went off without a hitch. Unfortunately, that was not how it went down. I will have a detailed report typed up and I want you all to read over it carefully, scrutinise it, and think of any way this information may have left the control room."

"What about our other cases?" Bert piped up.

"All units are going through the same process as us, each one has been assigned a case to take care of. Naturally, we are sticking with Matt on Operation Killjoy. The only person outside these walls that receives any Intel is Sir Robert, and that comes through me only. He will coordinate all the Teams."

He stood. "Any other questions? Right then. We may as well try to make some progress before dinner arrives. From now on we work in pairs. No one uses any electronic devises without a partner to verify what they are doing."

CHAPTER TWENTY SEVEN

Kellee jerked awake, startled by the rattle of the knob and the squeak of the door opening. Even in her uncomfortable position on the floor, exhaustion had won. Sleep made her eyes heavy, as she forced them to stay open. Fatigue had almost overwhelmed her. Wafts of delicious aromas surrounded the familiar frame of Matt as he strode through the door, laden with food and drink. She cut straight to the chase. "Jules took off with a heap of your precious cargo."

"What! When?"

"Immediately after you left." Kellee almost drooled as he plonked the bags on the bench top above the fridge. Her stomach rumbled like a thunderstorm in full swing.

"Why didn't you stop her?"

Her mouth dropped open in disbelief at Matt's unreasonable response. She rattled her cuffed hand. "What did you expect me to do?"

"You could have talked her out of doing something so stupid."

"Pfft. Do you think I didn't try?"

She sighed with relief as he unlocked the cuff and hauled her upright. "I need a shower. In case you can't see, I'm wearing a glass of coke. I'm cold and sticky, and more than a little pissed off with Jules myself."

His jaw clenched tight, and a small tick flickered near his eye.

"That can wait. I need to find the stupid girl."

Kellee dug in her heels, pulling back with the strength she could muster. "Fine! You go and do that; I want to clean up this sticky shit."

Holy heck he was strong, never had anyone ever lifted her off her feet before. In the time it took to blink, she found herself unceremoniously dumped on the bed, her wrist attached to the bedpost.

"What happened to trust?" She sprang up, pulling against the restraint to no avail. "Trust me you say. Well, what about trusting 'me' not to go anywhere?"

"No time for theatrics." The door slammed as he stormed out.

Not intimidated by the empty room she shouted back. "Theatrics? Good grief, I'll show *you* theatrics." He probably didn't hear her words, but she felt a moment of satisfaction as they echoed around the room.

She shivered as cold air raced over her skin. Her temper may have fired her up, but the air-conditioning was putting goosebumps on top of her goosebumps.

How long would he take? How dare he abandon her like this. Kellee went to war with her thoughts.

'Why in hell did she have faith in this man?'

'Cause you recognised he is a good soul, her inner voice soothed.

'But not once has he given you the opportunity to escape.'

Be real, opportunities are not falling from the sky.

'What about right friggin now? Would it hurt to pretend you escaped with Jules?'

"Oh, get over it and move on." She snapped aloud to the empty room as she pulled back the bed covers and crawled inside, not caring if her sticky coke residue messed up the sheets. What if she started yelling to see if anyone came to her rescue? Knowing her recent luck he would storm straight back in. Besides, she didn't possess enough energy left to scream. Cold and tired, with very little sleep in the last forty-eight hours, now cocooned in the warmth of the doona, she didn't even try to stop herself from drifting off to sleep. She would wake up again when he came back.

CHAPTER TWENTY EIGHT

K ellee looked comfortable snuggled under the covers. When he had removed the cuffs a few hours ago, she hadn't stirred, but from that moment on, seemed to sink into a more peaceful place. She'd slept soundly most of the day, relaxed and breathing in a deep, peaceful rhythmic pattern. At least now she was restful. The furrow lines on her face and tension radiating from her body had disappeared.

When he'd returned to find Jules and half the drugs gone, a dark anger had exploded. Kellee, wet and shivering in the cold air-conditioning, irritated him even more with her own fury and annoyance at something beyond his control. That frustration faded with the long afternoon.

He needed Kellee to rouse herself. He'd come to a decision while he witnessed exhaustion inching out of her body the deeper and longer she rested. It hadn't made an ounce of difference when he banged things around, hoping she would wake. She didn't stir.

Finally accepting his only course of action, he found himself anxious to talk to her. With the decision made, he was impatient for her to awaken. The thought of telling her about being undercover and the details of his mission, felt so right, he couldn't wait to share it. He wanted her to be free within hours, as soon as his team had arrived. He hadn't worked out how to contact them yet, but he would.

To pretend Jules and Kellee escaped together was not an option. Despite the security precautions, this whole scenario didn't sit right. As he handed over the goods at the servo as instructed, the man acted far too casually, and he couldn't shake the sensation of being under surveillance the entire time. The bloke at the bus stop reading the paper hadn't turned a single page.

He was pretty sure Jules had walked out the door, straight into danger. There was no sign of her, but a small broken branch on a tree and scuffed patch of grass indicated there had been trouble. His gut never lied. The conclusion he came to... abort the mission. Kellee's safety took top priority. A twinge of regret surfaced at the thought, but he felt a deep relief that she would soon be safe.

In the quiet room he recognised the moment the rhythm of her breathing became lighter. Kellee moved, letting out a little sigh, indicating she might awaken soon. He churned over the emotions she provoked. He was treading in unfamiliar territory with these feelings. They were certainly something he had never experienced before.

A totally different feeling from his love of family. Deeper, stronger, sitting in a space created for the two of them. Possessive, obsessive, protective; and he couldn't bear the thought of her getting hurt. He needed her to be free. The jug boiled, and he poured a strong black cup of coffee.

"Hey, that smells so good. Is there one for me?" Her husky, sexy as hell voice ignited the broad smile he felt compelled to use whenever he looked at her. She ran a hand through tousled hair as she sat up, swinging her legs over the side of the bed. Stretching her arms up over her head, she let out a throaty purring sound. So erotic. He added it to the growing list of things he loved about her.

She embodied all that was sensual and hot. Sure, his libido might be in overdrive, but his feelings went deeper than that. His desire to pull her into his arms and hold her took him by surprise. The urge to hug her tight and tell her everything will be all right, overwhelmed him. This was the first time since this innocent lady had been taken hostage that he truly felt relaxed with her. And with it came the freedom of his own emotions and he almost floundered over to say or do. With a sexy tilt to her head, she came to his rescue.

"Before you say anything, I need to apologise. I understand you took the only course of action you could with what you did, and I acted like a spoiled brat."

That was the last thing he expected her to say, and as the apology sank in, he smiled deeper. "Accepted. Your actions were perfectly understandable." His words sounded rather lame to his ears and her response sent him chuckling in delight.

"Oh, did you think I apologised? I just said I needed to." The cheekiest of smiles graced her face. "Is that coffee I smell?"

"Then there is no need, and yes. How do you like it...your coffee that is?" The endearing light flush rising to her cheeks warmed his heart.

"Black... three sugars, but in a minute. I need a quick shower."

A quick shower proved to be just that. It reminded him of his sister. No nonsense, no fuss, in and out in a flash, hair washed and all. He barely had time to finish making the coffee.

The small table acted as a buffer between them. His heart skipped a beat as long legs clad in shorts filled his vision. He would love to kiss every inch of those legs. He'd thought about what to say most of the afternoon, now his rehearsed words flew right out the window. His concern for Kellee was clouding his clear analytical mind. All he craved was her safety, at all costs. Even at the expense of the mission. He didn't want her anywhere near that Compound.

As he opened his mouth to speak, she sat down opposite him, finished brushing out her wet hair, and spoke up first.

"You asked me to trust you and I'm sorry, I will from now on. In the car my past consumed me, then being able to do nothing about

Jules messed with my head. Knowing my record for falling for the bad boy, kinda freaked me out, about it happening again."

His heart pounded. Did that mean she had fallen for him?

"Anger clouded my judgment. I was engulfed by a desperate need to inform the authorities about the Compound, the drugs, the human trafficking. But we won't go there just yet. There are things I need to say."

"Kellee..."

She held up her hand and kept on talking. "I want you to understand, I believe your promise and I have every faith you will do the right thing and let me go."

"Kellee. I want..."

"Please. Let me finish, then you can say whatever you like." Steam rose from the untouched coffee. She lowered her head as she said. "You may even hate me after this."

He intended to interrupt again, but the seriousness of her tone and his own intrigue at what she was about to tell him held him in check. She glanced at him, uncertainty battling with courage.

"I need to tell you what I did back at Granny's house." Her voice quivered slightly, what she wanted to say obviously didn't come easily. He resisted the urge to pull her into his arms and tell her everything was going to be fine, sensing the importance of what she wanted to say, realising she needed to deal with it in her own way. He made his body relax, casually picked up his coffee and took a deep, satisfying drink.

For a moment she toyed thoughtfully with her own cup, placing her hands around the warmth. She glanced back up at him, her jaw line firm and determined as she locked her eyes on his.

"I left my mp3 player, with a detailed description of the gang, the bunker and what information I gathered about Compound and human trafficking back at the house. I thought Fuzz might discover it when he checked the room, but he didn't. I was terrified he would."

Now he understood what all her nervous behaviour had been about. He remembered her tugging on the cuffs, but things happened so fast, he had dismissed it. God, he loved the spunk of this woman.

"Who knows how long it will take someone to find it - if they ever do - after that explosion. I did protect the device well though. It was small enough to squash inside a fancy metal cotton ball holder in the closed cabinet." She paused, holding her breath.

His heart raced, such a beautiful woman, and he was impressed with her courage, then, and now. He hated the way she looked at him with so much apprehension and needed to ease her fear by telling her that everything was going to be ok.

"Can I say something...?"

"No." She interrupted, shaking her head and looking confused. "Why are you smiling? This is not a joke. Please let me say all I need to. You should listen to the whole context. Then the ball will be in your court."

He leaned back in his chair, adoring the strength of her attitude, not only beautiful, but smart and resourceful as well. Behind closed eyes she was obviously thinking through what she wanted to say.

She took a steadying mouthful of coffee, placed the mug carefully on the well-worn table, then reached out for a second one, savouring the taste before she drew in a determined breath. "Help me Matt. The plain fact is, you shot the policemen and by the sounds of things, your reputation as the Reaper is pretty violent." Subconsciously she rubbed at her little finger. "I know you are not a bad person at heart."

"Ok Kellee, let me speak." Before she could open her mouth to protest, he leapt to her side pulling her close to him, ignoring her startled gasp.

"Matt. Let me..."

He gently touched her lips and said. "Shhh."

"But..."

She fit perfectly in his arms, a soft, warm contrast against his solid frame.

"But..."

He felt her melt into him, and his body hardened in response. His craving for her grew with every passing moment; not only sexual, but a yearning need to discover everything about her.

"My turn to talk, now." He watched her tongue as it flickered out to moisten her lips.

"Fine." She pulled away and stepped back a few paces. "I'll just say one last thing." Her breathing came in short sharp breaths. "There is no use pretending nothing is happening between us. I respond every time we touch, every time we look at each other." She held up a hand as he took a step forward. "I don't want this relationship to go any further. Under different circumstances, I guess things would have happened naturally."

"I am an undercover agent." His words flew over her head. She hadn't heard them as she backed towards the door.

"I want you to let me go. With a bit of luck, someone got my message and help is on the way. They might not be coming to this address, but I remembered the original one. We are in the same area. I should be able to find my own way. You can just walk away. Start a new life, do some good with your time. I'll assist you if I can. Won't tell them anything, except how you protected me and let me escape."

So intent on making her point, she seriously hadn't registered a word he'd said. Her hand rested on the door handle and if he took another step towards her, he knew she would bolt out into the night and possibly danger.

"Kellee." She stared right through him.

"Hells Bells Kells."

Her eyes snapped back to his with a frown. He grinned. "Listen to me. Please! I hope they got your message. Great move by the way, risky, but well played."

He slowly inched forward and held out his hand. "My name is Matthew Brennan. I am an undercover agent with MICO." She went a funny shade of pale and stared at him open mouthed. "Kellee, we are on the same side. The shooting of the police was a well organised sting, put into action by my Team. No one got hurt, I used blanks. As soon as I make contact, I can ensure your safety. I have a plan."

Too late he realised how much she must have been holding herself together. That she believed the truth of his words proved evident in the way her body crumpled, an expression of happy relief sprang across her features. Without saying a word, she found refuge in his arms. She laid her head on his shoulder and let out a prolonged sigh.

"I knew deep inside you weren't bad."

Her passionate kiss surprised him. Last night she had set his pulse racing, now she was kissing him without reservation, reaching into his soul, flooding him with fire. His emotions were in turmoil as she pulled back, half of him wanted to drag her back into his arms, the other part sighed with relief.

Wiping at the silent tears falling down her cheeks, she said, "What if they don't find the message? It may be burnt to smithereens in the explosion, or they just may not look at all." Kellee scanned frantically around the room, clamping a hand over her mouth whispering, "What if this room is bugged?"

Matt reached out, placing a reassuring hand on her shoulder. "I am ninety nine percent sure the room is clear. I gave it a thorough check while you were sleeping. More than once." He smiled, "I can't find anything."

The phone in his pocket started to ring. Reluctantly he stepped back, "Yo." The voice coming over the receiver was one he didn't recognise. "The servo man says thanks." He repeated the code phrase he had been given and listened again as the man spoke.

"We got the problem sorted. Pick up is midnight. The streets will be quieter then. Be ready."

"Slight glitch at our end." Matt kept his voice neutral.

The tinny phone voice questioned lazily, "and what might that be?"

The lack of surprise in the voice fuelled Matt's apprehension. His gut screamed caution. "While I was out dropping off...supplies, Jules took off. No idea where she is now."

"She's not important. Stupid bitch."

His instinct blasted into awareness, adding to his suspicions this might be another test. Jules had seen a lot and heard even more, had information about Granny and the Compound. No way would they not be concerned at her disappearance.

"She took a loaded bag of goods with her."

"What about the hostage?" The voice demanded.

Damn. Not a word about Jules taking what he estimated to be close to a million in street value. All the signs told him his gut was right. He let go of the last element of hope he would be able to save Kellee and be able to continue his mission. Saving Kellee took priority. Matt glanced at her, she stared at him, her head cocked to one side, trying to work out what was being said.

"Safe and secure." Saying the words out loud ripped at his heart. "She's with me." Her expression dropped a fraction. He gave her an ok sign, noticing her hands were shaking ever so slightly as she picked up her coffee cup and took a sip.

The tinny voice gave him no chance to reply as the man snapped out his orders. "Good man. Ok, that changes plans. Settle in for the night and be ready at five am. And don't leave the room." The phone went dead.

Matt turned to Kellee as he spoke. "Ok, we have until five tomorrow morning." He checked his watch; eleven hours from now. Sitting back down on the chair, needing a bit of space between them, he watched her move to the bed.

"Hey Kellee, things are not as bad as they sound. My decision to abort the mission was already made. There's no other way to secure your freedom. Their security precautions are complex and tight. I am convinced this is a ploy to prove my loyalty. I can only hazard a guess here. It's also possible they are on to me, and if they are, they won't hesitate to put a bullet in my head and yours. But if that was the case, I think they would have killed us by now."

"You trust your instincts, I trust you."

" Thanks. I must follow my gut; it hasn't let me down yet. Something's not right." He loved the way she didn't grumble about not being freed immediately, but sat quietly as he sorted through his thoughts.

He caught her intense gaze and gave her a twisted smile. "You know what I think?"

Her eyes opened wide as she raised her brows, tilting her head slightly to one side and down a fraction. God, he adored that questioning look.

"One thing I have learnt about this Gang over the last year is their extreme caution with security and in covering their tracks. That's why they are so darn impenetrable. I am sure this is a test to judge my reaction when being faced with the opportunity..." Three quick strides and he was at the wardrobe, pulling out the remaining backpack... "To take off with a small fortune."

"If they are testing trustworthiness, I guess Jules failed big time."

"Surely not the tunnel collapse, that's way over the top, and totally detrimental to their business."

"No. I believe that took them all by surprise. Granny has her own agenda, I think. This Gang is extremely organised. I think they are dealing with problems in their own way, but what's happening with us is close to their original idea."

"You said you had a plan?"

"My intention is to abort the mission. I'd hoped to use a phone I saw on the way in. If I can call my Team, discuss options with them, and arrange a pickup time, we should be at Headquarters by morning. I can disguise the move by heading out for a jog, I am known for my runs, so it wouldn't have aroused that much suspicion. I don't think they would have followed me, just kept an eye on this place. Now we have a problem.

Matt paced restlessly, voicing his thought process out loud.

"After that phone call, it's no longer an assumption. I believe this is a test. Too many indicators are pointing in that direction. New orders are to stay inside, so the run idea is out. There is no way to contact my Team, so the best course of action will be to wait until about three in the morning. They should be relaxed and complacent by then. Be prepared beforehand so we won't need any lights, then slip out and melt away into the night. There is only one way out of this cul-de-sac, so we will need to find a way out behind us first. If not, I might have to take out a sentry or two."

"Can't you use that?" She said, pointing to the phone still in his hand.

"Nope, a non-credit burner phone. Can only receive calls and they took my wallet. No money or cards."

"Can we use this sim?' She put her pack back on the bed, fiddled with the strap and held up a small chip. "I took it from my phone. Once we activate it again, they can trace where we are, even if we are unable to call?"

Matt's eyes opened wide in shock. "When in hell did you do that?" He racked his brain, trying to think of any opportunity that may have come her way, gave up and said, "Not only are you beautiful and smart. You can add resourceful and quick thinking."

Slight colour rose on her cheeks, and she dropped her gaze, looking embarrassed by the compliment. She spoke softly. "I think survival kicked in big time." Then, for the first time since she'd become a hostage, she flashed him a genuine smile. Her whole face lit up, her eyes sparkling with life. It was far too brief, and he was disappointed when it faded. He resisted the urge to pull her to his lap as she walked past him to sit on the chair on the opposite side of the table, sliding the sim in his direction.

"You slept quite soundly for a short while, after..." Her voice trailed off as he flicked off the back of the phone, took out the sim and replaced it with hers.

"Fingers crossed." He kept his tone light. Something was bothering her and all he wanted now was for her to feel at ease and safe. After a few minutes, the card activated.

They sat in silence looking at each other.

"Ok, let's do this." He punched in MICO's contact, looking up at Kellee in surprise when the phone answered on the first ring. "Shit, an automated message, can only mean there is trouble." He dialled again. "This is our emergency number. It should go straight to Stephen." He tried to keep the concern out of his voice for both their sakes.

∾

Kellee heard the tension in his voice as he spoke into the phone. She reached across the table and clasped hold of his hand in support. The seriousness of his expression kept her on edge and her heart racing.

"Four Zero Six."

There was a short pause before his body relaxed and he gave her hand a light squeeze. Whatever was happening on the other end eased some of his tension.

He listened for a while, then said, "Code blue," I can't see any other way. Doing an ambush like the diamond heist for early morning, it's too risky, to pull the same sting twice. They are not stupid people. I could take a couple of you out and..." His thumb began its soothing rub on the back of her hand and his eyes softened as he said, "you rescue Kellee."

Once the words were out of his mouth, Kellee had a weird sensation she wanted to stay and help. The thought of him going on alone was a frightening aspect. It increased her need for him to be safe and the more it rolled around in her mind, the less she wanted to abandon him. Assessing her emotions, she had to admit she had fallen for him big time. He was her perfect bad guy, and being honest with herself, she didn't want to let him go. Maybe together they could bring down this gang.

He shook his head slightly, as though he could read her mind. She kicked herself for the silly notion as he finalised the call. "No, I say we go ahead as planned. We've come so far, no point turning back just as it starts getting productive."

Stephen must have agreed. Matt gave a sharp affirmative to call back at 0300 to confirm their final plan details and hung up. Her hand cooled instantly as he released it to remove the chip. He replaced the original and slide it back across the table. She looked at him quizzically.

"You may as well keep this until we need it again. Stash it where you had it before, it's a great hiding spot." His attitude, cool, crisp and business like, smothered any warmth she'd felt. Like a dance, one step forward, two steps back, she returned to uncertainty of her emotions.

The coffee cups clinked as he took them one handed to the kitchenette nestled against the far wall. "When I check in with my Team again, it will be all go,go,go, so we should be rested and ready. They need to work this op on the quiet, not through their normal channels. As I suspected, they are in lock down. Stephen didn't go into detail, but it had something to do with Jo's mission. She is my sister," he explained. "I will find out more and pass on my Intel in person. I don't really want to trust the phone lines with some of the information."

He spoke calmly and professionally. Her heart sank. Had everything that transpired between them been an act? She went over to the bed and put the sim back in its hiding spot. Embarrassment crept to the surface. She had thrown herself at him. Again. What must he think of her, sleeping with the enemy?

He finished clearing up, wiping his hands down the back of his jeans. A kind smile warmed his face. Her heart skipped a beat and a tingling settled between her legs. That overactive mind of hers. Stop evaluating and start thinking.

"What do you think will happen to Jules?"

"A lot depends on her. If I am right, and they'd set a trap and she got caught, sad as it is, I don't think she would survive. I know how they work, and it wouldn't be pretty." He ran a troubled hand through his hair. "Should she evade them, and we find her, a lot will depend on how she reacts when arrested. There is one thing I have learnt, however. You can't help someone who does not want to be helped."

"You sound sad. Is this personal experience talking?"

"Yeah." He let out a sigh as he slumped on the edge of the bed. "I knew a young girl once. I kept her safe from the rougher members of the Gang. Protected her and tried to get her to see that a different path would give her a more beneficial future. Even took the risk of telling her I had a friend outside of the Gang who would help get her a job."

Kellee saw the pain seeping through his words, his face etched with sorrow, and she was just about to respond when he continued.

"She stayed with me a while, then wanted to move up in rank, closer to the leader, more excitement, more fun, prestige. The Police pulled her out of the river. Classified it as another junkie death."

His face took on a mournful expression She rose and stood in front of him, hands resting on his shoulders. He looked up at her as she said, "Not your fault. One thing I have learned, especially over the last few months. We all have choices. Good or bad. You are not responsible for what others do."

The truth and passion of her words came straight from the heart, and she could read the conflict in his eyes. Clearly, the pain had dwelled within him for a long time. Placing a hand over her hers he stood, so her hand stayed on his shoulder. With his other arm he pulled her close and she wrapped both her arms around him.

Perfection. Their bodies fit together like the last piece in a puzzle, hip to hip, chest to chest and cheek to cheek.

Knowing he was on the right side of the law made everything right about him. She relaxed, appreciating the warmth and comfort his arms offered. The undercurrent of sexual attraction bubbled gently beneath the surface, and although she sensed his growing desire, he kept the embrace to one wrapped in security. Lifting his cheek from hers, his eyes sparkled with a natural light-hearted expression. At that moment, she knew she was seeing the real man. Kindness, honesty, and passion shone bright, and she savoured the feeling as it flowed through her entire body.

Gingerly, she leaned forward placing a light kiss on his lips. It was barely a meeting of two surfaces. Tingles of pleasure danced through every nerve ending as he responded, moving his lips softly over hers.

She shivered as he ran the back of his fingers over her cheek, light, sensual, and she wanted nothing more than to step back into his arms. Instead, she turned away, picked up her pack and started rummaging through it. For what? for nothing really, but it gave her something to do with her hands.

"I really need a shower. The tunnel grime feels embedded into my skin. There's food in the fridge It's not much, but it will keep the hunger at bay."

All she could manage was a sharp nod, not trusting herself to speak. Had she just thrown herself at him again?

"Lighten up Kells, it's nearly over. Soon you will be safe, and all this will be behind you."

"I know," she responded.

He seemed almost unwilling to leave the room as he stood with his hand on the door handle. She smiled reassuringly at him. "I am fine. And yes, I will be glad when this is over." Her voice choked with emotion. "Have your shower in peace, I am not going anywhere."

She stood staring aimlessly at the door as it clicked behind him. He was her rescuer; her saviour, and it was only natural for her to bestow a lot of affection and gratitude on him. Now she knew they were on the same side, her whole perception of him was changing. She wanted his arms around her, craved to hear all about his undercover life and what his plans were to bring the scum to justice. When she searched deep inside herself, she realised she had no desire to rush home and be safe. The reality was she harboured a horrible fear that he might be found out and executed.

Her stomach protested its empty state. Kellee decided to eat and headed to the fridge. Picking off the salad, then replacing it after reheating the bun and meat in the microwave, the burger became edible, and it helped take her mind off the man in the shower. She brushed her damp hair, allowing it to hang loose around her shoulders. One thing for sure, that appalling wig would not be worn again.

External things were easily erased, but not the image of the pile of dead bodies in the tunnel. A shiver raced down her spine. These people didn't mess around. They played dirty, and they played for keeps. There were too many people out for a quick buck, ready for them to use and abuse. She couldn't help but have some sympathy for them. Remembering the desolation of being down to her last dollar and not knowing from where or when the next meal would come. At least she had found the strength to stay on the correct side of the law.

Dumpster diving into commercial waste bins she had classed as a necessity at the time, not so much a crime. Food to survive, and the amount of still packaged, pristine food that was thrown away shocked her, but she was still grateful. She only did it when her parents were on a real bender and the purse was empty. She considered herself more fortunate than some, always appreciating the roof over her head and a relatively safe place to sleep at night.

There was still the fact she had virtually thrown herself at Matt. Looking back, she acknowledged she was guilty in instigating their love making last night. The first time he had kissed her he had pulled back and apologised at the first available opportunity. What had she done? Taken it a step further by being so turned on, she totally rocked her own boat.

Still, no denying their attraction to each other. The passion, visible in his eyes, ignited her own desires. The signals rising from his body sang to her libido. Then again, his line of work held probably limited opportunity for him to...or maybe there was? Oh gosh, she was overthinking things again. Stay cool. In a few hours it would all be over. Her thoughts sent a wave of sadness washing over her soul.

CHAPTER TWENTY NINE

Kellee appeared subdued to him since his shower. She smiled readily enough and seemed just as shocked as he was at the extent of the damage to Granny's house when they watched it on the news. He sensed her withdrawal. Probably counting down the hours until she could finally be free. Not that he could blame her.

He found it hard to stop looking at her and even harder to control his thoughts. She was quite a contradiction. Her demure image combined with her bold assessment of his every move, kept him alert and attentive. She formed a sexy vision, sitting on the bed, leaning graciously back against the headboard, long legs stretched out in front of her, sending all sorts of exotic images racing around his head. Not that her legs were exposed, but the sarong she had thrown over them like a sheet, might be covering the skin, but not the shape nor length.

Underneath the large baggy shirt that swung mid-thigh, he knew she wore her own clothes. Flashes of her shorts winked enticingly as she moved about the room earlier. The shirt may hang like a sack, but it did nothing to hide the strength and suppleness of the body nestled inside. If he kept thinking like this, it would be hot shower time. The last thing she needed now was him making advances towards her. She had been through enough. Inexplicably though, he couldn't help himself.

His sexy, lopsided grin accompanied by a raised eyebrow as he sat down on the end of the bed, ignited the vibrant alive look he found so appealing.

"So, you have fallen for the bad guy again hey?"

"I happen to know you're no bad guy," she wagged her finger at him, "but then again, you do wear the image to perfection." She prodded at him with her outstretched foot, the sarong slipping to reveal a subtle light pink nail polish.

"Checkout those toes. I didn't peg you for the painted nails type."

The sarong slipped further as long perfect legs were extended. She admired the paint job on her toes. "I dislike my feet; they are big and ugly. Hard to buy shoes for, so I paint my nails to remind myself they are all I have and to appreciate them."

Her smile softened and her voice became husky as she wiggled her feet onto his lap. "So Matt, what type did you peg me for?"

"Where do I begin," he smiled. "Intelligent, sexy, resourceful, loyal, and the beautiful woman of my heart." He lifted her foot, placing a delicate kiss on her painted nails. "You are a surprised package of strength and warmth."

A small, "Oh" escaped before she could place a hand over her mouth.

"I think your feet are beautiful," he murmured against her skin, as he rained small kisses all the way to her ankle, moving aside the rest of the sarong in the process. "Your legs are so sexy. I could stare and play with them forever." He ran his hand over her smooth skin. "Long and sexy and check out these muscles." He bent, smothering them with tender kisses. She made a strangled sound of pleasure as she flinched and pulled her leg backwards.

"Sorry darlin', did that tickle? or would you like me to stop?"

"Err, no it was lovely Just a silly over reaction from me, I don't want you to stop."

He found it endearing that she blushed slightly. "Is it the lights. They are a bit bright. Are you worried I might see your scars?" He decided blunt and straightforward was the best way to go.

"No..er maybe. I am kinda over them now. They will be part of me for the rest of my life. It was quite a revelation when I realised they are not as bad as the scars in my mind that I had to get over. Which, by the way, I am ok with now. Mostly. My therapist worked wonders in the few short weeks I saw him. What happened to me was *not* my fault."

Her words carried conviction and Matt let her keep talking, realising it would prove cathartic for her to say things out aloud and to another person. He still wondered what was holding her back. Perhaps she tended to be naturally shy while making love, but he didn't think so. Everything about her personality opposed that idea. "So, what are you scared of?" he whispered softly.

"She lifted her arms, pulling her t-shirt over her head. I am not scared, you...you do things differently, approach lovemaking so openly, I am unsure how to respond. Not saying I don't like your style. She purposely wriggled her shoulders, attempting to distract him.

Matt resisted the urge to reach out and touch her perfect breasts as they moved. "The idea is to act naturally; however you want. There's no right or wrong way."

She took his hand, placing his fingers over her breast. "Do you always talk so much?"

"Ah...does my talking about what I am doing bother you?"

"Make love to me."

"No need to rush my beautiful woman, I want to appreciate what's before me."

She sighed, "This is where you're different. No one...well I admit to sleeping with only two others, neither of them wanted to take their time."

He raised an eyebrow in surprise, but kept his face neutral and let her continue.

"I mean, my first time, the kids at school set me up with the local heartthrob to be a victim of a class prank. They uploaded an embarrassing video of a gangly teenager losing her virginity. I swore off men for years."

"Bastard. No one should have to deal with something so cruel." Matt lent down to kiss one perfect toe, blowing cool air where he moistened the skin. "I can find him and give him some pay back. " He caught and held eye contact. "I am certainly not perfect. The bad boy in me likes to come out and play and I don't like the idea that he hurt you in any way."

"The past is the past. My point is, I never experienced any talk during sex, and I am not sure how to respond. It has always been a wham bam thank you mam. It is what I am used to. My fiancé, he always grumbled about my cold fish attitude, but he never took the time to enjoy the journey. Another in and out, finish the job quick type thing."

"You stayed with him for how long?"

She let out a small sigh. "Let's not think about him, let's err...make love and if I am quiet, you'll understand why."

He stopped and studied her, mesmerised by the depth of emotion in her eyes. "Well, I like to talk, and I like to take things slow...sometimes." He grinned, dropping a soft, cheeky kiss on her nose. "I don't expect you to answer. You relax and go with the flow and if you discover something you don't like, or you want to stop at any time, just let out a grunt."

Her laugh shimmied through his body. She chuckled deep and long, stretching luxuriously as she said, "but what if my grunt is a grunt of approval?"

"Of course, you may choose to use some words, or put a little inflection into the grunt, like this." He smiled as she burst out laughing again. God, she stole his heart.

CHAPTER THIRTY

The moment Matt's hands touched her skin, Kellee felt alive. Delicate fingers traced a ribbon of pleasure from her toes to her thighs. Soft, sensual, leaving no part of her flesh unexplored. Shivers of delight travelled throughout her entire body as his mouth followed his exploring hands. She almost jumped off the bed as he kissed the delicate spot behind her knee and although she tried to suppress any noise, small moans of intense pleasure escaped her throat.

His hands and mouth provided breathtaking sensations. After each lavish stroke of his tongue, he softly blew cool air onto her moist skin, sending arrows of lust straight to her groin and tremors of delight dancing along her nerve endings. The trailing of fingers, the lapping of moisture and the cooling breath repeated its unhurried journey until it met the hem of her shorts.

She watched him as he nestled between her legs, his cheeky grin and mischievous eyes holding contact with hers. He lent forward, pushing her limbs wider, leaning so he covered the most sensitive area with his lips, pressing down firmly and blowing air straight through the cloth, filling her with incalculable pleasure as she raised her hips to meet his next move.

"His grin widened at her response. Jumping up, he grabbed her, encouraging her to stand. "Let's shed these clothes."

In the blink of an eye, he stood before her in all his naked glory, flexing muscles and striking poses to show off his strength and vitality. She burst out laughing at his comical bodybuilder renditions.

"You are a funny man, Matt. Sexy as hell and extremely funny." Her words sounded loud in her ears, as they bounced around the quiet room, the heated burn of a self-conscious blush rising to her cheeks. Slightly embarrassed, Kellee turned to the side as she stripped off her own clothes. She stood naked before him.

Warm, tender arms embraced her as he spun around pulling her closer to his solid body. He took her completely by surprise, as he lifted her off her feet, twirling her until the back of her knees touched the bed. His hungry mouth met hers and she passionately duelled back with her tongue. Man, what a kisser. An inferno raced through her veins as she angled her head, thriving in the sensation.

To be standing head-to-head, body to body was an exotic release of endorphins. She let herself relax, sinking into the moment. Her hands refused to remain still, as did his. It became a contest to see who could explore the most territory. He trailed strong fingers over her back and down to her buttocks, as she investigated his rippling shoulder and arm muscles. His body sublime under her touch.

"Ahhh, Kellee," he sighed, breaking the kiss and stepping back a pace. Slowly he turned her around, feasting upon her with his eyes, "you are so beautiful." He leant forward sucking on her nipple, looking up at her as he made the whole area glisten.

A small sigh escaped her lips. And she was mesmerised by the way his eyes never left hers, they sparked a connection, running deep into the core of her being, wrapping around her heart and holding it secure. The anticipation rose as he lavished attention on her other nipple. Giving it identical treatment, he moistened her skin, blowing coolness, until he settled to suckle on her breast.

He tugged gently with his teeth, releasing the tip only to excite the pebbled peek more with his breath.

Sensation ignited sensation as he whispered words of passion and expressed his delight at how sexy he found her and the things he wanted to do to her. With a gentle push from Matt, Kellee dropped back on the bed, legs dangling over the side. And she couldn't help smiling back at his playful expression.

There was nothing more she wanted than to be with this man, to be wrapped in his arms and enjoy the feel of him inside her. She angled back, reaching up, urging him to come to her, to finish what they had started. He allowed himself to be pulled into a push up position over her, dropping his head to smother her with a kiss filled with unbridled passion.

"Let's not rush this darlin."

Matt kept himself poised above her, so there was no contact except for his kisses travelling down her flushed skin, between the valley of her breasts, dipping into her navel. "I can't wait to taste you, to spread your legs apart and drink your essence." His head drifted closer towards the triangle of downy hair at the junction of her legs. "I want to stick my fingers into your warmth, as deep as they will go, enjoy your muscles contracting and tightening around them."

Kellee burned from the inside out, her body jumping and responding to his delicate caress. Her heart was yearning for him to put into action his sensual narrative. She heard herself moaning, tried to suppress the sound, but the sensation of fingers and his mouth tasting her, made it impossible to remain silent as he pulled back, cooling her fevered skin.

"Omg, that feels so..." Her words faded away as she arched to meet his lapping tongue. He lifted his head and looked up at her up from between her legs with lust filled eyes and a lopsided grin. "You are the most amazing woman I have ever met." He travelled her length again, long and slow before pulling back, repeating the cool, teasing air. "You are gourmet and delicious."

His hand joined his mouth's journey. She jerked wildly as he inserted a finger with infinite slowness deep into her. He withdrew it with equal finesse, before thrusting back into the pulsing depths.

She groaned, twisting and turning at the sheer bliss of her heightened awareness and she wanted more. Lap, blow, insert, heat, cool, intense pleasure. Another finger joined the first, and he thrust them with a deep steady rhythm finding and connecting to her erotic centre. A place she never realised existed.

His mouth settled on her nub, his wandering tongue creating magic as his fingers worked back and forth, in and out, fastening the pace to match her rapid breath. She grabbed at his shoulders in a bid to pull him towards her. She needed him deep inside her, but back came the sexy grin and his words of encouragement.

"Come for me darlin', come for me."

His words were all it took to send her into rapture, as rolling waves of rippling ecstasy shot from her groin, spreading through her entire body. Full of liquid energy she was pulsating with radiant joy. Never in her life experiencing such extreme pleasure. Never before had her partners bestowed so much attention on her. She rode the raw emotion as he kissed his way up her body, pulling her close to him in the process.

Wave after wave of overwhelming emotion enveloped her. She loved this man, with the wild, curly hair, sparkling eyes, and cheeky lopsided grin. The man with a heart made for loving. She could relax and be herself with him. A weight lifted off her soul and radiated through her mind.

Happiness burst across her face, reflected in the twinkling in his eyes. "Come here my bad boy." She laughed her command. Squealing in delight as he continued kissing every square inch of her skin on his slow journey upwards. "Come up here and kiss me. I want to feel you inside me."

He paused, placing small kisses on her breasts, then in one swift move loomed over her, putting his hands on each side of her body. Matt leaned down, placing tender kisses upon her cheeks, her eyes, her lips. He moved gently on her lower lip, murmuring, "Is this what you want?"

Kellee lost herself in the depth of expresso eyes filled with passion as they held hers. She wrapped her legs around his hips, pulling him towards her.

I want you to make love to me." she whispered against his lips, "Take me to paradise Matt."

"I am already there Kellee. You are my paradise."

He entered with slow purpose, pushing himself in fully before leisurely withdrawing. "Ride with me darlin'."

CHAPTER THIRTY ONE

M att fought for control, he wanted to go hard and fast, seek the pleasure he sought. The sound of her soft emotional voice almost made him come on the spot. She was so sexy, vibrant, truthful, baring herself to him emotionally, it proved hard to contain his own need for release.

He held back momentarily drinking in her beauty, before slowly entering her again. Her actions invited him to withdraw and thrust again, but he held still deep inside her, savouring the moment and the desire etched in her passion filled face. He couldn't fault her, she felt perfect to him in every way.

For the first time in his life, he found himself at a loss for words. They weren't necessary. Riding high on an emotional level entirely new to him, he slowly started to move, showing her how much he loved her and what she meant to him.

The way she let him take total control blended perfectly with how his heart felt. He wanted total control of the situation they were in, and he couldn't wait to extract her from danger. To take her somewhere safe to be open and honest and see where this feeling took him.

All he could do for now, was control as much as he could in the present. Make love to her in the best way possible, create memories that would see them through a lifetime.

Her moan of delight clutched at his heart as he dipped his head, feasting upon the soft hollow of her neck, loving the way she moaned deeper, arching as she wanted more. Her arms around him, she used her hands and fingers to rake lines of pleasure from his shoulders to his buttocks, sending the desire he was struggling to keep in check, into fever pitch.

He kept it sensual, rotating his hips after every plunge, savouring the feel of her rising excitement. This gorgeous woman beneath him. Their bodies were a flawless fit. A primal cry of delight echoed around the room as long supple legs wrapped around his hip, urging him deeper and faster, to ride the rhythm of joy that would bring them release.

Their bodied slick with sweat, were working towards a climax. Matt, gasping deep breaths, held back his own release in exquisite pain, knowing she was close. Her body arched off the bed to meet his thrusts. He lifted his head slightly to see the rapture on her face. Her eyes were closed, head thrown back, and her breaths were coming in short sharp bursts. One more thrust and her moan of pure pleasure burst into the air. Finally, he let go and joined her song of love.

Spent, he flopped on top of her, then raised himself gently onto his elbows, so he could see her face. Misty eyes smiled at him as he leant forward to give her a delicate kiss. Pulling back, he whispered words of love and beauty against her lips, before he rolled to one side, pulling her into his arms, so they were nestled close.

She moulded perfectly against him, and he loved the way she burrowed as close as possible, and as she relaxed, her warm breath tickled at his neck.

He grinned, knowing she was woman of his heart.

CHAPTER THIRTY TWO

B ANG!

Kelle scrambled out of bed clutching the sheet close to her body. Matt was a tad faster, not worrying about covering his nakedness. He leapt across the bed, gun in hand and stood protectively in front of her at the sound of the door crashing against the wall. Flight or fight battled, neither won, rationality took control. Just before the light blinded them, she grabbed Matt's phone from the bedside table and tucked her hand inside the fold of the sheet. There was no time to ponder where this calm strength came from, as her eyes adjusted to the overhead light.

"What the fuck Fuzz!" Matt's words exploded around the room. "You got a death wish?" Matt clicked on the safety and tossed the gun onto the bed, picked his boxers up off the floor, moving slightly away from her as he stepped into them. At the same time, he kept his body between her and the three men who had burst through the door.

"Always living on the edge, bro." Fuzz's voice had a sharp edge to it as he surveyed the room, eyes flicking to Kellee then back to Matt. "And you're living a fun life." His bawdy laugh grated on her ears, "Sorry to spoil your party bro, but the boss changed the orders. We move out now."

Emotions rolled. Fear was smothered by the need to help Matt bring these bastards down. In all her Police years she had never felt such clarity. Clear headed, she prepared to follow Matt's lead. His broad wink, as he turned his back on the men, boosted her morale even more. As a team, they were invincible.

"Bathroom. Do what you gotta do and get dressed pronto." Matt's voice was sharp and void of emotion as he gathered her scattered clothes and pack and thrust them into her arms.

She had no idea if Matt realised she had picked up the phone. She'd been hard pressed not to drop it as she juggled the sheet and clothes in her shuffle to the bathroom. Now, with the door closed, she moved with lightning speed, inserting the sim, and making sure the light and sound were turned off. Ablutions first, then dressing in record time, thankful, not for the first time, that the present for her boss, the big baggy shirt hid the phone in her pocket perfectly.

Anxiety kicked in just a little. She was about to re-enter the danger zone, when Matt pushed past her, with a hasty whisper, "Abort, we escape first chance." There was no opportunity to pass him the phone, or even answer back, as Fuzz and a towering six-and-a-half-foot muscular sumo wrestler stood in the doorway, hurrying her along.

Stale tobacco and dried sweat clung to Fuzz's clothes and sour warm breath coated his words as he leaned in close, grabbing her pack. "You won't need that where you are headed sweetheart." His wicked laugh set her teeth on edge.

Kellee resisted the urge to look back to see where Matt was as they ushered her out the door and into the balmy night air. After the cool of the motel room, it took a few moments for her breathing to adjust to the thick humid atmosphere and she felt instantly hot and clammy. Rough hand shoved her towards a couple of parked motor bikes and before she could see if Matt was close, thick tape was put over her mouth and darkness engulfed her.

Panic and reaction were instant. Wild flaying hands flew to her face only to hit the hard surface of the helmet, the protective plastic shield must have been blackened out. Cruel sumo hands squeezed her upper arms hard to stop her from struggling, "Utter one sound and I'll slit your throat." She believed him. Never had she heard words so cold, she felt like she was being sliced open by a razor-sharp knife. She was stuffed into a heavy leather jacket and the same hands promptly lifted her with ease and plonked her on the back of the bike.

Her muffled scream echoed in her ears and as the bike took off, she had to clutch at the rider's waist for some form of stability. Panic, fear, and claustrophobia were competing for attention, and it took all her will power to keep them under control. Adrenalin flooded her body and she admitted to herself, she was terrified. Once acknowledged, her emotions seemed to settle down, and some semblance of rational thought began to fill her mind.

The bike maintained a steady pace. Under no illusion it was for her benefit, she knew her rider was keeping the throttle low and sticking to the speed limit to avoid notice. She thought about throwing herself off, even making the bike topple, but without vision it would be a frightful and fruitless manoeuvre. Basically, there was nothing she could do but hang on and hope Matt was close by, able to act when the opportunity arose. The best she could do was remain alert and ready.

It was a lengthy trip. Try as she might to pick up some idea where they were headed, straining her ears and attuning her nose to any distinct smells, there wasn't much to go on. Once she thought she smelt strawberries and a couple of times she guessed she heard dogs barking in the distance, but it was hard to decipher sounds over the throaty beat of the bike's motor. At times, through the bottom of the helmet, she could see small reflections of light. Sometimes bright, other times just a dull glow, but mostly the blackness was complete. The bike finally slowed and did a couple of quick turns before coming to a stop.

The lights of the bike behind them filled the bottom part of her vision momentarily before plunging her world back into darkness the silence rang in her ears as both motors were switched off. Her heartbeat kicked up a notch as she was unceremoniously dragged off the bike and the helmet ripped from her head. Her eyes did not need much adjusting, it was oppressively dark. She tried to look behind to see if Matt was anywhere close by, but rough hands grabbed her arm and propelled her towards a building, which was half hidden by the surrounding rainforest. An element of relief settled over her when she heard Matt's laugh behind her. She was not alone.

Silvery streaks of light burst through the clouds as the moon found a space in the open sky. The unfamiliar soft freshness that had been teasing her nostrils, as she stumbled along the uneven dirt pathway towards the house, was revealed as a vast expanse of shimmering water. Six steps up onto the veranda and she felt like she was on the water's edge. The dark, mysterious lake appeared to be circular in shape, shrouded by rainforest, hugging the distant edges.

Once again, the moon sought the cover of the clouds, as the last shards of light faded from the silvery surface. Kellee caught a glimpse of Matt's face. It wasn't reassuring. He looked drawn, and although he must be trying to conceal it, his look held concern. Surely this was not the Compound? It was just a house on the edge of a lake. There must still be time to escape. She tried to convey confidence with a twitch of her eye, but had no idea if he caught it as she was propelled inside.

Eight to ten people lounged around a large living space. The lighting was subdued, and it was hard to determine what they were up to as impatient hands pushed and pulled her down a narrow hallway and into a bedroom. The moon chose that time to burst free again, as if to bath in the glory of the panoramic views of the moonlit lake. No one had uttered a word since they had left the motel, and the big hulk who had been assigned to her just grunted as he flung open a massive wall to wall wardrobe's double doors.

"Nice pad," Matt's voice was close behind her. "so, what now, we stay here the night?" Kellee held her breath, ears straining for the answer.

A beefy laugh accompanied a rough shove to her back. She stumbled forward towards the wardrobe. "Ha ha ha, welcome to the Compound bro." The big, beefy man crouched down, tossed some fallen clothes to one side, and lifted a hatch revealing an almost vertical ladder leading down into a semi lit hole.

Kellee balked and pulled back to no avail, as a forceful shove to the back sent her sprawling onto all fours. She almost went headfirst down the tunnel. She spun around and lashed out with her legs, at the same time pulling the phone from her pocket, flinging her arm out straight into the pile of clothes on the wardrobe floor.

She was under no illusion. There was no way she could escape the strong hands that grabbed and yanked at her ankles, but she could bury the phone deeper into the clothes as she flipped over onto her belly. It was their only hope. No doubt the signal underground would be non-existent, but up here on the wardrobe floor there was a chance MICO could find it.

"Hey, take it easy," Matt's voice rose above the fear clanging in her head. "she's claustrophobic."

"Who gives a fuck man. Back off, it's our turf now."

She didn't recognise the gravely cold voice that had answered Matt and she could only catch a glimpse of those around her as she was unceremoniously dragged feet first down the ladder.

Fighting for a foot hold, she clutched on tight to the cool metal rungs. It was a long way down. Although the hand on one of her feet never let go, they allowed her to gain her balance and she climbed down one rung at a time. Automatically, she counted.

One hundred and fifty-four steps of hell. The tube-like rock tunnel closed around her, making breathing difficult. The dim lighting was adequate for seeing what was required to continue the downward climb, but the clamminess of her palms had her clutching tightly to steel rungs to prevent her from slipping. Worse was the smell. Hot, musky, oppressive and heavy with body sweat. She was hard pressed to keep her panic at bay.

The logical side of her brain was keeping her sane as her thoughts ticked over, analysing and assessing. But the hopelessness of her situation became obvious as she scanned the small cavern at the bottom of the ladder. It was more like a jetty, with a landing platform hovering above gloomy, inhospitable water. Two small boats bobbed up and down, straining to break their ropes as they bucked against a moderate current.

How in the blue blazes were they going to get out of this? She shot a look towards Matt, who had just finished his descent, realising she was thinking in terms of *we* not I. They were a team and although she felt like there was no escape, as long as Matt was close, she knew he would do his best to find a way to protect her. To get them both out of this mess and hopefully, bring a few bastards down in the process.

"Shit, watch it. I nearly fell in the water." Kellee's voice fell on deaf ears as she was unceremoniously dumped onto the bench seat in the closest boat. As the brooding hulk sat down next to her, she grabbed the side of the craft as his weight made it rock and tilt even more.

"Shut your mouth and stay put." His scowl deepened as he shoved a square, broad hand on her knee to hold her still. She rolled her eyes. As if she was going anywhere! That water looked dark and foreboding. What did he think she was going to do, jump in and swim away?

"Matt, shift ya ass to the opposite side. Balance the load and don't mind me sitting close to you. Titch has got his side covered." Fuzz's accompanying laugh echoed, bouncing off the surrounding rocks.

The electric motor buzzed quietly, and a bright light lit up the darkness as they glided through the inky waters towards the current in the middle. The boat bucked as the swift current caught it in its grip. Kellee almost gasped at the speed they were travelling. Rocks and dark formations sped past, silky smooth. Wet crevices, highlighted by the light beams flashed by, deep and mysterious. Kellee started to shake. Whether it was from the cold or the fear, she couldn't determine, and not for the first time in the past forty-eight hours, she struggled to control her breathing.

"Woohooo" Matt's hoot of excitement gave her courage as they burst out of the tunnel, into a moderately sized cavern.

"Ready Fuzz?" The man behind her at the tiller raised a cranky voice. "If you leave it until the last-minute man, I'll kick your ugly face in when we dock."

Fuzz chuckled and stood, feet part. He lifted a large grappling hook and deftly snagged it onto an overhead rope. "Hang on tight." Spinning almost ninety degrees, the boat bucked against the current.

Kellee screamed, clutching at the side of the boat as it swung wildly. The thug next to her tightened his hold on her leg. Pain was the only thing his grip offered.

"What the..." Matt queried as the boat found calmer waters out of the swift main current and chugged sedately towards the caverns shore edge.

"That's our insurance, a death-defying security precaution that only Compound dwellers know. Anyone finds the wardrobe tunnel and tries to follow..." His manic laugh made Kellee shudder, as fear gripped her entire body. "...If you don't catch the rope, it's goodbye assholes as they get sucked into the raging tunnel up ahead. No coming out of that alive, it's a ripper."

"That's why I said don't leave it till the last-minute you moron." The man with the cranky voice snapped. "It nearly backfired on you once before. Dice with your own life not mine."

The boat bobbed gently as they docked at a small jetty, soft lanterns giving the rocky cavern a warm gentle glow. It did nothing to calm Kellee as she half tumbled, almost sprawling onto the wooden planks. Her system was overloaded with panic. What if MICO did find her phone and followed through the wardrobe? OMG she would have sent them to their deaths.

She made frantic eye contact with Matt as he exited the boat behind her. A rough hand pulled her forward, causing her to break contact, and she knew at all costs she must get a message to Matt so, if possible, he could warn them. Without thinking of the consequences, instead of resisting the yank on her hand, she went with it, causing the goliath of a man to stumble as she threw him off balance. Swinging her right arm in a wild ark and clenching her fist tight, she connected with his jaw using all the force and body weight she could muster. It was like hitting a solid brick wall. Fingers crunched, and pain shot through her arm like spikes of fire.

Her plan had been to follow through with a swift knee to the groin, but before she could react, a stinging blow to the side of her face sent sparks flashing behind her eyes. Her cry of pain echoed around her as her knees slammed into the hardwood. Kicking her legs, trying to gain traction, she was dragged along as the giant strode to the end of the short jetty, almost wrenching her arm out of its socket. Once he stopped, she attempted to scramble to her feet. He dropped her hand and grabbed her by both shoulders, pulling her upright. A man stepped in close, jabbing a needle into her neck. Almost immediately she felt the effects. She saw Matt striding towards her, but he seemed so far away. He called out, but she couldn't hear what he said. Her legs began to crumble as dark swirls swam in her eyes. Reaching out, she clutched at thin air, then felt herself falling into the black void of oblivion.

CHAPTER THIRTY THREE

Matt was sure the cool facade he was trying desperately to project was non-existent. Kellee's eyes had scored a pathway to his heart. First desperation, then pain followed immediately by panic. Her struggle was short and fierce. By the time she crumpled to the rough stone floor, he had only just scrambled out of the boat, achieving only a few determined steps in her direction.

Out the corner of his eye he saw a flash of movement. A hairy, clenched fist came towards him, thumb poised on a syringe, ready to plunge downward. As it swung close, he could see the needle with its glistening bead of liquid wobbling precariously on the tip. Adrenaline kicked in as he ducked sideways, blocking the aggressor's arm with an upward thrust, his own arm twisting outwards at the last minute. The needle went flying. He followed through with a sharp, powerful uppercut to the man's chin. His opponent went down like a ton of bricks.

"What the fucks going on Fuzz?" He strode to the end of the short jetty, pulling up just as he stepped onto the cavern floor, leaving a moderate space in-between him and the man he questioned.

Fuzz ignored him, addressing the giant who stood next to the unconscious Kellee. "Idiot! The pig was meant to be taken down to the pens first. Now we have an angry boar to contend with."

The giant shrugged. "She wasn't meant to put up a fight. I improvised. No big deal, I can take down that foul-smelling grunter easily."

Fear shot through Matt's body, not so much for himself but for Kellee. He had failed her. His hands began to sweat. The cold dread of his cover being exposed activated his flight or fight instinct. His eyes scanned the surroundings as he planned an evasive course of action. Attack, grab Kellee, take the boat and motor back to the house. He had to get them out of the Compound at all costs. They would kill him, but Kellee...escalating fear assaulted his senses, metallic, smoky, like an electrical wire fusing out.

Matt directed his attention to the man standing near the woman he loved. He was big, but clumsy looking. Adjusting his stance and forming tight fists, Matt poised with bent elbows, one by his waist, the other a little higher over his chest. He drew on all his strength; failing was not an option.

Fuzz was closest and Matt caught him off guard as he leapt in his direction rather than at the giant, landing a knuckle cracking punch on the side of his jaw. Stumbling backwards, Fuzz's eyes widened with painful surprise, before they took on a superior squint as he issued an order with this hand.

Matt spun around just in time to dodge a blow from a small, agile man. He jumped back towards him, landing a solid blow to his gut, followed by an uppercut to the chin. The man crumpled like a building imploding.

"Get him lads, rough him up, but don't kill him," Fuzz shouted with smug victory as he backed away, "the boss wants to question him...in depth."

No longer able to hide the despair flooding his mind, Matt shot a panicked glance in Kellee's direction. The giant, who had been standing next to her, now had her lifeless body draped effortlessly over his shoulder as he strode away. A cry of anguish escaped his lips. He had failed her, failed his mission. Even though deep down he knew it was pointless, he squared his shoulders and prepared to face the onslaught from the men racing out of a nearby passage towards him, determined to take down as many as he could.

In Rambo reborn style, he threw his fists left and right, attacking, defending, ducking to avoid blows, twisting this way and that in a bid to diminish even a few of the men around him. Muscles flooding with lactic acid gradually became too heavy to lift and he was unable to defend himself against the brutal blows that were pounding his body.

Defeated and struggling to catch a full breath of air, he dropped to one knee, lungs heaving from exhaustion. Bodies of his foes were scattered about him, some out cold, others groaning as they struggled to their feet. The smell of pungent sweat, both his and his opponents, mixed with the tangy odour of the blood dripping from his mouth onto the floor cemented his despair. There was nothing more he could do to help himself or Kellee. His body slumped in defeat. It was over.

Matt clenched his gut as a boot clad foot lifted backward to strike.

"Enough." The boot stopped mid-air. "The boss wants him alive and coherent." Fuzz was victorious. "Drag him to the cell boys."

Rough hands dug under his arms, half hoisting him to his feet. Hopelessness flooded his mind. How could he save Kellee? He couldn't even get his legs to work properly. He stumbled as the hands dug painfully into his flesh. A savage laugh added to his pain as his head was jerked backwards by the hair and Fuzz's fist filled his vision, "ahhh, what the heck you traitorous cu...," were the last words he heard before everything went black.

A steady drip, drip, drip, hitting the side of his face, accompanied by a deep, prolonged moan nudged him back from the world of darkness. At first he thought he was responsible for the groan, but as he became more aware of his surroundings, he realised the sound was too far away from him. He coughed and spat blood, gagging from the foul stench rising from the cold stone floor he lay on. Pushing himself halfway up, he leaned back on his arm, waiting for the dizziness to pass. Gagging again as the reek of raw sewage made his breathing taste foul. He huffed out a breath and shook his head. In the dim light, blood flung from his lips with the movement. He rubbed his hand against his swollen skin and stretched out his jaw, wincing with pain. Gradually, he tested his limbs one by one and was relieved to find they were all in working order. Painful but working. He may have been unconscious when they put him in the cell, but the grazes down his arm showed they had not been gentle.

The groan came again, somewhere off to his left and deeper to the back of the stone cell. Kellee? Fear shot through his body. He half stood, cursing as his legs crumpled beneath him. "Kellee?" He compromised, half dragging, half crawling to the moaning bundle of rags.

"Oh my god, Jules," he tried to wipe her matted hair out of her face, "what have they done to you?"

She cringed.

"No, no leave me..." Her voice cracked with an hysterical sob "d..d..do..don't hurt m...m..me." Pitifully she clawed with bloodied, torn nails at the stone floor in a bid to scramble away, her twisted, swollen legs sprawled out uselessly behind her.

"Jules, it's me, Matt. I'm not going to hurt you." He didn't try to touch her again until she quietened, squinting at him through bruised and swollen eyes.

"M...M...Matt, oh Matt," she sobbed. The dried blood caking her lips cracked as she spoke, causing fresh bright red drops to dribble down her chin.

Matt looked frantically around the cell, scanning for anything he could use to ease her pain. In utter dismay he looked back at the battered woman, knowing there was nothing he could do to help her distress, except let her know she was not alone. He grabbed the filthy blanket she had been half lying on and bundled it into some semblance of a pillow and tucked it under her head.

It was impossible to get her into a more comfortable position. Both her legs were broken, dark bruising already pooling around the jagged angles above and below her disjointed knees. She kept sobbing his name over and over, clutching at him with shaking, weakened fingers. Gently, he pulled the matted strands of hair away from her eyes and smoothed her tattered clothing the best he could.

"It's ok Jules." He lied soothingly, "I will get us out of this." He had never felt more defeated. His thoughts drifted to Kellee and his heart seemed to be ripping into desperate fragmented pieces. Drawing on all his inner strength, he hardened his resolve. He needed to pull himself together and find a way out of this mess.

"Rest up Jules," he whispered close to her ear, "I am going to go over this cage with a fine-tooth comb. Find a weak point somewhere." The heat coming off her forehead as he gave it a compassionate stroke worried him. Fever was setting in.

Looking around their dank oppressive prison, he decided the bars that ran the full length of the front of the cell would be the best place to start. The back wall held several chains with manacles, and horrid images filled his mind as he saw the dark stains on the walls and floor around them. He shuddered. Steadying his breathing and trying to push all thoughts of Kellee out of his mind, he started rattling the bars in the far corner, feeling them top and bottom, testing for any sign of weakness or decay.

Each bar stood firm and solid, and he became more despondent and desperate as he made his way along the cell. Vivid thoughts of what had been done to Jules and what might happen to Kellee encroached with every bar he checked. A mantra screamed inside his head. This one will be weak for Kellee. Each bar, as strong as the next, fed his frustration to a fearful pitch. He started pulling violently on them, cursing, and swearing as each failed to give way. Using his foot as leverage, he tugged with all his strength.

Hands slippery with sweat his grip faltered, and he landed flat on his buttocks with a bone jarring thud. It took a moment for him to fight through the pain then he slowly rose to his feet.

"There's no way out of this cell grunter."

The sound of water splashing, and the cold callousness of the voice made him turn to it's source. Fuzz stood a couple of meters away, tipping water from a bucket into a tin container that was attached to the inside of the bars at floor level. Water was going everywhere, most of it missing the container, but Matt's eyes never left the man's face.

"If you wanna drink, you will have to get on all fours like the bastard pig you are." The dim light exaggerated the anger and sneer lines on Fuzz's face, giving it a vicious, evil look. And the hollow echo of his words bounced around the stone prison, wrapping themselves around Matt's soul, smothering it in despair. "Don't waste your time. You ain't getting out of here. Just hope the boss lets me hang around while he strips the flesh from your face, and that's after he has broken every bone in your body."

Matt refused to verbally respond. Instead, he drew upon physical and mental strength he didn't really have. Slowly, standing tall and strong, he narrowed his eyes, turned his granite face towards Fuzz, gaining some satisfaction when he took an involuntary step backwards. It was all show. Inside he felt like yelling, grabbing the bars and yanking them with all his might. Kellee, oh Kellee, how was he going to save her?

Fuzz seemed to take courage from behind the protection of the bars. He struck out at the metal with a wooden club, screwing his face into a sneer. He spat the words. "You think you're tough, gunna be rescued? Think again, grunter."

His sick, twisted laugh caused Matt's eye to twitch as he fought to remain impassive.

"I saw your slut ditch the phone in the wardrobe. Couldn't have planned it better myself. It's gunna lead your rescue squad right into the waterways, except they won't know to catch the rope."

His taunting laugh echoed around the stone walls, feeding the fear deep within Matt's gut. "And while they are drowning, we will be using the back door, taking your slut with us. Boss reckons he has a couple of buyers already outbidding each other like fuckin' crazy trying to get their hands on a stinking six foot pig."

Fuzz cupped his balls and made a rocking action. "But first I wanna have my fun while you rot in hell."

Matt breathed rapidly, fighting to remain impassive. Trying to calm his thoughts, he almost muttered out loud, 'I love you Kellee.' His thoughts raced to his family and work team. He couldn't even warn them. Shit. What in the hell could he do? Without realising it, he had been clenching and unclenching his fists. He suddenly stopped, leaving them deceptively loose at his side. "How about you and I have a go, one on one?" He jumped forward, grabbed and rattled at the bars. "Right now," he taunted, "if you're man enough."

There was just a grain of satisfaction in seeing the momentary spark of fear in Fuzz's eyes. Matt had no doubt he could beat him. Fuzz spat in Matt's direction, but it fell well short of the mark as he kept his distance.

Matt goaded him. "You always were a 'yes' man, and a fucking coward. Only capable of hitting a man when he is down, or his back is turned, you yellow bellied bastard." He rattled the bars again. Not that it did any good. Fuzz's confidence had returned, and Matt regretted the outburst when there was not a damn thing he could do about any of it.

"When the boss gets around to you, it's going to be a real pleasure to hear you scream and beg for mercy." He grabbed at his crotch again. "I'm off to have some fun. Stay put grunter, your time will come. Maybe the boss will let me have you too. I couldn't care less what I fuck."

Matt watched him walk away. Jules whimpered in the background. She hadn't made a sound since Fuzz showed up. He bent and cupped his hands in the water bowl, scooping as much as he could, dribbling a few drops into her parched lips. She was obviously dehydrated and there was no way she could get to the water herself. He knew there was nothing more he could do for her either, he doubted she would last much longer.

Returning to the bars, he pressed close, looking this way and that, all the while listening for any external sound. Convinced they were alone, he squatted near the water bowl, looked again, then lay flat on the cold, wet floor and stuck his arm through the bars as far as it could go. Fuzz had been so intent on being the bad guy, he hadn't noticed when a piece of wood had splintered and flew off when the bars were struck with his club. He flattened his shoulder against the bar and stretched, his fingertips just tickling the wood fragment. Not enough to be able to grasp it.

Sitting back, he removed his shoe and repeated the procedure, gradually rolling the wood close enough to grasp. It wasn't much, but it was better than nothing. He had been afraid Fuzz would see it, which was why he had grabbed the bars when he did. Anything to keep his attention away from the floor. The shard of wood was only about five centimetres long, but it was reasonably sturdy.

A plan was a plan, no matter how small and futile. Positioning himself next to the water bowl, he started to scrape at the base of the water-soaked bar. Being continuously wet had softened the stone and loosened the hard packed dirt and small bits started to flake away. He concentrated on the job at hand, determined to succeed, unsuccessfully blocking thoughts of Kellee and his family. For the first time in his life, he was seriously scared, frustrated, and close to panic at not being able to warn or save those he loved. Let alone himself.

CHAPTER THIRTY FOUR

Kellee screamed, cursed, and attempted to kick out to no avail. The rope binding her hands behind her back bit deeply into her skin. Ignoring the pain she continued to struggle. The shackles on her ankles were restricting her movement but didn't stop her body from ramming the short little dweeb who was trying to fondle her breasts. She head-butted him in the belly, savouring his grunt of expelled air that left him wheezing and gasping for breath. She took the small reprieve to steady herself and assess the situation.

Coming to with strange hands groping her body, she had snapped awake and sprung to her feet in fighting mode. Catching them by surprise, fists flying, she had downed a couple before they had known what hit them. A wave of nausea and dizziness had left her vulnerable and a well-aimed fist to her cheek had sent her reeling. And once the shackles were on her feet, they had unceremoniously dumped her on the floor and tied her hands behind her back. Now they were attempting to put a chain collar around her neck.

The giant of a man with the body of steel had been laughing at his comrade's demise. He was standing by the door, the only exit to the room, unperturbed by her escape attempt. It was obvious the room had a purpose. It was large, windowless, and looking at the white painted walls, you wouldn't know you were in an underground cave. There were showers down one end, a wardrobe holding silky lightweight clothes, in sizes from horridly small to adult. The men had joked that they wouldn't find anything to fit her. Then re joked about painting her blue like an avatar and she not needing clothes. One side of the room was set up like a photographer's studio, with makeup, lights, cameras and to her horror, a bed. Some of the walls had chain loopholes. Again, some were positioned horribly low. She shuddered. This was a room of terror. Even the air smelt of fear and despair mixed with perfumes and soap.

She was terrified, exhausted and at the end of her strength. When they came at her again, she didn't think she would even be able to lift her arms to fend them off.

"For fucks sake hurry up and put her collar on." The man sounded nasally, as he swabbed at his nose, trying to stem the flow of blood. He kept his distance, a wary eye on her.

"Shut up you moron." The man with the chain gave it to the giant. "She's all yours Titch. We don't have time to mess around, everyone is clearing out. The Compound has been compromised and we are meant to be moving fast." He sniffed deeply and sounded disappointed. "The boss wants her in chains and up to his office asap."

Just as the giant stepped forward, chain in his hand, Fuzz burst into the room. "Titch, get her into these clothes." He tossed a pair of blue jeans and a blue checkered shirt at the giant. "They are the boss's; they will fit the lanky bitch. He wants her to look as normal as possible for the outside part of the move. Then tie her back up and fast."

He yelled when they didn't move quick enough. "Everyone knows what their orders are, we are just doing it faster. We need to get out of here pronto. Pack up and clear out or you will be pig food. Titch, hurry it up, I gotta take the bitch to the boss."

Titch held the chain around her neck, while they released her hands and feet. She chose to be compliant while she swiftly put on the clothes provided, glad of their protective feel and warmth. She didn't bat an eyelid when they bound her wrists again. At least her feet were free. She decided to conserve what little strength she had left for the outside part of the move. It would offer the best chance of escape. Probably the only chance, and hopefully Matt would be there. With him around to overpower the guards, they could pull it off.

Titch passed the other end of the chain to Fuzz. "Do you need me any more boss?" He cocked his head in her direction and raised an eyebrow. "Nope, get moving, see you at the bunker. You'll get more directions there."

They pumped fists like old friends, before he turned and walked through the door, leaving it open. The hustle and bustle outside was like a busy city street at peak hour.

"Come here," commanded Fuzz, and when she didn't respond quickly enough, he yanked on the chain, so she stumbled towards him. Then he yanked again, bringing her so close she almost bumped into him. The chain's rattle snapped close to her ear as the link tightened around her neck. Her breathing became restricted before it released again, and Kellee could not find the courage to meet him eye to eye. She was trapped. Helpless and worried sick about Matt. And cold. Despite the warmer clothes she started to shake. There was nothing she could do now but bide her time for an opportunity to present when she was outside.

"Matt sends his love." Fuzz laughed at the words. "Wish we had time to play. Maybe at the bunker."

"Where is he?" She surprised herself with the steadiness of her voice. Inside she was panicking, and his next words turned her world upside down, flooding her with despair.

"Oh, you don't have to worry about that traitor." He wrapped the chain around his fist, giving it a quick hard tug. "We got that pig locked up so deep no one will ever find him." His face revealed pleasure as she coughed and spluttered, stepping closer to him to relieve the tight pressure around her throat.

"That's right, come to me sweetheart."

Kellee resisted the urge to spit in his face. Things were bad enough as they were.

"Can't wait till there's more time to see what you got, see who's going to bid the highest for you." He flashed a rotting teeth grin at her, and she kept her breath shallow, not wanting to smell the foul stale smoke that surrounded him whenever he spoke. "Think I will ask the boss if I can be the one that puts your portfolio together. Look forward to taking photos of your pussy, maybe I will get a pig to sniff..."

What the heck. She spat a big juicy gob on his face and braced for the impact of his fist.

The loud beeping of his radio handset, cut off his swear word. He dropped his fist and answered immediately. "Yeah boss, already on my way," he lied.

He snarled, wiped the spit away with the back of his hand, then wiped it down her shirt, yanking unnecessarily hard on the chain as he strode out the door.

It took Kellee just a few choking steps to catch up with him. Her long strides clipped at his heels. She took a small grain of satisfaction when he tried to pick up his pace, but he was no match for her powerful legs. Her mind was racing. From Fuzz's remarks, Matt's cover had obviously been blown. She feared for him, for what they would do to him. The only consolation was they were on the move. He must still be alive. She was certain Fuzz would have rubbed his death in her face. If they didn't intend to take him along, then surely they would have killed him outright.

"Hey Fuzz, want me to take her? I got room in the van?"

"Nope. Special delivery for the boss. Take off as soon as you're ready." He shoved Kellee forward, then yanked her back, with a twisted laugh as she choked. "You're gunna regret spitting on me bitch."

Kellee took in as much of her surroundings as she could. They were moving away from the general direction of the departing people. A few were in chains like her, being mercilessly dragged away. Thank goodness there were no children that she could see. It looked more like a cave now, rocky and uneven under her feet, and cold. Even though she was moving, she felt chilled to the bone. Once or twice she stumbled, but quickly caught back up again before the chain tightened. They turned down a narrow passage, then up a small flight of stairs. Fuzz was breathing heavily because of the fast pace she was setting, and he scowled at her. "You'll keep bitch. May even bid on you myself."

Reaching a thick wooden door, he knocked and looked up at the camera, flicked a casual salute and waited. His phone rang.

"Yeah boss, where are you?" His tone always seemed polite and respectful when talking to his boss, almost worship-like. "Shit! ok will do. Be there as quick as we can."   "Come on bitch, we have to hustle." His laugh sounded manic and not altogether sane. "Looks like you ain't getting rid of me anytime soon." Yanking her back down the stairs, he took off as fast as he was able.

"Where are you taking me now?" Kellee didn't really expect an answer. It wasn't difficult keeping up with his short legged stride, but she could sense his urgency. Something had not gone to plan, and she prayed with all her might that somehow MICO had made it past the cavern's waterways. Her hopes were dashed with his next words.

"The first pig squad were sucked away just as planned." He laughed, "Man I wish I could have seen that. Boss said they were yellin' and a screamin' as they got sucked through the tube. He yanked hard as she had almost stopped dead in her tracks. "Keep it movin' bitch. My boys could hear a second lot behind them, calling out." Haha Haha. "Fuck I wish I could have seen that."

Kellee hit rock bottom. She instinctively knew if she didn't make a stand right now, she would be lost forever. Her heart was grieving for Matt and the MICO crew and it was grieving for her and what lay ahead. She stumbled. He retaliated by pulling harder on the chain without letting up his fast pace. The pain of the chain digging into her neck and that momentary lack of air kicked in Kellee's fighting spirit. She would not go down without a fight. With no Matt coming to the rescue, her best chance was going to be while it was one on one. Her best chance was now. Her legs were free. She had been trying to loosen her wrist bonds. There seemed a little bit of give, but not much. Best chance would be to fall over, resist the tug on her neck and fake injury. Grab him with her legs and hopefully squeeze the breath out of him. No doubt she would go down, but it certainly would not be without a fight.

The rocky passage was getting thinner and full of twists and turns. Always steadily climbing upwards. Every so often, when they came to a junction, Fuzz would stop and think, as if remembering directions. It was obvious he was in new territory. She thought she noticed a natural brightness creeping in to overtake the dimness. The air was gradually changing from a musty cold smell to drifts of clean freshness. They must be getting close.

The ground was rough and uneven. Kellee was working herself up to take the tumble. It was not an easy thing to do. To deliberately throw yourself onto hard-stone ground, knowing the chain would cut off your air supply, and it would undoubtedly hurt. She psyched herself up, tensed ready to execute her plan, when they came to an abrupt halt. Deflated, she realised she left it too late. Just in front of them she could see a man packing something into pre prepared holes in a natural arch like structure. The tunnel narrowed to little more than a man's width and she thought she could see explosives being set. What hit her most though, was the sweet freshness of the air. They must be so close to the surface.

"Hey Boss, didn't know this tunnel existed. Fucking cool man. What can I do to help, looks like you're gunna' blow the place sky high."

"You made good time Fuzz. Yep, bring her here. We are going to blow her along with the tunnel." The boss growled as Fuzz shoved her towards him. "Too much of a liability now. We need to seal this cavern, and quickly. This part of the operation is over. I am going to the next level and you, my right-hand man, are coming with me." He gave Fuzz a high five. "What a buzz. A promotion and we get to blow up a cop all in one day."

The Boss was slightly taller than her, muscular, commanding and intimidating. As he pulled her towards him, she felt powerless. Her heart was pounding in her ears. Taking a breath was almost impossible, as her chest constricted with fear. Looking into his face was like looking at a frozen picture. Totally devoid of emotion. His eyes were dark cesspools of emptiness, his mouth a tight, unforgiving line.

Before she could think, her legs were kicked out from under her. Instinctively, she tried to brace the fall with her bound hands and cried out as the rope cut into already raw wrists. She grimaced, preparing for impact with cold hard stone. Instead, strong hands caught her, pushing her into a sitting position. There was no time for thought as those same hands swiftly tied a bag of explosives to her ankles and snapped out the order to set the timer.

There was no use begging and screaming. A minute was all she had left. A whirlwind of memories flew through her brain, each competing for the chance to be her last memory. Matt's face won. He brought peace to her inner turmoil and with a slight smile on her lips, she counted down the seconds.

CHAPTER THIRTY FIVE

Matt dug frantically with his chip of wood, cursing again as another small splinter broke away, and he prayed it would last long enough to get the job done. Progress was slow. With each scrape of the moist stone, only a little crumble came away. It wasn't enough. The wood broke again, it was almost too small to use. He sat back on his heels sucking in a deep breath. He wasn't used to feeling this helpless nor defeated. Panic was sitting close to the surface in the form of rage, almost unbearable and uncontainable.

Breathing deeply again, he rubbed at his cramping hands, ignoring the abrasions and broken nails.

Jules moaned.

Looking back at his work he finally realised he was delusional. There was no way he would be able to dig deep enough to make a difference. The bars were solid and held strong, obviously made to last. He must have been working on this for at least an hour and he had barely scratched the surface.

Jules moaned again. Her groans were almost constant now. At first, he would go and check her each time, dribbling more water into her mouth. Now he didn't respond. He was too deep in his own world of pain and anguish. With every moan he thought of Kellee, and he was terrified at what might be happening to her.

A rage he could no longer contain let fly like a whistling kettle left to boil at full steam. He jumped to his feet, yelling, and cursing with fury at the prison that contained him. Focusing on the bar he had been trying to loosen, he grabbed it with both hands, using every ounce of strength he possessed and throwing his head back with a mighty frustrated roar.

The bar held strong. Solid. Unmovable.

He sat down resting back on his heels, the cold silence around him ringing in his ears. Earlier, muffled noises filled the background. Now, silence reigned, as if the cavern were empty. He had never felt so alone. Picking up the remnants of his piece of wood, he twisted it around and around in his fingers, sifting through the fragments of information he knew.

Somehow, smart resourceful Kellee had grabbed and activated his phone so MICO could follow. In this line of business, you took every opportunity when it arose. He would have done the same thing if he had thought of it. Although in deep trouble, Kellee was quick-witted, tough, and he knew she could fight. If a chance arose, she would take it. He took some small comfort in the fact they wanted to sell her. At least that way she wouldn't be harmed, despite Fuzz's taunts. You don't miss handle precious goods. And every moment she was alive held a chance for escape.

As for his family and the MICO Team, all he could do was hold onto the belief they would see the wire. It was a long shot. He hadn't seen it at all, but there was still a possibility. Their senses would be sharp and alert. Anything could happen.

He must remain positive that Kellee and his Team would find ways, and confidence in himself that this bar would eventually yield. They were good thoughts to hold onto as he started scraping again.

As if to reinforce his belief, another bigger chunk crumbled away. This one had a small stone attached to the side. Placing the tiny, almost non-existent stick aside, he tested the stone. It was adequate. Better than the stick and sturdier. He could apply more pressure with it. The process was slow and painful, but he felt he was finally getting somewhere.

He looked over his shoulder at the filthy, bloody lump that was Jules. She had been quiet for a while now, her breathing shallow as she drifted in and out of consciousness. When he got out of here, he would have to leave her behind, at least until he could find help. The thought saddened him. No one deserved to be treated so cruelly.

"Hang in there Jules," he called out, "I'll have us out of here in no time." He almost jumped as his words echoed around the stone prison. He shivered, the cold of the cell starting to seep deep into his bones. The cell no longer stank like a sewage pit. His nose had adjusted to the foul air, but he remembered the gag producing reek, disliking the fact he was about to add to it. He had no choice. He was busting. Moving to the furthest possible spot, he relieved himself, "better than wetting my dacks," he muttered.

Matt needed to keep his mind blank, continue pushing away errant thoughts before they could surface. He raised his arm over his head, twisted side to side, then dropped one arm at a time over his shoulder; down his back, pushing on the elbow with his other hand in a bid to stretch out the cramps and kinks, before settling down to start digging again.

The scraping sounded loud and out of place after the silence. Cold dread crept over him. What if they intended to leave him to starve to death, never to be found. He stopped scraping and looked at the bars, shut his eyes and leaned forward to rest his forehead against the cold steel. Even if he could get one bar loose, it wouldn't be enough for him to get his shoulders through, let alone his whole body. He breathed deeply, trying to find the will to keep on digging. Never give up. He repeated his family's motto. *Never give up.*

Matt froze. Held his breath and listened, willing his heart to stop making a pounding racket. He wasn't mistaken. Footsteps. More than one person, heading his way fast. Adrenaline kicked in, heightening his senses even more. The noise grew louder. He jumped up, instinctively looking for somewhere to hide, somewhere that would give him an advantage. Maybe this was it. Maybe death was just around the corner.

Well, he wouldn't go down without a fight. Stepping in close to the bars would give him the best position. Further away and they could put the muzzle of a gun through, easy shot. If he was closer, they would be less inclined to stick a weapon within his reach. If they stood back to fire, they risked the bullets ricocheting off the bars. Yes, he decided. They would have to open the cell, and regardless of how many people, he would try to disarm one and take out the rest.

Using his foot to scrape the bits of rubble back around the bar, he prepared for the worst. The footsteps were clear and defined now, running at a solid pace. Trying to detect how many proved hard. There were at least three, possibly as many as six. His hands tingled and he shifted lightly on his feet, keeping his weight balanced. He positioned himself close to the archway entrance so they wouldn't see him until they came right into the cavern, hopefully giving him enough time to check out their weakest link.

"He's here." The sweetest words he had ever heard. There in all her redhaired, fiery glory stood his sister Jo, chest heaving as she tried to catch her breath. Close on her heels was an imposing man he had never seen before. Matt reached out and clasped his hand through the bars, leaning heavily on the cold metal. All his pent-up fear and emotion boiled to the surface and for the first time since he had heard of his brother's death, tears moistened his eyes.

"Right where Willow said he would be." His sister's voice was just as choked as his as she clasped her hands over her nose. "My gosh, it's rank in here." She stood back as one of the men in MICO's camouflage greens snapped the lock with huge bolt cutters, swinging the cell door open wide. Jo rushed in. She launched herself into his arms, giving him a vice-like bear hug, before pulling away wrinkling her nose. "You stink."

"Love you too Jo." He laughed, before his face went sober. "First, we need a medic...." He cut his words short, as two burley men rushed in with a stretcher. His next words raised hopeful questions, "Kellee? And is Robert here with his men?"

"We don't know where Kellee is yet," interjected the tall, imposing stranger by his sister's side.

Matt raised a questioning eyebrow, looking between Jo and the stranger who continued to speak. "And yes, Robert and his men are approaching from an exit point you probably don't know about. It's around the other side of the lake. We are hoping to hear from him about Kellee. Our only contact with him has been via our phones. There was no time for him to come to us first and then get around to the other side of the lake. He sent two medics and an armed guard to help us get to you. Willow told us about Jules. She doesn't look like she will make it." He shook his head. "That's rough, man."

"Yeah, these bastards don't mess around." Matt was itching to get going now Jules was being looked after. "Let's move." He staggered slightly as he stepped forward.

"Slow down!" ordered Jo. "Obviously, you have no major injuries, but heck, you look like you have been hit by a truck... Medic!" She stood firmly in front of him, waving her hand, pointing at Matt.

Under the medic's swift attention, Matt flinched as the antiseptic stung the wounds on his face. He felt marginally better once the major grime had been washed away, and as the long high from adrenaline subsided and the feeling of safety hit home, he began to shiver.

The thick beige shirt his sister placed over his shoulders helped regulate his body heat. He put it on, grateful for the warmth it provided.

"Drink and eat." The man at his sister's side passed him a nutritional bar and a sports drink. "It will replenish lost electrolytes and give you a boost of energy. According to our directions, we have a fair hike ahead of us." He raised an eyebrow. "So, if you're coming with us instead of heading out with the medics, you will need your strength."

Matt quickly assessed the man as he took the drink from him, downing it in half a dozen rapid gulps. Stepping aside so the men could manoeuvre the stretcher out the narrow cell entrance, he wiped the back of his bandaged hand over his mouth. "I really am fine. What's our next step errr...?" he questioned, looking between the man and his sister.

"Matt this is Axel. We worked together on my assignment to infiltrate the Range Riders." She smiled. "I guess you could say he is my partner."

The sparkle in her eyes as she nodded in Axel's direction was not lost on Matt, but there was no time to dig deeper. She pulled a folded piece of paper out of her pocket and held it closer to the light. "These are instructions from Willow" she stated.

"And who is Willow?" Matt, glanced at the map, switching from foot to foot, impatient to be on the move. He stopped and took a breath when Axel put a supportive hand on his shoulder.

Mutual respect passed between the two men as Axel spoke. "Willow was my contact when I was with The Range Riders and was the key coordinator in bringing the gang to their knees. I trust her with my life. I can tell you more on the way. All I know is for now, our best bet is to follow Willow's instructions."

Axel leant over the map and Matt was amazed to see his strong headed sister let him take the lead, just adding points in here and there. "We haven't had time to really look at it ourselves," he started, "Things have been moving so quickly there has barely been time to take a breath."

Jo leaned forward and said, "Not that we have time now, but we need to bring you up to speed and then head off to where we have to go next."

Matt munched on his protein bar as they continued to pour over the map. Axel was right. He did need this. With every mouthful he felt much better.

Axel double tapped his finger. "We are here." He tapped again, "Robert and his crew are coming in the second entrance which we think is around here. This is where we hope he will break through and rescue Kellee. We can't see any other way in or out of these caverns." He placed his finger on a spot that completed the triangle. "We must go here."

Matt looked puzzled. "Why? For what reason.? Nothing is there? Shouldn't we head towards where Robert is coming in? That way the scum will be trapped between two forces, better the chance of finding Kellee."

Axel took a deep breath. "When Willow phoned, it was rushed and urgent. We were about to go down the wardrobe stairs Kellee's phone led us to. Thank goodness we were warned in time. We were given directions on how to find you, and this place." He tapped the map. "If this is where we were told to go, there must be a reason. Willow was time pressed, said there wasn't much further intel, but hoped we would find more directions when we got to this spot. I trust Willow with my life." He tapped the map again, reinforcing his statement.

Jo interrupted, "Willow was briskly apologetic at leaving us with no clear direction, except this. Information was still coming in. So, are we ready to move? Let's find this next place."

They set off at a steady jog. The medic team already making their way out, moved to the side to let them pass. They would have to go back out the way they came in. The three pushed on alone, following narrow uneven stone passageways full of twists and turns. Old lava tunnels, made thousands of years ago, were dimly lit by an unknown source and Matt prayed the soft glow would hold out long enough for them to get where they needed to be.

Axel must have memorised which tunnels to take as he steadily zig zagged towards their goal. "Next tunnel on the right, then third on the left and we will be there," he called over his shoulder as he picked up the pace. All Matt could hear was the pounding of feet on hard stone, and his heart pounding the same beat in his chest.

CHAPTER THIRTY SIX

A xel abruptly stopped, holding up his hand in warning. An eerie vibe hung in the small chamber. The same dim lighting illuminated a small flight of roughly carved stone stairs leading up to a door. There seemed no other exit other than the passage they had travelled along. The cool damp air and the silence wrapping around them was unnerving.

Matt watched as Jo and Axel worked in perfect union, as if they had been together for years. Guns in hand, they covered each other as they navigated the ascent. He took the gun they had given him and covered their backs, standing at the bottom of the stairs, gun pointed toward the way they had come, secure with a stone wall at this back.

"Clear."

On Axel's cue, he raced up and into a compact office lined with computers and surveillance cameras. Most were still running.

"Are you ok Matt?" Jo placed a concerned hand on his arm.

To be honest, the last twenty-four hours had taken its toll. He felt battered, bruised, and emotionally exhausted with worry. Seeing the empty office added to his fears. Where was Kellee? He had been hoping beyond hope he would find her here. Looking at the concern in his sister's face made him realise his worries had been lessened with her arrival. At least Jo and the MICO team were safe. Now was not the time to give up on the faith that everything would be ok.

"I am fine Sis." He gave her a gentle hug and couldn't help thinking how tiny she felt in comparison to Kellee. "Tired, sore, worried, but fine." He chuckled as she squeezed him tight for a moment before pushing him away, wrinkling her nose. "No hugs bro, you stink."

"Right," Matt took charge. "Let's figure out why 'Willow' directed us to this spot. I don't like the fact we are so vulnerable in this position. This is a dead-end tunnel, and I don't want us trapped." He walked over to the row of monitors. "Jo, stand guard at the bottom of the stairs. Give a low whistle if there's any activity. Axel, you and I will scour this place and see what we can find."

The burnt ashy smell which had been noticeable as they entered the room, came from a metal bin. A shredder was close by, so it was a no-brainer that the important and incriminating documents had been destroyed. Nothing but fine dust remained. As Axel rummaged through the drawers and filing cabinet, Matt turned his attention to the row of monitors, his eyes drawn immediately to the cell in which he had been held captive.

Shocked by the knowledge his every move, and futile attempts to escape had been on camera, it also gave him an indication how long the office had been abandoned. It must have been empty when he was rescued, otherwise reinforcement would have shown up. He said as much to Axel.

"Unless too many of their crew had gone by then. It was deserted when we docked at the jetty. Haven't seen or heard a soul since." Axel replied. "And there is nothing here of any value that I could find." He shut the last drawer with a frustrated bang.

"You need to see this." The tone in Matt's voice had Axel at his side in an instant. "Jo, come back up." He raised his voice loud enough to bring his sister running. "Look at this monitor. Someone is down there."

"Are they setting explosives?" Jo put her hands over her mouth in horror.

"It looks that way. We need to picture this as a whole scene, so we can work out where they are. Let's start with what we know. These camera feeds run in sets of three. This group," he pointed," is the Jetty area; there is the landing bay." Axel interrupted, tapping the second screen, "this one is the tunnel to the right where the cells are," Matt nodded, indicating the next screen, "the third would be the tunnel to the left where they took Kellee." His voice strong, steady and determined. "These three cover the cells. This is where I was." He tapped a screen. "This one is the tunnel leading to the cell and this one connects to the Jetty feed. See this area here is the same."

Jo interjected, "So this group show the other side of the Jetty feed, and these up here connect to them." Stepping back a pace she observed the bank of screens and exclaimed, "They are a visual map of the whole complex." She stepped back in, "Look, this is where we are. This one here shows the door to this room."

"Yes, I saw you go down the stairs, which is why I looked more closely."

Matt held back his fear and checked again. In none of the screens could he see any sign of Kellee. With no time for worry or speculation, it was imperative they activated a plan now. Time was running out. He focused his attention back to the screen that showed some activity. "Three men here setting explosives, no activity on the next screen and the next screen is either broken or turned off."

"I think this is the control panel," guessed Axel as he counted the corresponding monitors against the panel in front of him. "By my reckoning, that is camera eight." He pressed the number eight on the keyboard panel, giving an elated *"yes"* as the screen flickered to life.

"It's an escape tunnel. You can see the light at the entrance in the distance." Jo's tone held both fear and excitement. "There's

Robert and his squad just coming into view. It looks as though they have arrested some of them and are now entering the tunnel. We must warn them. Find out if they have Kellee." She took her phone from her back pocket. Tried it and shook her head. "No signal, we are down too deep. Last time I spoke to Robert, he feared that might happen and he wasn't prepared for an underground rescue. He had only just returned to his Base north of Bamaga after saving us," she flicked her hand in Axel's direction, "when he got a call to haul ass back down here."

"There doesn't seem to be any other directions from Willow here, unless we are meant to approach the exit tunnel from this end." Matt tapped at his chin impatiently with his index finger, aware the clock was ticking. "Axel, what about these two screens, any chance of powering them up?"

"I have been trying...hang on..." he grappled about under the desk and held up a power cord, "hopefully they've only been unplugged."

The monitors hummed to life.

"I think this is what we were meant to find" exclaimed Matt, "Look, the top one shows a small steep third exit, looks like it has rarely been used."

"A secret escape route perhaps?" Jo looked at Matt with raised eyebrows.

Matt nodded his agreement, "This middle screen must connect to the secret escape and to this room, but how? It's just a blank rough stonewall."

Axel backed out from under the desk and stood, "Look what I found." He held up two walkie talkies. "They are both powered up as well." He tossed one to Matt, who caught it deftly.

"Is that writing?" Jo incredulously pointed to the middle screen.

Matt shifted his angle and leant forward. "Yes, it is. I thought it was a shadow on the rocks. It's faint but says, "push. L1 R2, L1 R2, R1 L3."

"Ok, that's like the instructions Axel and I were given to find you, but not the first part. So, the L1 R2 are where to turn, first left, second right and so on." Jo paused thoughtfully, "but why 'push'?"

Matt shifted impatiently restless to get going. He disliked cryptic clues. They reminded him far too much of Patrick. He scanned the room, his eyes drawn to a mirror image of the blank wall off to the side. He almost bumped into Axel as he leapt forward and pushed on the stone wall in between two cabinets. It was obvious now that something had been moved recently. There were scratch marks on the stone. It gave way and swung inwards. He let out a cry of triumph.

"The wall you can see on the monitor opened," Jo grinned with excitement. "Matt, I can see you on the screen. This must lead to the secret exit. And these are the directions: which tunnels to take."

Returning the grin, Matt stepped back towards the screens. "Robert is still advancing but slowly. They are in combat formation taking every precaution. I can't see the men who were setting explosives though."

"They disappeared down this tunnel here, maybe to hide until Robert and his men have passed, or maybe there is another exit. Either way, Robert will find them; his team are checking every tunnel branching off this main one." She turned back to Matt. "So what's the plan? We need to hustle."

"I don't know how Willow pulled this off, even down to supplying us with walkie talkies, but there's no time to think about that now." Matt checked with Axel to make sure the radios were on the same frequency and channel.

"Jo, Axel, you two head off to warn Robert and his men about the explosives. We can't risk them walking into a trap. And it is still possible they already have Kellee somewhere safe. The Compound is not that big, it's just a complex maze. You should make it in time. As soon as you meet up with Robert, we will all have contact. We can fill each other in on what we find." He held up his walkie talkie when he thought Jo was about to protest his plan. "I'm taking the new tunnel." He ran his fingers through his hair. "It's our best chance of finding Kellee."

If Jo noticed the hitch in his voice when he said Kellee's name, she didn't let on. After giving him a brief hug, she flicked her head toward Axel. "You're right Matt." She slapped Axel on the shoulder. "Come on big fella, let's get this done." She turned at the door. "Take care bro, the camera was obviously redirected to the secret door. You don't know what lies ahead. Check in every five minutes, code word 'GO.' We'll do the same." And with that, they were gone.

Matt stood momentarily stunned. His sister's decisive action, her strength and conviction as she agreed to his plan, was a contradiction to her usual personality. Strongly argumentative at any orders given, he had expected her to protest his going on alone. Even though it was the only option. To see the teamwork between her and Axel spoke volumes. When this was over, and Kellee was safely in his arms, he looked forward to a debriefing on her recent assignment.

He took one last look at the monitors. He could see Jo and Axel making steady progress, Robert and his men were still some distance away from the explosives. He turned each screen off before disconnecting the keyboard completely. The room darkened and the electronic hum ceased, plunging the small office into a cold silence.

Once through the door, Matt pushed it shut and left the keyboard on the ground. Knowing he had done all he could to protect their backs and they were now taking the best course of action. He spoke softly into the handset, "Go." He sighed with relief when Jo responded in kind. The communications worked. He set off at a brisk, but cautious pace, following the turns he had memorised.

CHAPTER THIRTY SEVEN

Matt's smiling face filled Kellee's vision. Eyes closed, she clung onto it. If she was going to die, she wanted it to be the last thing she saw. His cheeky, lopsided grin and those sparkling expresso eyes warmed her heart, and she felt her lips break out into a smile.

A strangled gurgle of pain and a sudden thud caused her eyes to fly wide open in shock. She screamed as a body slumped next to her, feeding her fear as she tried unsuccessfully to scramble away. Blood seeped out in a growing circle from a wound somewhere under Fuzz's fallen body. There was no doubt he was dead. The knife in the boss's hand dripped blood and she cried out in desperation as he moved towards her. Her breathing shallowed as panic surfaced. He bent, wiping the blade clean on the dead man's shirt before turning his attention to her.

"We don't have much time. I can't stop the detonation, but I have delayed it slightly." The knife sliced through the bonds on her feet, and he hauled her upright before cutting her hands free. "When I say run, I want you to take off as fast as you can back down that tunnel. With a bit of luck, help is not far away."

Kellee rubbed at her wrists, willing her body to stop shaking.

"Listen carefully. If I have timed this right, any second now Matt is going to come bursting around the corner. I need to be gone and you *must not* let him follow me. He lifted her chin, so she had direct contact with his eyes. "It's imperative you lead him away. When the tunnel branches right, keep veering right and you won't lose your way. I have opened one of our emergency exits. It is a narrow opening but once you are through and around the curve you will see a wide cave entrance that will lead you outside. If you don't run like hell, you will both be caught up in the tunnel blast. Do you understand?"

She nodded quickly as she searched the hard lines of his face for clues as to who this man might be. Then he smiled. The lopsided grin and espresso eyes came alive, and recognition dawned. As clear as day she saw the resemblance of the brothers. "Patrick?" she questioned softly.

The seriousness of the situation chased his grin away and urgency was back in his voice. His words came out fast and clear. "Don't let Matt follow. Tell him I am close to busting the top hierarchy of this crime gang. It leads all the way into the higher levels of political corruption. It also points towards whoever killed our mother. That was no accident. She overheard something she shouldn't have and was killed for it." He grabbed her hand, placing a usb stick in her palm, closing her fingers into a fist around it. "This is all the intel I can share without damaging my cover. Tell Stephen he is in danger. Mantis is the code name for the head man I am after. He has put a contract out on him. Trust Willow, my only contact to the outside world."

"Come with me Patrick." Kellee took a step towards the tunnel. She could hear footsteps pounding. Becoming louder as they came closer. "Come on," She tugged at his hand.

She watched his face close over with pain.

"No. There is a child I have to save." Regret engulfed his voice and features. "She was meant to be here, so I could give her to you, but they took her on ahead." He shook his head as if trying to clear it and looked at his watch, then looked up sharply at the tunnel and swore.

Kellee watched things unfold as if in slow motion. Matt skidded to a halt as he rounded the corner, his eyes flew to hers immediately, held for a few seconds before they lifted to Patrick's. Her heart went out to him as his facial expression changed from shock, anger, relief, love and back to anger again.

"I am beyond redemption for what I have done. NOW RUN!" Patrick hissed in her ear. "Twenty seconds, count down as you run, take Matt with you, save him." A strong hand shoved her in the back propelling her forward.

Without further hesitation Kellee sprinted, counting Sixteen in her mind as she grabbed Matt's hand and yanked him after her. He resisted for only a microsecond as she swung to the right down a narrow tunnel, before she finally felt him put his faith in her lead. "Twelve...Eleven...TEN..." she shouted.

Matt took charge. He surged forward as she pointed towards a rough stone doorway. One at a time they went through. He grabbed her hand again, sprinting towards the daylight he could see as they rounded the next bend. Almost at the entrance, he pulled her sharply to the left as she yelled THREE. He yanked her down low and shielded her with his body as the count headed towards zero.

Kellee listened to his heart racing next to hers. A couple of seconds felt like long minutes. The shock waves hit them first, followed by a series of deafening explosions. Coughing and spluttering they hugged each other tight as small bits of debris and dust fell around them. Matt's arms hugged her tight and his whispered words of love healed her heart.

Matt's handset crackled to life and Jo's voice heavy with exertion and concern came through, "Talk to me Matt. Is everything ok? Over."

"We are fine, I have Kellee. Fairly sure the tunnel up ahead is now just rubble. We will check as soon as the dust settles. Over."

"Robert's orders. Stay put. The tunnel could be unstable. We are with him, and have backtracked to the office. Be with you soon. And great news about Kellee. Over and Out."

Matt lifted Kellee to her feet, studying her as if he could not believe she was standing unharmed in front of him. His voice filled with emotion. "They told me they painted you blue and...Patrick?"

"We are both safe Matt." She interrupted. "Patrick will be safe as well. He had just as much time as us to run."

They stood together, the brilliant green foliage at the cave entrance symbolising freshness and freedom. At the same moment, they both smiled.

"Come here my wise little avatar."

He pulled her tightly into his arms, his lips meeting hers with a kiss of tender love. Holding a promise of things to come, his kiss went on forever, as if he never wanted to let her go.

Finally, unable to breathe, she pushed gently at his shoulders and smiled her love at him.

"Let me up for air you big lug, or I *will* turn blue"

Their mutual laugh echoed around them, settling into their hearts, ready to grow into a lifetime of happiness.

The End.

AFTERWORD

Help The Author

If you enjoyed this, or any one of Brenda's books, please pop over to amazon.com.au, goodreads,

Ingramspark or any platform you like to use and leave a kind review. A simple I loved it, goes a long

way to helping the author.

We know all books get borrowed, whether from the library or a friend. If you borrowed this book,

thank you. I hope you enjoyed your journey into one of my stories. It would be appreciated if you

could help me by also leaving this book a kind review.

And please take a picture of the book and post to social media, I love seeing where my babies end

up.

ALSO BY

All Roads Lead To Love series by Brenda May
Six siblings. Six stories. The setting. MICO. Military Intelligence
Covert Operations. Founded and operated by the Brennan family
who are all involved in one way or another. Set in the Tropics of
Northern Australia, each book is a standalone, with a subtle crime
arc running through each story before coming to its conclusion in
book six.

RELEASED

Book 1 A Wild Ride to Love - Josephine Brennan. Jo is the
youngest and only female in a house full of testosterone. She is as
rough and as tough as her five older brothers. Call her Josephine
and you're likely to meet her fist.

Book 2 A Hostage to Love – Matthew Brennan. He mourns
the death of his twin brother by staying deep undercover in
a connected MICO operation. His aim is to find the bastard
responsible for his murder and shut the organisation down.

TO BE RELEASED

Book 3 The Signs of Love – Kevin Brennan. Youngest of the brothers. Unsure of where he fits into the family run organisation, MICO. He is always trying to be as good as his older brothers. At the same time, he inevitably ends up doing things his own way.

Book 4 The Secret of Love – Stephen Brennan. The brains behind the undercover operations section of MICO. He has no time for a personal life when so many depend on him for their safety.

Book 5 A Stranger to Love – Robert Brennan Jnr. He operates an elite training camp for the best of the armed forces, supplying MICO with the agents they need. Strict, Military to the core. The oldest sibling takes his responsibilities seriously. Life is too short for laughter.

Book 6 The Redemption of Love – Patrick Brennan. He feels he is beyond redemption for things he has done. In his mind, he died the day he faked his own death. His goal, to climb to the top of the gang he has infiltrated, and destroy them, one by one, from the top down.

About Author

Brenda May worked and lived on a tropical Island and in a remote Cape York Wilderness area, before
    settling down in Far North Queensland with her partner to raise their two daughters. After
    successfully owning and running a wildlife tour business for twenty years, she now lives in Innisfail
    caring for her daughters two Papillons, who may just appear in one of her books. Her passion is
    writing and interweaving it with her love and knowledge of the Australian landscape.
    You can find out more about the author and her books from her website brendamayauthor.com
    From there you can sign up to her newsletter, check out her social media, and keep up to date with
    new releases.

Acknowledgments

As always, a huge thanks to my daughters, Jenna and Caitlin, for their ongoing support andencouragement. To my writer's group Licuala Winq, for the fun, laughter, and positive feedbackthrough our monthly meetings. To Jeanette Smith for rapping my knuckles and laughing 'a mile a minute' at some of my prose. Huge thanks to Ken Allen my ever-patient IT help, things are slowly sinking in I promise. And to you my readers, may you find enjoyment and adventure with each new story.